Born in France to American parents, Katia Lief moved to the United States as a baby and was raised in Massachusetts and New York. She teaches fiction writing as a part-time faculty member at the New School in Manhattan and lives in Brooklyn with her husband and two children.

Also by Katia Lief:

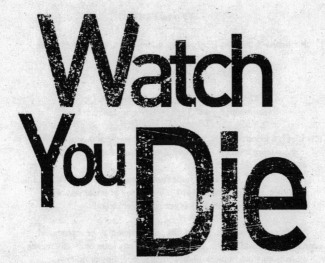

Watch You Die

Katia Lief

EBURY
PRESS

5 7 9 10 8 6 4

Published in 2013 by Ebury Press, an imprint of Ebury Publishing

A Random House Group Company

The Random House Group Limited Reg. No. 954009

Addresses for companies within the Random House Group can be found at:
www.randomhouse.co.uk

A CIP catalogue record for this book is available from the British Library

ISBN 9780091939212

To buy books by your favourite authors and register for offers visit
www.randomhouse.co.uk

The Random House Group Limited supports The Forest Stewardship
Council® (FSC®), the leading international forest-certification organisation.
Our books carrying the FSC label are printed on FSC®-certified paper.
FSC is the only forest-certification scheme supported by the leading
environmental organisations, including Greenpeace. Our
paper procurement policy can be found at
www.randomhouse.co.uk/environment

Printed and bound in Great Britain by Clays Ltd, St Ives plc

For Eli

ACKNOWLEDGMENTS

I am deeply grateful to my wonderful editor Gillian Green, along with her talented crew at Ebury/ Random House in London, for giving this novel its first life in the English language. To Matt Bialer, Stefanie Diaz and Lindsay Ribar, for their dedicated efforts to make that happen. To Dan Conaway, for guiding the book from here on out. And to my husband, Oliver, who read it and (for the first time ever) liked it just the way it was.

'When I hear music, I fear no danger. I am invulnerable. I see no foe. I am related to the earliest times, and to the latest.'

—*Winter*, from the journal of Henry David Thoreau

PROLOGUE

The phone rang at a quarter to six.

I was making dinner. Lemon chicken, sticky rice, salad.

Nat was doing homework at a friend's house. Through the kitchen window I saw the green tips of crocuses pushing up through the late winter soil. A wind had started up that afternoon. I had left my husband Hugo a message to swing by after work and pick Nat up so he wouldn't have to walk home in the cold. He had gone to school that morning in only a sweater, eager for spring, though the air was still bracing. Martha's Vineyard, surrounded by ocean as it was, released winter stubbornly.

I figured it was Hugo calling me back. Felt it. I dried my hands on a dishtowel – a red rooster proud on nubby white cloth – and answered the phone.

"Mrs Mayhew?"

"Yes?"

I tossed the salad. Greek olives and carrot slices tumbled with ripped pieces of soft Boston lettuce, all glistening in an oily vinaigrette. So it wasn't Hugo – it was not the first time my sixth sense had fooled me. I would try him again when this call was over.

"This is Tuesday Miller. I'm a nurse . . . I'm calling from the hospital."

Tuesday. What an unusual name. And today *was* Tuesday.

Tuesday. A quarter to six. Dinner was almost ready and the table still wasn't set. I had rushed from my desk and started cooking immediately because Hugo had an eight o'clock deposition in town and we were loath, from years of habit, to miss a family dinner. I felt suddenly frustrated by this phone call. I didn't have time for it and wanted to hang up. The feeling was quick and large and even at that moment I knew it was out of proportion.

I turned off the burner under the rice. Leaned against the counter.

"Yes?"

"I'm very sorry to have to give you this news."

And then there was a moment, an abrupt chasm of time, an ocean of silence that opened between us. Between me and this woman Tuesday who had called me on the phone when I was busy, in the middle of something. I didn't have time or patience for this woman who had called to interrupt me.

"Your husband is Hugo Mayhew."

Not a question. A statement. An introduction? A *forewarning*.

"Yes."

"Mrs Mayhew, I'm sorry to have to tell you this . . . he was in an accident, driving on Middle Road. I'm afraid—"

And then . . . and then a storm at sea. And the sea was my heart, my soul, my brain, my life. The dark, cold underbelly of the ocean rose into my eyes as I crumpled onto the kitchen floor, oblivious to the rich aromas of a meal no one would eat.

PART ONE

PART ONE

CHAPTER 1

His eyes were pale brown with streaks of darker
brown and flecks of green. I recognized them before
I recalled any other element of his face. It was the
three-dimensional luminescence of the green, like
floating chips of granite, that made the eyes so
memorable along with the right pupil, which hovered
slightly off-center and stayed partly dilated regardless of how bright the light was. Once you noticed
the pupil – and I had noticed it back on the Vineyard,
in the office supply store where he used to make my
copies – it established in your mind a sensation of
off-kilteredness. And then you shoved that thought
away because it was so unkind. He was just a young
man with a gimpy eye doing a menial job – no need
to judge him. He was always efficient and polite if a
little over-friendly. I never knew his name.

All that came back to me now, looking into those eyes across my desk in the newsroom beside a window whose blue-skied view was halved by the vertical edge of a neighboring skyscraper. It was the second autumn since my life had been upended by Hugo's death. How, I often wondered, could this be the same sky I left behind on Martha's Vineyard, a sky that had sheltered, taught and broadened me over fifteen years of a comfortable life, a career as a journalist, the astonishing joys of motherhood and a happy marriage? But I couldn't bury my husband there and stay on the island. I tried but found it impossible; the geography was too open. Here, in New York, constant boundaries buffered the sensation of emotional vertigo that follows an unexpected loss.

He stood in front of my desk, smiling as if he had found a long-lost friend.

"Darcy!"

Well, he knew *my* name.

"You work here too?" he asked.

"Staff reporter." I nodded. "Metro section. They've got me on a new environmental beat. You?"

"Mailroom. Today's my first day. I feel like I'm well positioned to go somewhere from here. Right place, right time, you know? I want to be a journalist just like you. I used to read all your pieces in the *Gazette*. You're an amazing writer, Darcy."

The way he said my name again, like he knew me. As if we'd met, actually met, and traded names. Had we? Had we introduced ourselves over the copy counter on the Vineyard? Had I forgotten his name? Or had I failed to listen in the first place? I smiled and nodded, feeling mean and dumb, finally managing a lame apology.

"I'm sorry; I've forgotten your name."

"We never officially met. I'm Joe Coffin."

I put out a hand and we shook. "Hi, Joe. Nice to officially meet you. Actually it *is* nice. I haven't seen a soul from the Vineyard since we moved here. I miss it."

"I don't. I lived there my whole life and I feel liberated to finally be in America, you know, for real."

America was what the islanders called the mainland, which was essentially the entire rest of the country from the coast of Cape Cod to California. That's how separate, special and isolated you tended to feel living on the Vineyard after a while.

"So, are you one of legendary Coffins?" It was one of the Vineyard's oldest family names, dating back centuries, and you saw it everywhere – on street signs and roadside mailboxes. Another ubiquitous island name was Mayhew, Hugo's family name, although in his case any connection had been lost long before we moved there.

"More or less. It's my mother's name, but she's not that close to the rest of them. What about you? You're a Mayhew—"

"My *husband* was a Mayhew. He did some research into his family tree once and it didn't intersect with any islanders. Apparently his branch came a little later and landed farther north, in Plymouth."

"Right, your husband. So you and I probably aren't distant cousins. They say the Coffins and Mayhews intermarried a lot back in the old days."

"Nope, no chance of us being distant cousins."

I couldn't tell if that disappointed or pleased him . . . and briefly wondered why it should matter at all.

"You know what?" he asked, and as he formulated his proposition his face came into focus in my memory. I had seen that face in exactly this pose of thoughtfulness, seen it, digested it and remembered it now: "I read all your articles," he had said to me once before, handing me my collated copies over the counter at the Vineyard shop – Martha's Ships, Clips & Copy Cats – a yellow clapboard house that had been transformed into the island's only full-service office support center. "I'd like to be a journalist one day, too." He had shared his intentions with me once before and I had failed to contemplate or even acknowledge them. I was always so busy being a wife and a mother and a freelance writer for the *Gazette*. And then, when I won that prize for my series on the wind farm proposed for the coast of Nantucket, I became even busier, writing for other papers, gaining the traction that had ultimately landed me here at the *Times*. I had failed to listen to this young aspiring writer once before when he had reached out to me and I had not an iota of time or attention for him . . . and here he was again, with that same look on his face. Some things are fate. This time I would listen.

"We should have lunch," he said.

"Absolutely."

"It's such a nice day today. We could get sandwiches and eat them outside somewhere."

I wanted to say *no, not today*, to plead deadlines and short hours, something with my son Nat this afternoon that would prevent me from catching up with my work later, but in fact there was nothing special on my agenda. The truth was, today was a perfect day to break for lunch. I was waiting for return emails and calls about a few different stories I was working on: an update on the touch-and-go resurgence of the Gowanus Canal in Brooklyn, rescheduling an interview with the deputy mayor about the city's efforts to limit cars and therefore gas emissions in midtown Manhattan, and the start of an environmental cleanup of a lot in downtown Brooklyn where the site of a small chemical factory was being prepared for inclusion in the massive

Atlantic Yards development for which hundreds of residential and business tenants had been displaced via eminent domain. This last one was a hotly contested urban renewal project that was already being covered by many reporters. My part was strictly the environmental cleanup element of this single vacated lot and I figured I could get about two stories out of it. Basically my work today was what I thought of as *mining*: like oil drilling, you stuck in some probes and saw what came up. These were all relatively small stories the *Times* had put me on to test my mettle as one of their newest reporters. I may have been a prize-winning journalist but to them I was still a freelancer they had taken into the holy fold. I would have to prove myself. And so, under the radar, as I worked on my assignments my antennae were up for a story I could really fly with. But today I was not under deadline pressure. I could have lunch with Joe; I just didn't want to. However, I had been a bad listener, a poor human being, so I would do it anyway.

"Sounds good," I said. "Meet you at one o'clock in the lobby?"

He smiled. I swear his eyes even widened a little, and I thought, *Cute kid*. I put him at about twenty-two, twenty-three years old. At thirty-nine I wasn't quite old enough to be his mother but maybe his mother's younger sister.

"I'll be waiting," he said.

And he was. He was standing against the wall near the security guard when I reached the lobby five minutes late. When he saw me he smiled and stepped forwards. He was a nice-looking young man, with pale skin, dark brown hair and those riveting eyes. We were about the same height but a kind of intensity, you might even say charm, compensated for his smallish stature and made him seem taller than he was until you were standing right next to him.

As we walked through the lobby he wove his arm through mine, a move I escaped by stepping into a diminishing opening in the revolving door. He was forced into the slot behind me. It had been an inappropriate gesture, a sign of his immaturity I assumed, and on the sidewalk I made a point of keeping a good distance between us.

No matter what people say, anyone who sees a single man and a single woman out together assumes it's a date or at least acknowledges the possibility. This was not, of course, but I had to recognize how it might look to a passing colleague and the thought made me cringe. *Dating*. Never in my wildest dreams had I ever thought I'd be back to that. But I had been a widow for nineteen months and loneliness worms its way into you. I had already accepted that I would never replace Hugo, whom I loved and love and would always love. But I was still a youngish woman with, presumably, half my life ahead of me. Even Nat, my son, had encouraged me to "move on", in his words, and facilitated an obvious attraction between myself and his eighth-grade art teacher Rich, a divorced father, by hinting to the man that his "single mom" had a lot of free evenings. I was never really free; I had Nat, and I had work. But just to please my son I had accepted an invitation to meet with Rich for what I thought of as a parent–teacher conference over dinner. And then another. I liked Rich the more I saw of him. Period. That was where my social life stood at the moment. As for Joe, I hoped he didn't think of this as a date – though the arm-weaving indicated he might. I would simply never have considered dating a man so much younger than me. And it was flat-out inappropriate, taking my arm like that in the lobby of our workplace. The more I thought about it, as we navigated the lunchtime crowds along 43rd Street to the deli on the corner of Seventh Avenue, the more annoyed I felt. But I didn't want to be rude and so I hid my reaction.

We entered the bustling store and took our place in line alongside a refrigerated case of prepared foods and cold cuts. "This is my favorite deli," I said. And as if to prove I wasn't lying, one of the sandwich makers, Brian, looked at me and winked.

"Tuna on rye, lettuce and tomato?" Brian asked. It was my lunch whenever I ate at my desk, which was most days.

"Bingo."

"And for your friend?"

I resisted an urge to explain that Joe was not exactly my friend.

"I'll have the same thing," Joe said. Then, to me, "What do we drink with this perfect sandwich?"

"I drink grapefruit juice." I stepped aside to pull a small carton from the refrigerated display.

"Mind reaching one for me while you're in there?"

I got Joe his drink and stood back in line next to him to wait for our food. His insecurity – ordering everything I ordered, agreeing with whatever I said – annoyed me. But I didn't want to make this more awkward than it already was so I hid that, too.

"I didn't see you this morning," Brian said to me as he handed Joe our paper-wrapped sandwiches.

"I had breakfast at home with my kid today."

"Poppy bagel, chive cream cheese, coffee regular!"

"Actually, at home I usually have cereal."

Joe tipped his head slightly forwards as if awaiting more information, such as what *kind* of cereal I had eaten at home. Behind us, the line was getting longer. I carried our juice cartons to the cash register.

Joe set down the sandwiches and got out his wallet. I got out mine.

"It's on me," he said.

"Thanks, but absolutely not." I handed the cashier a ten-dollar bill, saying, "We'll pay separately."

"Next time, then," Joe said. I didn't want to openly contradict him in front of the cashier, fearing he'd feel emasculated because I earned so much more than he did, or because I'd never date him and didn't want him to act as if I would. Why I should care what this guy felt about any of that, I had no idea; gender reflex, maybe. Like so many women, I had been raised to be a *nice girl* and couldn't seem to shake the habit.

We walked the few blocks to Bryant Park, talking the whole way. It was October and getting chilly out. Soon autumn would give way to winter. Until recently I had looked forward to it, yearning for the cold and early dark as a cave-like place to crawl into. Winter was a time when a person who wanted to understand their aloneness could really dig into it, whereas the warm beckonings of spring, summer and fall were difficult, almost burdensome, when you were unhappy. The first shifting of seasons without Hugo had been agony; the second time around, the pain had been duller but still there. I was stronger now and yet I had welcomed the rigors of another lonely winter, if only to prove to myself that

I had developed the grit to survive widowhood. I had wanted the challenge, anticipated it, until the move to New York – and meeting Rich – had jolted me awake.

"So how do you like it here?" I asked Joe.

"It's OK. Everything's new. I guess it takes an adjustment when you come to a new place."

"I thought you were happy to be in America."

"I am. Don't get me wrong. It's just all so different and I'm taking it in slowly. You?"

"I grew up here," I told him. "In fact a big part of the reason I wanted to move back is because my mom's still here."

"Do you live with her?"

I almost laughed. I hadn't lived with my mother for twenty-two years. "No, she's in a home for Alzheimer's patients. It's on the Upper West Side."

"I'm sorry."

"I imagine your parents miss you on the Vineyard."

"My mom does. I never knew my dad."

"Any siblings?"

"No, it was just me and my mom growing up." He stopped abruptly, which made me curious, but I let it go.

"Me too, after age nine, anyway."

Joe looked at me, awaiting an explanation. When I was nine years old my father Karl committed suicide by jumping out of his office window in midtown Manhattan. He was a wonderful man, a creative director at an advertising agency, successful, loved and well off; but more than that he was a survivor of the Holocaust. A child survivor. My parents in fact had met in the camps. Both were child laborers: he, digging and burying, she, mending and ironing for the commandant's wife. Clearly, of the two, he had had the worse job. The scars from that time ran so deep and hurt so much, the resonance was so painful – and he suffered. Finally, he stopped the pain and the noise and the memories all at once. When he died, despite aching hearts, my mother, Eva, and I agreed that we understood why he had made this terrible choice. "He couldn't listen to it anymore," she told me, making a familiar circling motion around her head with both hands, meaning *the echoes*. In the same conversation she assured me that she would never make such a choice; she would never, ever leave me. My mother was very strong and I didn't doubt her for an iota of a second. She moved us from New Jersey to Brooklyn – just as I had, widowed, with my only child – and started a new life. For years she worked in the garment industry as a seamstress of couture bridal gowns – I could still see her muscular fingers negotiating a wisp-thin steel needle through bead after tiny bead – while I grew and blossomed into a regular American kid, hard-working and optimistic as only an immigrant's child can be. Now we were reconvened in the city of mended lives. But none of that was Joe's business.

"My father passed away," I said, and left it at that.

At Sixth Avenue we entered the park. It was crowded, thanks to the lovely weather. People were perched on the round edge of the fountain, and on the Great Lawn it took a few minutes to find ourselves a spot. Joe took off his denim jacket and spread it on the grass for me to sit on. It was a sweet gesture and completely unnecessary. Even my beloved, considerate husband hadn't done stuff like that, though I admit it was nice knowing my skirt wouldn't get grass stains. I tucked my legs beneath me and positioned my lap to hold my sandwich. Hungry, I dug in.

"So where are you living now?" Joe asked.

I struggled to answer through a half-full mouth: "Brooklyn."

"A realtor stuck me in Washington Heights but I'm thinking of moving."

"Don't you have a lease?"

"Yeah, but my landlord's a sweet old lady. She'll probably let me out of it if I ask her. Where in Brooklyn are you?"

"Boerum Hill. We've got a duplex with a big back yard. It's really very nice. Good for my kid." I caught a pickle slice as it tumbled off the wax paper spread beneath my sandwich, and ate it.

"I'd love to have children some day." In a burst of sun his smile looked bright white but I could also see, just visible toward the back, a tooth that appeared dark and rotted. That, or it was an empty space. As a reporter I was trained to read stories in such details. In Joe's mouth I saw that he grew up poor on an island whose economy, I knew from having lived there, was driven by tourism and high-end real estate. Full-time inhabitants without specialized educations and skills tended to scrape by. I already knew he was an only child of a single mother. Now I also knew that they couldn't afford dental work, at least for the part of the mouth that didn't show. "But first," he added, "I want to concentrate on building my career."

"A good choice. You're young. Build your career, get yourself settled, then have a family."

"That's what you did, right?"

"Not exactly." I smiled, remembering. "Hugo was just out of law school when we had Nat, and I hadn't even started freelancing. But it worked out in the end. Sort of." I closed my eyes for a moment and then opened them to the sun so it could burn off any intention of tears.

Joe leaned toward me. "I'm sorry you lost your husband. I really am."

"It's not *your* fault." I bit my sandwich, chewed and swallowed. Mechanically, against emotion, hunger now evaporated. "You must have read about that in the *Gazette*, too."

He nodded. "Everyone did, didn't they? It was on the front page."

Of course it was. Hugo Mayhew had built a name for himself as an environmental lawyer based on the Vineyard. His clients, at first mostly on the Cape and in Boston, had ultimately encompassed the whole planet. Not yet forty, he had become a treasured citizen of the island and the world – a treasure of my heart – and his death brought real sorrow to many. Nat and I had known enough about his work during his life to be proud of him – *he* was my inspiration to write about the environment in the first place – but it was his death that really opened our eyes to the scope of his work. He had toiled as a champion of environmental issues for years, on the legal front, before the world caught up to his vision and when it did he was set to ride the very crest of the wave. I often wondered if, had he lived, he might have ended up in a position of power in the government where he could have had a real impact on our country's direction in relation to environmental issues. But he didn't live. He died. He lost control of his car on a dark bend of road on his way to pick Nat up from a friend's house, after which father and son were due home for dinner. Because of his stature there was an inquest into his death, but it was a formality. People died in car accidents. They just did. I was told his obituary ran not only on the front page of the *Vineyard Gazette* but around the world. I couldn't read it.

Hugo and I had met in Boston right after finishing college and soon before he started law school. We called it our "fun summer", our only piece of time together when we were really footloose and fancy-free. We'd sleep late, take trips on the spur of the moment and while away whole afternoons. I dabbled in job hunting that summer but didn't really try that hard; I was too distracted and thrilled and absorbed by falling in love with Hugo. We'd looked like siblings, he and I, with our slightly olive skin, hazel eyes and thick auburn hair. It felt, from the very start, like a natural fit. And we loved so many of the same things: traveling, long meandering walks, ping pong, margaritas on a hot beach, milk and cookies before bed, nature hikes, morning lovemaking. We lived together throughout his law education while I tripped from job to job. After we married we settled on the Vineyard, where he opened his law practice against the better judgment of everyone we knew. Only after we had Nat and he started preschool did I discover my vocation as a journalist. I took baby steps at first, but found good subjects and had good luck. I'd liked the flexibility of freelancing and loved working at home. Never had I imagined myself back in New York, working at the *Times*. *Never* had I imagined my life without Hugo.

"So, do you have a girlfriend?" I had to change the subject.

Joe blushed. "Kind of. Not really. I'd like to."

"Don't worry, you will." He *was* sweet. His innocence and hopefulness recalled the good feelings, the excitement, of that time in life when you're young and starting out.

"So, I was wondering," Joe said, just as a cloud opened above us and sun blasted into our faces. I shielded my eyes with a flattened hand but Joe just sat there literally taking the heat. His left pupil contracted to a pinprick against the brightness while the right pupil, off-center, stayed mostly open. "Maybe you could recommend me for the *Times'* internship program? If you felt comfortable doing it, I mean. I know it's hard to get into."

"Oh, sure, if I can. I'll ask around about how that works. But shouldn't I read something of yours first? Do you have any writing samples?"

"Definitely. I'll send you something."

I folded the wax paper around my remaining sandwich and shifted to reach into my purse. "Here, I'll give you my email address." I fished around for my business card holder.

"It's in the company directory," he said. My heart jumped at that: had he already looked me up? "Isn't it?"

"You're right, it is." I dropped the card back into my purse and looked at my watch. "Better be getting back, don't you think?"

"My supervisor would think so." Joe laughed and so did I.

As we left the lawn behind us and were on our way out of the park, past the fountain, my cell phone began its ragtime ring. The call was coming from a cell phone number I didn't recognize but I had left a lot of messages that morning and so I answered it with my workaday greeting: "Darcy Mayhew speaking."

"You have questions about Atlantic Yards." It was a man's voice, one I didn't know.

"Yes, just the one lot. Who is this?"

"Not now. Meet me at the lot, tomorrow, six a.m. I have something to tell you."

Before I could protest – *Who are you? Why so early? Can't you tell me on the phone?* – he hung up.

My heart raced as I closed my cell and walked alongside Joe through a lunchtime crowd that hadn't thinned at all since we left the office.

"Everything OK?" Joe asked.

"Yup."

"If I were a parent, I think I'd always worry in the back of my mind about my kids, you know? When I wasn't with them."

I looked at him. He wasn't a parent so how could he know about that? Had his own mother over-worried about him? I did think about Nat when we weren't together, but he was thirteen years old and already, two months in the city, knew how to get around on his own. And I was learning that it was time to start giving him some space and independence.

"I try not to worry about him too much," I said. "He's a good, smart kid. And trust me, you learn early that if you worry too much you'll go insane."

"So the call wasn't him."

"They're not allowed to use their phones during the school day. Is that why we're talking about this?"

"Because your phone rang."

"My phone always rings." Though not with anonymous callers.

"I wish mine rang more."

That was a remark I simply could not respond to. I was out of gas for Joe. My mind was already back at work: *Who was that caller? What could he possibly have to tell me that couldn't be said on the phone?*

We passed through the revolving doors into the lobby of our office building. It was relief to be back, to have finished with that lunch. I had done my duty by Joe. I would complete my duty by reading his writing sample when he gave it to me. If appropriate, I would pass along his name to the *Times'* internship program. And then I would be finished with any obligation I might have to this earnest young man.

We waited for an elevator, I for one going up to the newsroom, he for one going down to the mailroom. The indicator lights above the elevators showed us that mine would arrive first.

The door opened with a *ding*. "That was a nice lunch," I told Joe as I stepped inside. "Thanks."

"Maybe we can do it again."

"Maybe. Work's about to get pretty busy, but we'll see." The elevator door scrolled shut. *Finally*. It really had been kind of a pleasant lunch and I wasn't sure why I felt so glad to be away from him. But I did.

The newsroom was busy when I returned just after two o'clock. Afternoon was the time when every work shift intersected. Morning reporters were finishing up. Evening reporters were getting started. Regular nine-to-fivers like me were eating at desks or returning from lunch. (Nine-to-five being a misnomer, of course, since most of us never stopped working. We tended to carry our company-issued laptops everywhere we went. Some reporters even claimed to sleep with them in their beds.)

Keyboards clacked, voices hummed and even in this age of cyber-documents papers littered desks like fallen leaves. Desks were pressed together, separated by aisles punctuated with support columns decorated by clocks, calendars and maps. Personal muses, things like family photos and children's drawings, were positioned low to give a sense of individual space and also to spare everyone else your idiosyncrasies. One desk, however, stood out. A political writer of some renown had built a castle wall out of Lego pieces glued together along the aisle edge. Incredibly, with all the activity, with people whizzing along the aisles in pursuit of late appointments or extra coffee to fuel whatever story they were chasing at the moment, that Lego wall was never compromised. Not even a dent. I had come to think of the newsroom as a stage where a kind of dance took place. Despite the clutter, there was a sense of precision here, a Pilobolus of highly intentioned actions and reactions which each day resulted in one of the world's most-read newspapers.

I walked to my desk, greeting anyone who wasn't absorbed in something. On the way, I ran into the city editor, Elliot Lee. A skinny man of about forty-five, with sleek black hair grey-dusted at the temples, he was the most formal person in the newsroom and looked terrific in the handmade suits he wore, like today, when he had meetings with outsiders. Other days he tended to dress down in pressed grey pants, blue shirt and no tie, trying to fit in by being more relaxed without compromising his authority. It was a delicate balance, which I understood perfectly. Like me, his parents were immigrants, in his case from China, and he was always on the lookout to squash any tendency that might set him apart. One day, without explanation, he wore a peace medallion around his neck, an experiment he never repeated.

Approaching each other in the center aisle, Elliot smiled. His teeth were crowded, with one top front tooth slightly overlapping the other. He raised a flat palm to give me his customary greeting, a stiff high-five.

"How's it going, Darcy?"

"Great."

"Need me for anything? I'm out the door in half an hour so now's the time. Won't be back until after you're gone."

"Nope, I'm good. Thanks."

We slapped hands, smiled and kept on going.

A knot formed in my stomach. Shouldn't I take the opportunity, before he disappeared, to tell him about the mysterious call? Certainly it would earn me a point or two that I had been singled out for a scoop. And it never hurt for someone to know where you were at any given time, particularly at odd hours of the early morning or late night . . . No. I wasn't going to vanish, and I didn't need to tell Elliot about the call. Not yet. There were more seasoned *Times* reporters than I already working various angles of the Atlantic Yards story. What if Elliot decided to hand my source over to someone else? Besides, it was not unusual for people to contact reporters with tips that were dead on arrival. I would see what it was all about before deciding how to handle it.

Settled behind my desk, I listened to voicemail and checked email. Nothing important. Meanwhile I kept replaying that call in my mind: "Meet me at the lot, tomorrow, six a.m. I have something to tell you." The tone was confident. From the moment I answered the phone, he directed the conversation. I assumed he wanted to meet early, before anyone would be at the site, so that we wouldn't be seen together, which meant he wouldn't want to be associated with the information he planned to give me, which meant it had to be good. I had always wondered how reporters cultivated sources whose assured anonymity promised the best scoops. Now I saw that maybe it was the other way around: maybe the source cultivated you. Freelancers who weren't famous did not receive such calls. It was because I was here, at the *Times*, that I had been selected to be the recipient of sensitive information and I admit that this new sense of position, of nascent power, gave me a small thrill.

"Mom, *be there*." Nat slapped a blue photocopy onto the table next to my dinner plate with its little heap of chicken bones, bits of yellow rice and smears of whatever sauces and spices made this Dominican takeout so good. *Variety Show*, the blue paper announced. Nat had been putting his all into practicing a song from *Guys and Dolls*.

"They scheduled it for *tomorrow*?" I said. "Does that say five p.m? On a work day? They tell us *now*? I guess they don't really want people to attend."

"They sent it home last week. I forgot to give it to you. Sorry."

"Oh, *Nat*."

"Can you come, Mom?" Nat, stationed in front of me with his blue bookbag splayed open on a chair beside him, spilling textbooks, notebooks and papers. Nat, who had recently matched my height and was growing by the minute. Nat, with a pimply mustachioed face his father had never seen. Nat, who showered nightly but could never get his suddenly oily hair clean enough. Nat, who was growing that sticky hair into a mop. Nat, my baby, his every vulnerability exposed by hormonal chaos, standing wobbly on the bridge to manhood.

"I'll be there." I got up and stuck the paper to the

fridge with a hamburger magnet that was one of a comfort-food set Nat had given me as a stocking stuffer two Christmases ago. Hugo had taken him to shop for me. "Afterwards we'll celebrate by going out to dinner."

"Great." Nat grinned. "We can grab a bacon burger at Gravy."

"Ha ha ha," I said in my most deadpan voice, which set Nat chuckling. It was the hamburger magnet: a constant reminder of my legendary lapse from sort-of vegetarianism. During pregnancy my cravings had centered on red meat. Right after Nat was born I went back to drawing the line at chicken and fish but I was never able to shake off Hugo's amusement at seeing me consume those late-night half-pounders. He had loved a good steak and my sudden intense relationship with burgers validated his carnivorous appetite. After that, I never again tried to sway him on the issue of red meat though he made a point of buying the organic version, for whatever it was worth.

"I'm thinking more like Japanese or Mexican," I said. "Pacifico maybe. But it'll be your night so you can decide – as long as it isn't Gravy or the diner."

"Or Boco or Raja House. Mom, there are like a million choices along Smith Street and you've outlawed half of them."

"With so much good food around, we can afford to be picky."

"If that's your defense, stick with it." He winked, zipped closed his bookbag and hoisted it to his shoulder. "I'm going to do some homework."

"Clear your place first, please."

"Hey, Mom, *chill*."

"I am chilled. I just want you to clear your place."

"Obviously you can't hear your own tone."

But what had been wrong with my tone? Lately he'd been accusing me of being "neurotic". But I wasn't neurotic; just sad and anxious since losing Hugo. I believed my sensitivity was normal and hoped it would pass. Anyway I figured that my newly teenaged son was himself oversensitive, which was also normal, though lately both of our emotions had run very, very high. Which was also *normal*. Our shock and grief and loneliness for a dead man were *normal normal normal*. Knowing that didn't help us much, though I found myself constantly repeating the mantra of our normality to reassure myself.

Nat cleared his place with his two-ton bookbag lagging off one shoulder, dipping him to the right. I wanted to point out that this imbalance could someday lead to back problems but kept it to myself.

"How much homework do you have tonight, anyway?"

"I don't know. Some."

"I have to be out really early tomorrow morning, OK?"

"No problem."

"I mean *early*, about five forty-five."

"Whoa. Don't wake me up."

"I won't, just be sure to lock up and carry your cell phone to school and—"

"Yeah, Mom. OK. *Got it*."

I smiled at my son. He nodded and smiled back as he moved through the kitchen into the adjoining living room and the staircase leading upstairs where we had our bedrooms.

"I'll be up in a few minutes," I said, but he gave no indication that he'd heard me. It didn't matter. I had decided that this would be my tactic: *To be there for him*, a constant presence, whether or not he asked me to. *To love him* regardless of tone of voice or choice of words or style of clothes or level of attention or quality of attitude. *To communicate with him* without holding against him the silences enforced by unanswered questions or rejected cell phone calls. He was a teenage boy and he showed his love for me on whim. He was the child, I was the grown-up. He needed me and I knew it. And I never, ever forgot that this boy had lost his father.

I scraped my plate into the garbage can, the bones gathering atop a pungent cantaloupe rind from that morning. Mitzi and Ahab, our cats, came running as always on the assumption that sounds from the kitchen meant a feeding; they loved their food. I rubbed their faces, scratched their backs, petted their stomachs. When they realized they weren't getting a second dinner, they wandered away. I did the dishes and shut off all the downstairs lights.

Upstairs, Nat's door was closed and music was playing. I could see from the cracks around his door that the light was on. He was probably studying – or about to begin.

Nightgowned and washed, I settled into bed with my laptop perched on my stomach. I entered the time and address of tomorrow's early meeting on my calendar and then made an online order for a few pairs of jeans for Nat to replace the ones from six months ago he'd already outgrown. Then I checked my email – nothing important – and wrote one to my best friend Sara, one of the many treasures I'd left behind on the Vineyard. Moments after sending it the instant message box appeared on my screen telling me that she was online. We rarely phoned each other at night so as not to wake anyone; these late-night chats had become almost a habit.

"So?" she began, picking up wherever we'd left off last time we cyber-talked.

"Yes?"

"Did you see him again?"

"See who?"

"Did you?"

"No."

"Dating your kid's teacher is unprofessional."

"Motherhood isn't a profession, it's an art! ☺"

"LOL. If you keep seeing him I'm going to have to come down there and meet him to make sure he's right for you."

"Come soon. I miss you. Kids OK?"

"Great. Sleeping. Miss you too. So that guy is working at the *Times*? I couldn't believe your email . . . you sure it's him? . . . he was kind of strange."

"Kind of."

"Nice lunch date? ☺"

"Stop!"

"Can't say I'll miss him. Gave me the creeps kind of."

"Yeah, kind of, I know what you mean."

"Hmm. Exhausted. Goodnight, sweetie."

"Goodnight. Love you, Sara."

"xoxoxoxoxo"

After closing the IM box I ran email one last time. Speak of the devil: Joe had sent his writing sample. The file attachment looked small so I opened it, figuring I'd get it out of the way. It was a 750-word essay called "The Wild Life of Martha's Vineyard" which made me laugh. While the island was home to wildlife galore there was no place less wild than Martha's Vineyard, where our largest town Oak Bluffs was known locally as "sin city" but would qualify as a tame village anywhere else in the country. Nice double entendre in the title to set the tone right away. I read with high hopes.

Hopes which were quickly dashed. His writing was flat and meandering. Without irony or insight, he covered the various wildlife refuges around the island, where they were, their acreage, inhabitants, funding and so on and on and on that by the time I reached the end my brain felt anesthetized. Wildlife could be a most interesting subject and he had killed it. I wouldn't be able to recommend him for an internship based on this sample.

I wrote him back with what I thought was a fairly neutral email, thanking him for showing me his piece and saying that I'd enjoyed it but felt he should work on his writing some more before applying to the internship program because he'd probably only have one shot. I thought it was a sensitive note and that he would humbly accept my seasoned advice. Within moments I learned how wrong that assumption was.

"I thought you cared about me," he wrote in an email that arrived in my mailbox almost instantly.

Cared about him? I hardly knew him. A loud bell went off in the back of my mind: *Do not answer this, shut down your computer, go to sleep.* But I ignored it.

"I do care," I wrote back, not adding how annoyed I was to be lying in bed at night having this email conversation when I had to be up at 5 a.m. "Every writer has a learning curve and all I'm suggesting is that you take some more time with it so you can really perfect your craft." Which was bullshit. He was a terrible writer and if I were honest I'd tell him to find a new aspiration. "Please don't take my comments personally, Joe. And don't worry; you are going to be a great writer!"

"I don't think you mean it," he wrote back right away, "but thanks for saying so. Lies can be a kind of grease that's OK so long as it keeps the cogs and wheels spinning. Right?"

"I don't like lying," I lied. I *didn't* like it and yet I was doing it right now. "I think it's time to sign off for the night. I'll see you at the office."

"Maybe I should send you another writing sample, something you'd like better?"

"No, it's OK. See you at work."

"Here's one I think you'll like." A very large attachment came along with that email. I didn't answer. Shut down my laptop and turned off the light, hoping to get enough sleep before my alarm went off.

Moments later the phone rang. Caller ID on my bedside table listed his name, Joe Coffin, and my heart leaped.

I got up and opened my bedroom door. Nat's door was still shut.

"Don't answer that," I said across the dark hall.

"Why would I?"

It was true: Nat always answered his cell phone when it was one of his friends calling but rarely the home phone unless he saw that it was for him.

"Goodnight, honey. Sweet dreams."

It rang ten times before voicemail picked up. And then the ringing started up again.

CHAPTER 2

It was still dark out when I arrived on foot at a grouping of empty lots on Pacific Street near Flatbush Avenue, about ten blocks from my house. The edge of this nineteenth-century neighborhood, with its tangle of brownstones and stores, had been diagnosed with "urban blight" by the city and defended by a hearty opposition to the wrecking balls of eminent domain as a thriving mixed-use district. I stood in front of an open space that wasn't here last week, proof that the city had won the argument. Nine buildings had been demolished all at once, creating a toothless space that made you wish they could leave it empty as it had been hundreds of years ago before civilization came along to improve on nature. It always surprised me when I remembered that the islands of New York City had once been as pristine as Martha's Vineyard, the protection of which had been one long civic battle.

I stood there waiting in the darkness, hugging myself for warmth and craving coffee. I had planned on getting a cup of takeout along the way but nothing was open. I was exhausted in that brain-buzzy way, that I-might-lose-my-balance way, having been unable to get to sleep for hours after Joe finally stopped calling. He had called six full sets of ten rings each, each set truncated by voicemail, before finally giving up. Six sets, sixty rings. By the time my alarm clock turned on the radio at five o'clock I'd slept maybe two hours.

Quick, echoing footsteps drew my attention toward Flatbush, a normally hellacious avenue which at this hour was calm, with only the occasional car or truck rumbling by. A very tall man in a suit and tie walked in my direction. White guy, wearing a black backpack and a bright yellow bike helmet, which he removed as he came closer. He had sandy, thinning hair and wore rimless rectangular glasses. His hand was sweaty as he reached out to shake mine.

"Everything I say is off the record," he said.

"Then how can I help you?"

"I'm an 'anonymous source'. That's how you'll refer to me."

"And if I need to find you?"

He smiled. His teeth were straight as soldiers and tea-yellowed. Up close, in the waning moonlight, his skin had a papery glow.

"Abe Starkman. Project Manager, Department of Buildings. That's for your information only."

"OK. It's off the record. Why am I here?"

"Come."

He led me partway down the block to the empty lot where the chemical factory had stood. Orange lines had been spray-painted to mark out individual lots. At the front of the factory lot, my lot, was an uneven blue X.

"What's that?" I asked.

"All work's been halted."

"Just here?"

"Yes. Just this lot."

"Since when?"

"Yesterday."

In the passing light of a truck I saw that despite the chilly air a sweat had gathered on Abe's forehead. He drew a tissue out of his pants pocket to wipe it off. Glanced at the lot and the blue X as if to remind himself that he had made a decision to talk to me. And continued.

"Someone from Buildings is going to call you later."

"To say they filed a stop work order?"

"Yes, and to tell you why."

I took a small pad and pen out of my bag and
flipped it open. He stopped talking. Through his
glasses I saw that his eyes were a milky blue. Not a
muscle moved on his face yet the sweat had
regathered like a storm. I had a feeling that this was
a man of rules, a bureaucrat. Talking out of school,
watching me note his every word, clearly made him
uncomfortable. I put my pad away.

"The person who calls you will tell you that toxic
chemicals were found buried in sealed drums. He'll
tell you that the contents of the drums are unknown
and the department hasn't determined yet whether
it's seeped into the earth. He'll tell you they halted
work at this lot until a determination can been made.
He'll tell you they're acting on our behalf, for our
safety. You'll be referred to Russet Cleanup to
answer more questions. Russet will tell you more
lies."

Two cars sped past on Flatbush, racing each other,
trailing harmonizing notes of blowing horns.

"The truth is that the work was stopped because
one of the workers found bones."

"Bones?"

"Human bones."

"I see." Though I didn't, not fully. "Why can't
they just tell the truth?"

"Because the truth scares them. It could expose
more truth that could devastate the Buildings

Department and even City Hall."

I glanced at the lot, delineated in the darkness by bright orange lines, and saw now that the dirt had been raked smooth.

"How many bones?"

"Seventeen. All we know now is that they come from at least three different people."

"Did they make any identification?"

"No, not yet. The bones are old though they're not sure how old."

"Months? Years?"

"Decades. Possibly older."

"As in it could be remains from an early settlement? That old?" Though even as I suggested this, it seemed unlikely. How could historical artifacts possibly threaten today's City Hall?

"Unlikely, but anything's possible. The factory's been there since nineteen seventy-eight so the bones have been there at least that long."

"In your opinion, Abe, what are some other possibilities?"

"It's just an opinion, you understand that."

"Yes."

"Nineteen lots in this project, including this one, were sold to the developer, Livingston & Sons, by a company called Metro Partners. But Metro's a dummy company – it's a front for Tony Tarentino."

Tony T, as he was known, was a local mob boss.

One of his lieutenants had been arrested on racketeering charges last year and his trial was about to begin in downtown Brooklyn's federal court. For a few minutes last week it was the talk of the newsroom until we moved on to something else.

"But it wasn't an easy deal. The city had to intervene – help negotiate."

"Eminent domain battles are never easy."

"We expect that. But when Tony finally sold, it was at a considerable market value loss."

"Why?"

A half-grin crooked Abe's mouth and the sudden muscular shift cast his face in cynicism. Maybe not cynicism, exactly. Resignation. His was the disappointment of a public servant whose conscience was forcing him to discredit his own agency. At least that was how it seemed on the surface. I had never heard of Abe Starkman until today and couldn't know if anything he was telling me was even plausible.

"What was the deal?" I asked.

"I don't have any details right now, but I'm looking. Meanwhile it's no secret that the mayor has encouraged his people to do everything possible to push forward redevelopment of the Atlantic Yards – it's to be one of his signature legacies. And remember, he was a businessman before he got into politics; he doesn't mind hopping into bed with a developer if it helps him get what he wants, better yet if no traces of the encounter are left behind. But helping to broker a deal with Tony T, well, that was bound to leave a mess, sooner or later – and here it is."

"Where are the bones now?"

"Forensics storage. Shelved. Queens Property Clerk, voucher 12-84992."

I was meant to remember that but never would so I took out my pad and quickly noted it.

"If they're cold-casing it why stop work and why concoct a story?"

"To make sure they've got all the bones. They'll finish excavating so if they ever need the bones for future reference, they won't have to tear down the building."

"Like for a RICO investigation that reaches past Tony T."

"Et cetera."

"But they're not going to make it a priority to ID the bones now?"

Abe shook his head. "The bones could point back to the Tarentinos. If there was something untoward about the deal for the land, and if the city tries to backpedal now, in light of these bones, on some presumed promise of leniency in the racketeering trial, then Tony T would be . . . unhappy."

"God forbid."

"Well, I wouldn't want to be the person who made any promises."

"Were you?"

"No."

"Who?"

"I can't be sure."

"Guess."

"That's all I can tell you. At least three people were buried in this lot and we'll never know who. Their families won't have closure. That's what bothers me so much, I think. And the possibility that after twenty-five years working my heart out for a city I love they would sell out to the bad guys for a real estate deal that's going to make a few developers rich, and be the jewel in our mayor's crown if everything goes his way. It disturbs me. And the scheming going into the cover-up – that disturbs me, too." He wiped his forehead again and checked his watch. Tendrils of sunlight were reaching into the dark sky. He glanced over his shoulder at Flatbush Avenue. "Be very careful what you do with this."

"I will."

"But please don't turn your back on it." He caught my eye and I nodded, and implicit in that nod was a promise we both acknowledged in silence. Then he turned and walked away.

I watched him, tall and straight in the early dawn. He buckled his bike helmet under his chin and disappeared around the corner. I walked down to Fourth Avenue where I could catch a subway into Manhattan. On the corner of Fourth and Pacific I saw Abe Starkman whizzing past on a white racing bike, shoulders hunched over his handlebars and necktie flapping behind him.

It was easy getting a seat on the subway this early. I jotted notes all the way into midtown. Abe Starkman had tossed me a giant hot potato. I needed to think it through and do some preliminary research. When I had some information to bolster (or not) his credibility, then I would talk with Elliot, my editor. But my brain was buzzing in a bad way and thinking clearly right now wasn't easy. I slipped my notebook into my bag, sat back and closed my eyes until the train pulled into 42nd Street.

The first thing I did when I ascended onto Seventh Avenue was get coffee and a bagel at the nearest deli. While I had been in the tunnels the sun had fully risen and the morning rush had started. I took a few sips of coffee – the warm caffeine bursting awake synapses in my brain – then walked toward the *Times* building carrying my brown-bag breakfast in one hand and dialing Nat on my cell with the other hand. I had to call twice before he groggily answered.

"Mom?"

"Up and at 'em, Sonny Boy. Time for school."

"What time is it?"

"Almost seven fifteen."

"Where are you?"

"Walking into my office building. Pushing the elevator button. About to step into the elevator and lose this connection. Eighth floor, seventh, sixth, here it comes."

"Spare me the countdown."

"Are you getting up?"

"Hey, Mom, who kept calling last night? That was loco."

"Totally loco. In fact, better not answer it this morning if it starts ringing again."

"Trust me, I won't."

"Remember to lock up behind you when you leave and—"

"Mom!"

"OK! I love you, Nat. Have a great day. I'll wait for you outside school after the show."

"See ya later, Mom."

The newsroom was humming when I walked in and headed to my desk. Courtney, a young Metro crime reporter I'd befriended, was talking on the phone, leaning back in her chair with her long legs crossed at the knee. Her straight blonde hair was pulled back in a ponytail, which generally meant she planned to stay in the office writing until her shift ended midday. She had long, lustrous hair she always deployed in its full glory when out on assignment. Though I was older by a decade we had bonded in our agreement of how our femininity, though in some ways it held us back professionally, was inevitably part of our arsenal. Where we differed was in precisely how to use it. She was of a younger generation who wore high heels and short skirts and expected to go far. I was of an older generation who feared that if we dressed that way at work we'd end up nowhere. Plus I had life experience that told me that you went farther on brains and integrity. Courtney had those in spades but she also had the legs and the hair. I couldn't blame her for using them to her advantage though it worried me to think that her *feminine wiles* approach might cause some kind of professional backlash sooner or later.

I winked at Courtney and lifted my chin in hello, not wanting to disturb her call, but there was something she wanted to communicate to me enough that she gestured to my brown bag, shook her head and shrugged her shoulders. I had no idea what she was trying to get across.

Until I reached my desk. The roller shade was partway down, blanketing half my desktop in shadow. The other half looked stage-lit, accentuating the fact that a breakfast identical to the one in my bag had already been delivered for me.

The poppy bagel with chive cream cheese was

sliced in half and laid out on a white paper plate with crinkled edges. Beside it a paper cup, I LOVE NEW YORK with a red heart for *love* leaning along two sides, sat with its lid pressed tightly on. Coffee, I assumed. Coffee with milk, just as I liked it. What else had Brian at the corner deli revealed about my tastes yesterday when Joe and I waited in line?

Joe. Sleep stealer. I emptied my brown paper bag, removed the breakfast I had bought, put this other breakfast in the bag and rolled closed the top. Then I tossed the bag into the garbage can. Only now did I see the note he had left with the food:

Sorry about last night, Darcy. I was too eager for feedback. I feel terrible that my calling probably bothered you. It won't happen again. Promise.

That defused my irritation enough to stop and think. He realized he had made a mistake and he was sorry. He had bought me breakfast as a peace offering, which was actually a thoughtful gesture, wasn't it? I had a choice: I could hold a grudge and things would be really uncomfortable whenever I ran into him at work, or I could accept his apology and let it go. I ate my breakfast and stewed on it. Finally I decided on number two, forgive and forget. Hugo had talked a lot about the power of diplomacy, not getting self-righteously stuck on the finer points of a conflict, how important it was to stay focused on the larger picture. I wasn't sure exactly what the conflict with Joe had been about – had I bruised his ego? – but I would give him the benefit of the doubt. He was ashamed of himself. Wasn't that enough punishment? Anyway, I had other, more important things on my mind and didn't want to fret too much about Joe and his youthful preoccupations.

I checked email while finishing my breakfast. After a few minutes Courtney came over and leaned on my desk.

"So what's with the new guy from the mailroom?"

I shook my head, smiled, leaned back in my chair. "He used to live on Martha's Vineyard. We didn't exactly know each other but he recognized me and we had lunch yesterday. Yada yada yada."

"He's got a crush on you."

"I'm not so sure about that. I think he's just new here and he wants to make connections."

"I saw him drop off the breakfast. The way he set it up – he rearranged it twice. He likes you."

"Maybe. But if he does, he shouldn't."

"Puppy love," she said, and leaned in to needle me some more when her ringing phone summoned her back to her work.

I expected Joe to stop by my desk and continue the drama of his overenthusiasms, taking the temperature of his apology and so on. But two hours passed with no sign of him, which was nothing if not a relief.

I got to work on the bones story. The first thing I did was check out Abe Starkman, who on paper looked squeaky clean in a way that correlated with what my intuition had told me in person: that he was a whistle-blower, the real thing. Next I went to the Department of Buildings website and found the public record for the purchase of the nineteen lots: a deal between Metro Partners, the seller, and Livingston & Sons, the buyer, just as Abe had described. Then I checked out Russet Cleanup, a toxic waste removal outfit that had been in business under two years and had already racked up complaints with the Better Business Bureau though no city violations, which seemed a paradox as normally the two went hand in hand. Everything, so far, seemed to bolster Abe's version of events.

Just after nine, Elliot arrived. He whizzed through the newsroom nodding and helloing and high-fiving all the way to his corner office. His next move was always to review phone messages then make his way to the coffee pot that sat on a low bookcase across the newsroom. As soon as he installed himself behind his desk, I poured two cups of coffee and headed to his office.

"Thank you!" As he took the styrofoam cup he

quickly sipped to make sure it was prepared to his liking, light with half a packet of sweetener. One of the first things a reporter learned in Elliot's newsroom was how he drank his coffee; it was the surest way to snag his attention before other business did.

"Mind if I close the door?"

He raised his eyebrows. "Go ahead."

I shut the door and sat across from him. His hair was still wet from the shower and he wore a pristine white shirt open at the neck. I suspected he'd been up for hours as his wife also worked and they had young daughters whose nanny often arrived late. I could imagine the mad rush for the shower and the door. A portrait of his family smiled at me from an enlarged photo propped on a file cabinet behind him.

He took another drink of his coffee then set it down beside him and leaned forwards, arms folded together on his desk, ready to listen.

I told him everything about the phone call yesterday and my meeting with Abe Starkman to whom I referred only as an "anonymous source who works at the Department of Buildings".

"Did you get the call yet?"

"Nope. But it's still early. Buildings doesn't open until nine."

"Right. They'll want it to seem as normal as possible. When they do call, Darcy – *if* they call – treat it like you would any other piece of information

coming from a government agency. Take notes, get
contact info and thank them. If they tell you to call
Russet Cleanup, call Russet Cleanup. Then come
talk to me and we'll take it from there. No story until
we investigate this fully. Ticking off City Hall is not
something we like to do on an everyday basis. OK?"
He shifted to face his computer. I could see he was
itching to move his day along.

"One more question, Elliot."

"Yup."

"I'd like it to stay my story. I mean, after they do
their environmental bit with me about the chemical
drums and Russet. I'm very interested in this."

He considered me a moment. "I'm sure you are. It
could be very interesting. But government corruption
isn't your area of expertise . . . so we'll see."

"Some people think government corruption and
environmental issues are exactly the same thing."

He smiled, then repeated himself: "We'll see."

"Should I check out the bones in the meantime?
Make sure they really exist?"

"Not yet. Let me think on it. Just wait and see if
that call comes."

I got back to work, on alert for the phone to ring.
It didn't. Meanwhile I hunkered down to see how
much information I could wrest out of public and
private databases, LexisNexis and the *Times*' own
archives. I searched for stray facts, back story, local

history, mob lore, anything that seemed reasonably connectable to Abe's claim about the dug-up bones. For example, I learned that prior to 1978 when the chemical factory was built the city had seen 558 presumed mob hits to seventeen related murder convictions to almost ten thousand unsolved missing persons cases. Whole people had vanished off the face of the earth, thousands in this city alone, since they started keeping records in the mid-1800s. Prior to 1978 two other buildings had stood in that very spot, the first having been erected in 1795 and the second in 1871. For over two hundred years the only opportunities to hide bodies in that lot had been just after the American Revolution, at the birth of the industrial age and in the drug-addled disco-crazed late 1970s.

It was only a guess but I chose door number three, 1978. And I was intrigued by Abe Starkman's assertion that Tony T may have gotten a better deal than the developer-city silent partnership had realized when they (allegedly) brokered an agreement to buy his land for part-cash, part-favors. The city wouldn't have factored in that their blind eye would have to encompass three murder victims and leave them forever unnamed. No wonder they wanted the bones to disappear into the forensics stacks. It was safer for the city to sweep this one under the rug and leave it there. And it would be safer, for Abe and me and the

Times, to forget about it, too. Business–government–mob corruption was an old and dangerous story.

But the bones, if they were real, had a story to tell. Leaving those people unnamed and forgotten would be an unspeakable lapse in our own humanity. In my heart I knew that we had to find out who they were . . . and how they got there. Hugo's death had taught and was teaching me so many things, one of which was that you completely lose someone only when you stop remembering.

The afternoon came and went without the awaited phone call. I had to leave the office at four to make sure I'd be seated in the theater at Nat's school for the five o'clock performance. Park Slope's M.S. 51 was one of Brooklyn's most popular middle schools but every subway was at least a ten-minute walk away. Luckily I made it on time and didn't miss a moment of the show, an hour and a half of joyous small moments that got my mind off the bones and Joe and my exhaustion and onto what was most important. Nat was important. His song was important and especially important was his voice, booming and creaking as it swung through the raucous number his teacher had chosen. Nat had wanted to sing a ballad, slow and sad, but his teacher had given him this happy comedic song instead. I could practically see his bogged-down spirit lift as he sang, center stage, alone in a spotlight. When he was through, applause was thunderous. I clapped louder than everyone else, my eyes filling with tears. Before the applause had fully died down I heard a voice lean in behind me.

"He's awesome."

I turned around and there was Rich, sitting one row back: dark-reddish hair, soft blue eyes, freckly complexion, as always wearing jeans and a T-shirt so he'd be ready for anything in his art classes. I knew from Nat that Rich was a favorite teacher, not just of his but almost everyone. I understood why: he was warm and friendly and easy to talk to. He had an unusual openness that made him good to be around. At our second and last meeting – or "date" as Sara would call it though I had not yet had the nerve to think of it that way – we had agreed to get together again this Friday night. I was to meet him at his home studio where I could see the art he did for himself, his "real art" as he called it. We'd also agreed that, when we ran into each other at school, we would keep our personal relationship private.

"Isn't he?"

"You OK?"

"I always cry. Can't help it. I cry at everything."

The next performer cartwheeled onto the stage in a red leotard.

After the show I waited outside school for Nat.

Students and parents flowed out onto the street, and flowed and flowed, but Nat didn't appear until almost everyone else was gone. I nearly fell asleep on my feet, I was that tired, until the moment I saw Joe on the corner of Fifth Avenue and Fifth Street.

Adrenaline pumped into my blood and woke me up faster than any amount of caffeine could have. What was Joe doing here?

But no sooner did I see him than he vanished in a clump of people who moved across the street when the light changed. My eyes stayed with the people but when they dispersed at the next corner – no Joe. I stepped forwards, thinking I would go after him, if only to make sure I'd actually seen him and not someone else my sleepless brain had transformed into him. *Had* he been there? Had I *imagined* him? I got all the way to the corner when I heard Nat's voice.

"Mom?"

I turned around and waved as he caught up with me.

"Where were you going?"

"I thought I saw someone I knew."

"It looked like you were leaving."

"I waited a long time. Where were you?" But I shouldn't have asked. My darling son ignored the question. So I changed the subject by telling him, "You were great!" We walked to the subway, discussing the show and debating restaurants for dinner. As we walked I kept my eyes open for Joe but didn't see him again. I now questioned whether I had actually seen him in the first place. I was so tired, my eyes were foggy; it could have been any young man who looked even a little bit like him.

It was just this kind of uncertainty that had kept me on guard since Hugo died, this new and unwelcome insecurity in my own perceptions. It *was* possible that I only thought I'd seen Joe because I was so exhausted and aggravated with him for making me exhausted. Was my mind projecting ghosts of my disquiet onto the streets now? If so, it wouldn't be the first time. A little over a year ago, I was convinced I saw Hugo driving past me in a car. I was sure of it and, in a panic, called the Vineyard medical examiner's office to confirm that Hugo Mayhew had in fact died five months earlier. That was the moment I thought I might be losing my mind, and it was the beginning of a decision-making process that convinced me I had to leave the island.

I once read a book about widows called *Onto the Pyre*. I had grown up with a widow, my mother, and so the subject had long fascinated me before I became one myself. Psychologists had documented a wide range of feelings and reactions after the loss of a spouse, with wilder fluctuations among women, which is why widows were chosen as the book's focus. More men than women died within a year after the death of a lifelong spouse – they actually called it *dying from a broken heart*. Women overall appeared to be more resilient. Many grieved for a while and then set about rebuilding new, different lives. Others nursed their grief indefinitely, gaining strength from memory. A few refused to react much at all once the initial shock passed and put their energies into remarrying as quickly as possible. Some were broken in ways that never repaired fully but managed to live usefully. Some threw themselves into family, others into work. A few snapped completely and went insane. My mother had devoted herself to family (me) and work. I liked to think I was following in her brave footsteps.

Times like tonight, with Nat, were emotionally anchoring. Ultimately, I liked nothing more than being alone with my son, particularly when we were out of the house and away from all the stuff we needed to do. He reminded me so much of Hugo and yet he wasn't Hugo, he was himself, and regardless of everything that had happened he was blossoming before my eyes.

We ate Middle Eastern food in a packed restaurant on Smith Street. Then we walked slowly home, browsing in store windows along the way. He indulged me at the window of an upscale shoe store and I indulged him at the window of a comics store.

It was eight thirty before we got home. Nat started on homework and I called my office voicemail to check messages.

The call from the Buildings Department had come in at four fifteen, soon after I left for the show. A man named Ian Wright had left a message for me to call him back regarding the cleanup of the factory site. I would return the call first thing in the morning. Then presumably I would call Russet Cleanup. If what Wright and Russet told me corresponded with what Abe Starkman had said they would tell me, I would be back in Elliot's office seeking permission to look for the bones.

CHAPTER 3

It rained on Wednesday and I arrived at the office waterlogged in my raincoat, rain boots and with a soggy umbrella too wet to put anywhere without soaking everything it touched. Minus an umbrella stand, the women of the office took to using the bathroom on such days as this, devoting one sink to umbrella drainage. I dropped mine into the pile, fixed my hood-squashed hair, shook out my coat and went to my desk.

Where I found a bagel and coffee waiting, just like yesterday. And now Courtney's observation about the punctiliousness of the presentation really hit me. The bagel's slice was angled at a perfect diagonal and one of the cup's I LOVE NEW YORKs was positioned front and center. It was exactly the same except today's note was different:

Good morning! Don't let the rain dampen your spirits! Oh well, I guess today won't work for another picnic. Joe

I glanced at Courtney, who rolled her eyes but kept typing at lightning speed. I knew she was on deadline so didn't bother her. Dumping my bag on the floor and my raincoat over the back of my chair, I lifted the plastic-lined garbage can and with one sweep of my arm donated the breakfast to the janitor. Then I searched Joe Coffin in the company's online directory and dialed the mailroom's extension. His supervisor summoned him to the phone.

"Good morning!" he said when he heard my voice. "You don't have to thank me; it was my pleasure."

"I'm not calling to thank you, Joe. I want you to stop."

"You're cranky. Didn't you sleep? I didn't want to call last night because—"

"Don't call me at home again, please. And there's no need to get me breakfast, OK? It's nice of you but . . ." And here I caved. I couldn't bring myself to say what I really wanted to which was *it's worse than annoying, it's creepy*. "It's unnecessary. I've been trying to eat at home. It's a waste of food."

"OK." He said it simply, like a fence collapsing in a slight breeze.

"OK. Well."

"I'm sorry, Darcy. I guess I'm coming on too strong. I just don't have any other friends in New York."

"You will. Give it time. You just got here." All the platitudes I could think of to get this guy to leave me alone without outright hurting his feelings.

"I was hoping you could show me around the neighborhood. I'm moving to Brooklyn soon."

My insides thumped. It had only been two days since he'd mentioned he might look into it. *Had* I spotted him yesterday in Park Slope?

"Where?"

"Red Hook. Everywhere else was way too expensive."

"Did I by any chance see you in Park Slope yesterday evening?"

"No, I was in Red Hook, seeing my new apartment." But his answer came too quickly and sounded rehearsed. And yet why would he lie? He had already told me he'd been in Brooklyn and was going to move. "It isn't fancy but I think you'll like it. I thought maybe after I settled in, you and your son could come over for dinner."

"Joe . . . please listen to me. I'm a lot older than you and my life is in a different place. I'm a mother. I'm a widow. I've even got a boyfriend." I blurted out the part about the boyfriend, an exaggeration because Rich was *not* my boyfriend, but my defenses were up and I knew from lifetimes past that the claim of having someone else usually worked to dampen a man's unwanted interest. "And work keeps me so busy I just don't have time for anyone else."

There was a pause before he answered. "It's OK. I understand. We'll be friends."

It was exasperating talking to him. I didn't want to be his friend; I was trying to tell him I couldn't be his friend, so how had we come back to that?

"No, I don't think so. Sorry." I hung up before he had a chance to respond.

Courtney stopped typing long enough to look over at me. "Broke another heart, did you?"

I threw a paperclip at her, she laughed and went back to her story, and I checked my watch to see if it was nine thirty yet. I had decided to give it a little time before making my call to the Buildings Department so as not to seem overeager, as if I already knew too much. Which I did, or thought I did. Tucking away assumptions, I waited another ten minutes and dialed Ian Wright's number.

He answered his own phone which told me that he was not a senior employee, which either meant his higher-ups didn't know about this or they were overconfident. I introduced myself and Ian Wright launched right in, telling me everything Abe Starkman had said he would. Almost to the word.

Next I phoned Russet Cleanup and as instructed asked for Lenny, who confirmed everything Ian Wright had told me.

And so my job was done. Or it would have been if I lived in the land of Mickey Mouse. Did Buildings really think so little of *Times* reporters that they thought they could feed us information and we wouldn't question it? *Would* I have questioned it if not for Abe Starkman? The truth was, I didn't know.

Someone had already brought Elliot his morning coffee so I had to wait twenty minutes for an audience. This time he asked me to shut the door before I could suggest it myself, indicating that he had been thinking about this and took it seriously. And also, possibly, that he was nervous about where it might lead.

"They called?"

"They called. And I made the follow-up call to Russet. It was exactly like my source said it would be. It was like they were reading from a script."

Elliot leaned back and twirled a freshly sharpened pencil between thumb and forefinger. Then he laid it on his desk, picked up the phone and buzzed an in-house extension. Through the glass wall of his office I saw Courtney answer his call and react to his directive: "I'm teaming you on a story with Darcy. A *possible* story. She'll fill you in on the details. This is confidential for now so zip it up." As he said that,

I watched Courtney pull an invisible zipper across her smile.

So that was that. I was on the story. With Courtney. It was unnecessary to question Elliot's decision to pair us; Courtney had experience reporting on criminal cases and would be an excellent guide into that world. Her smile told me that she felt as I did: pleased that we'd be working together for the first time. And apparently she'd said nothing about her deadline, which only confirmed what I already knew about her: that she was a true and hungry reporter.

She filed her story at eleven thirty, half an hour before her deadline, and we went outside together to catch a cab to the Queens Property Office in Long Island City. The morning rain had stopped, leaving behind a humid and overcast afternoon, so we shed our raincoats and carried them with our drip-dried umbrellas under our arms.

On the Queensboro Bridge, high above the East River, Courtney told me a bit about where we were going. It was known as the Pearson Place warehouse and it was the New York Police Department's most notoriously unreliable evidence storage facility. She told me it was better and more organized than in the past but even so I should "prepare myself" and I "wouldn't believe it". When I had told her what we were looking for and why (again, without mentioning Abe Starkman's name), an expression of understanding dawned across her face.

"Pearson would be the perfect place to lose something you didn't want anyone to find until you were ready to help them find it," she said.

We drove off the bridge and along Jackson Avenue for a bit before turning onto Thompson and then Skillman, a long avenue banked on one side by a rail yard. After a few dilapidated blocks we turned onto Austell Place where our taxi pulled to a stop in front of a huge four-story warehouse. We paid and got out. Courtney had been here before, she knew the place and the people, so I held back and let her take the lead.

Which she did, in style. She had on tight jeans, cowboy boots and a tailored purple blouse through which you could see her black lace camisole. Her face was free of makeup but with the hair luminescent down her back and her long, confident stride she came on like a movie star. I followed her through the door into a low-ceilinged anteroom that smelled badly of mildew.

Courtney greeted the receptionist with familiarity, leaning her big white smile right up to the round hole cut into the foggy Plexiglas barrier. "Hey, Tanisha, how's it going?"

"Hi, Courtney." Tanisha looked up from a mound of papers she appeared to be collating very slowly.

"Anand here?"

Without answering, Tanisha buzzed an intercom and summoned Anand. While we waited, Courtney dug into her purse for a lipstick and applied some to her mouth: bubblegum pink. After a minute Anand appeared through an inner door. He was a portly East Indian with swollen lips and tiny eyes that glinted with humor, offsetting the authority of his police uniform.

"Princess!" His voice was the high squeal of a eunuch. He crossed the small room to greet us, one of his hands grasping Courtney's shoulder with sausagy fingers and squeezing the delicate fabric of her blouse. She held her bright pink smile. Behind the Plexiglas I saw Tanisha roll her eyes.

"How am I so lucky today? What brings you? You know I would kill someone myself if that is what it took to get you hunting for evidence."

"You don't need to go that far to get my attention, Anand. I always look forward to seeing you." And on his round cheek she planted a kiss that left a pursed set of bubblegum lips on his skin. He must have known it was there and yet he did nothing to wipe it off; in fact, that kiss stayed on his cheek throughout our visit.

"I see you brought a friend," he said.

Oh, this was ridiculous. We were *colleagues*. But I went along with it and introduced myself. We pressed our palms together in a damp handshake.

"Anand," Courtney said, "we're doing a follow-up on the Innocence Project. It seems like there's been a lot of activity in the past year on DNA testing of old evidence. We're working on a chart. Mind if we poke around in the stacks and check some of the voucher logs for dates?"

"Why should I mind? Come, come."

We followed Anand through the door and into a huge warehouse filled with metal shelving on which large cardboard barrels were stacked. There were thousands of barrels and on each one black hand-written numbers had been scrawled. Voucher numbers, I presumed, like the one Abe Starkman had given me. I wondered why Anand didn't question us for coming to the warehouse for this information when certainly it was available in a database. But the deeper we walked into the yawning space and the more I listened to him prattle with Courtney, the better sense I got of what she had alluded to on the taxi ride over. An atmosphere of unprofessionalism permeated this place. Which explained why someone had chosen to send the alleged bones here instead of to another one of the city's evidence storage facilities . . . because, as Courtney had explained, this was where it was easiest to lose evidence you weren't keen on being found.

The mildew smell in the giant warehouse was worse than in the reception area; here it had a ripe pungency that seemed to seep into my skin. The air itself felt soggy. The walls were raw cinderblock and the floor was covered in cracked linoleum that bulged upwards in places.

"Go to town, Princess. If you need me, you know where I'll be." Anand waved us toward the barrels and walked off in the opposite direction. At the far end of the warehouse I saw another officer seated at one of two pushed-together desks. He had what appeared to be a thermos. A newspaper was spread open in front of him. The other desk held an open laptop and this, I assumed, was where Anand intended to post himself.

"That was too easy," I said to Courtney when Anand was out of earshot.

She grinned. "You see what I mean about this place?"

"I do. So where do we start?"

"The barrels are stored chronologically, so we'll start with the latest arrivals."

We walked past four empty rows of shelving where evidence from as yet uncommitted crimes had been allotted real estate, until we reached the beginning edge of a sea of barrels. We checked each voucher number that had come in over recent weeks but the one Abe had recited, 12-84992, was not among them.

"It's not here," I whispered. "So maybe it doesn't exist."

"This is Pearson. We have to keep looking."

We finally located it in the third row on the ground level shelf, tucked behind another, older barrel that had arrived here over a year ago. One detail Abe had neglected to tell me was that someone had assigned this voucher number the wrong date. Unless he hadn't known about it.

"We need to open it," I said.

"I'll go talk to Anand and the other guy for a little while. You walk the aisles. Pretend to take some notes. Then see if you can get the lid off. Don't make any noise if you can help it. Here." She reached into her purse and handed me a tiny digital camera.

"Are we allowed to take pictures?"

She tilted her head and gazed at me in wonderment at my naiveté. "Darcy, welcome to New York City. Take pictures if you find bones. Quickly. Then cover the barrel back up and come find me."

She walked off, loudly saying, "Keep on going, Darcy. I'll be right back."

"OK!" My voice echoed three times through the warehouse.

I listened to her footsteps walk the long way across the warehouse as I moved slowly through the aisles with pen poised over pad, leaning in to see the long white activity tags on every barrel and scribbling as I went. It worried me that there might be a surveillance camera monitoring the aisles until

I looked up at the fifty-foot-high ceiling: an endless field of stained dropped ceiling but not a piece of electronics in sight.

I returned to the low shelf with barrel number 12-84992. Carefully and quietly, I slid out the barrel blocking it, then slid 12-84992 forwards enough to reveal the round lid. It did not appear to be sealed with anything more than pressure.

Laughter echoed across the warehouse. Courtney was keeping the officers busy.

Wedging my fingertips under the metal rim, I tried to pry it off but it was pressed tightly on and wouldn't budge. I reached into my bag for my house keys. After a minute of loosening the seal in minuscule increments with the tip of a key, I was able to widen an opening enough to fit my fingers under the lid's edge, and push. There was a slight popping sound. I waited, listened: no echo. My hands shook as I lifted off the lid and set it on the floor beside me.

Inside the barrel was a large brown paper bag with the same voucher number scrawled on its side. The top had been rolled down and sealed with a single band of plastic tape. I was afraid that taking out the bag itself would make too much noise so instead I reached in, detached the tape and slowly unrolled the bag.

I could see a haphazard pile of something stick-like inside the bag but it was too dark to tell if it was a pile of bones. I couldn't make out color or shape except that some appeared longer than others. Positioning Courtney's camera over the barrel, low enough to conceal a flash, I took a picture. And for the instant of the flash I saw them: the bones. I took another picture for another glimpse and saw them again: a heap of dirt-stained femurs and tarsals, costals and carpals, mandibles, tali, humeri.

To make sure the photos had come out I checked them in the camera and now saw the images in greater detail: some with a creamy natural hue, some streaked with black, some bulbous at one end, some jagged where they had snapped. In the bag, lit by the flash, they appeared vividly and irreverently tossed together. And I thought of the only thing such an image could evoke in someone of my background. I thought of my father and his boyhood job as a digger in the camps. How many heaps of bones had he seen with his own eyes? And then my imagination, my *memory*, though in fact this was not *my* memory, built the bones into the skeletons of people as my father might have seen them. Recognized them. Friends, neighbors, colleagues . . . family. How had his young brain processed so many thousands of bones? Had he rebuilt them, given them flesh and sight and sound and language? Had he given them the music of life as he dug and buried, dug and dug and buried and buried and buried? These random bones in the bag in the barrel came to life before my eyes as I imagined my father's skeletons had come to life before his. Know them or not, you recognized them, these people robbed of life. They were his echoes.

"Why had *I* survived?" my father had asked me rhetorically when as a girl I snuggled in his lap as he revealed verbal snapshots of his history. He believed in sharing it, teaching it, so its lessons wouldn't be forgotten. "Why me and not them?" And then, after a pause, "Some questions have no answers."

I put the camera on the floor next to my purse. Folded down the top of the bag and resealed the tape. Replaced the lid, tightly. Took two no-flash photos of the outside of the barrel, making sure to get the whole voucher number. Pushed the barrel back on the shelf and carefully, slowly moved the other barrel back into its place as concealer of a mystery. But not for long.

Emerging from the aisle into the cavernous space, I could see Courtney far away at the other end of the warehouse sitting on the edge of Anand's desk swinging her crossed legs. The three of them were playing cards.

"Done!" My voice echoed in two, three, four, five waves of sound.

Courtney slid off the desk and said something that made the men laugh. Then she strode across the space and joined me. We didn't speak until we were outside, walking to the main drag where we hoped we could find a cab. The clouds of earlier had vanished and a strong sun now burned off the residual humidity. We hailed a livery car, got into the ripped back seat and gave the driver our office's address. Then I handed Courtney the camera and she looked at the pictures I'd taken in the warehouse.

"Wow," she said.

"I was tempted to take one of the bones to get it dated at a lab."

"But you didn't, I hope."

"Of course not."

"Good. Though I understand your temptation." Courtney scrolled again and again through the four photos, a deep vertical crease forming in her pretty brow.

"We don't know if the bones are from the site," I said, "except that my source said they are."

She looked at me, the crease deepening. "Exactly."

"How do we find out?"

"I'm thinking we try to get our hands on the transit records for the supposed toxic drums dug up at the site. Mr Livingston and his sons didn't cart the drums or the bones or whatever off the site themselves, and neither did the suits at Buildings. They got someone else to do it. So we find out who did the transporting and see if we can connect any dots."

"All those jobs are bid out. It should be matter of public record."

"Unless they used someone else, to cover their tracks . . . which would look really suspicious, so maybe they didn't. It could go either way. But somewhere there's got to be a record of the delivery to Pearson, if it came from the site, so let's start with that."

I nodded agreement. Paper trails, computer records, voicemails: hard facts. It sounded good to me. For years, until recently, I had to work around the facts. Too many people didn't believe the scientific data about the environment until Al Gore's movie. Now, finally, facts were carrying some weight.

"Our goal is to expose this," Courtney said, "if there's anything to expose. If the city admits to finding the bones in the lot and gets them IDed, we'll have done our job. The whole mess will come spilling out, whatever the hell it is. After that all we do is write it up and collect kudos all around."

She was right. Pulling back the veil of secrecy was our only goal. If we managed that, it might even advance our careers a few notches. I had loved writing about the environment all these years and I intended to continue but I yearned to incorporate more of the larger picture. I had developed an awareness that behind every wind farm and every oil spillage and every organic farmer and every sewage disaster there was a human drama that had come to impact the environment. I had long wanted the opportunity to widen my scope to examine the social and political context of environmental issues. This story, I hoped, would give me the leverage I needed to make it happen on a national scale at the *Times*.

But it wasn't going to be easy. So far we had one anonymous source, two sets of lies and a bag of bones. Those things together didn't paint a complete picture. We had a lot more work to do.

"Listen," Courtney said, "before I knew I'd be on this, I made an appointment for two o'clock. Mind if I keep it?"

"Not at all. We don't have any deadline, to say the least. We might not even be able to sell Elliot on doing this story."

"With those bones? We'll sell him."

Courtney leaned toward the driver to give him her revised destination, the Cornelia spa on Fifth Avenue. Thus I learned how she liked to pamper herself after meeting a hard-won deadline as she had earlier today: with a massage and a facial. After she got out and shut the door, she leaned back in through the open window.

"Come with me? I bet they could squeeze you in."

"Thanks, but no. I think I'll just head back to the office."

Stationed at my desk in the newsroom, I ate a tuna sandwich and made some notes in my laptop, transferred the photos from Courtney's camera onto my hard drive and then emailed them to her and Elliot, who had gone out to a lunch meeting. Then I phoned Russet, thinking I'd give them the benefit of the doubt and let them prove they had received a shipment of drums full of toxic chemicals from my lot at the Yards. Instead of asking for Lenny, this time I spoke with Bruce, the guy who happened to answer the phone. I explained who I was and requested a copy of the bill of lading because I was "anal" and liked to "cross all my t's and dot my i's" before submitting even the smallest article to my editor. Most people accepted it if you claimed to be neurotic and afraid of a tyrannical boss; I had used this excuse many times to extract seemingly insignificant information from sources. As in the past, it worked this time, except for one thing: Bruce couldn't find a receipt of delivery anywhere. He said "it happens sometimes" and "our secretary stinks with paperwork". I accepted his claim of disorganization as easily as he had accepted mine of punctiliousness. We laughed and said goodbye. My next thought was to find a bill of lading on the other end, at the Pearson warehouse. If the bones had been brought there over the last couple of days, even with an incorrect voucher date, the delivery receipt might still be unfiled and if the people at both ends had done their jobs it would show point of pickup as well as drop off. But I would leave that to Courtney, given her way with Anand.

After that I tried to focus on more research but had trouble concentrating. I couldn't stop seeing the bones. In my mind they were becoming links in an Erector set connecting me to my parents and their histories. I kept hearing the echoes. I wanted it to stop.

Suddenly, sitting at my desk, I yearned to see my mother. But it was already after three o'clock and I generally liked to get home by five thirty so Nat wouldn't have to be alone in the house for too long. If I went to my mother's now, by the time I arrived and settled in the visit would be too short for her to have a chance to realize I was even there. My habit was to visit her for lunch on Fridays. I would have to hold on to my feeling until then.

At twenty past three, however, my cell phone rang. Nat was calling, asking for permission to go over to his friend Henry's house to do homework and hang out. It was as if he had read my mind. I told him to go and said I would therefore go uptown to visit Grandma. I promised to be home by six thirty and asked him to also be home by that time. Then I slipped my laptop into my bag, left the office and took a subway to the Upper West Side.

The assisted living community where my mother had lived for the past three years was in a huge pre-war building, formerly a hotel, on West End Avenue. The lobby, plush with red carpeting, reproductions of antiques and a crystal chandelier, was busy this afternoon with the usual combination of attendants and the elegant elderly New Yorkers who lived here. The Alzheimer's patients were sequestered on the seventh floor where a key was required to summon the elevator. I had my own key and was allowed to come and go as I pleased. My mother, like the other patients, did not have a key and could leave only in the company of family or staff. People with Alzheimer's tended to wander and this safeguard was for their own protection. Sometimes I took her out but more and more our visits were contained on the seventh floor, where she was comfortable and would not be confused by the unfamiliar.

Arriving during the time between afternoon snack and dinner, I first looked for her in the common room where she often sat with some of the other residents, chatting or staring through a particular window where a separation between two buildings revealed a slice of the Hudson River. Today she wasn't there and so after greeting the others – three women and one man who had met me dozens of times and acted as though they'd never seen me before – I found my mother alone in her room down the hall.

She was lying on her bed, propped up by pillows, with her eyes closed. But she wasn't sleeping. She opened her eyes as I came near and looked at me blankly, her only child, for what felt like too long. She seemed to wonder who this visitor was – until finally she smiled. Every time I visited now I wondered if this would be the time it happened: when my mother wouldn't recognize me. I dreaded it with visceral revulsion. And it would happen; it was inevitable.

The disease had been stealing my mother's mind bit by bit by bit for seven years now. At first it had been manageable at home with live-in attendants but eventually that arrangement became too tenuous. She had needed round-the-clock specialized care. I was living on the Vineyard at the time and wasn't around to supervise the help or visit often and so I found her this home, which had been wonderful. I had long grown used to the sense, when I stepped off the locked elevator, that I was entering an alternate universe. Even Nat accepted the radical shifting of expectations one experienced in this place. A patient might walk up to you and say anything. Or you could tell someone your life story and a minute later they would ask your name as if they had never met you.

My mother reached up her arms and I leaned down into them, resting my cheek against her velvety skin. Her familiar smell was instantly comforting, a unique perfume of musky body odor and baby powder. Then she lay her head back down on her stack of pillows, soft puffs of white hair fanning out behind her.

"You're a little bit late," she said with that marvelous smile that always warmed her face to counter a criticism.

"Just a little." I didn't bother pointing out that the visit hadn't been planned.

"Do you have much homework today?"

"Not much."

"Good. When you're through you can help me make dinner. Think about what you'd like to eat."

"I will. How are you feeling today, Mom?"

"Fine. I have nothing to complain about, do I?"

"No, you don't."

"There was a picture there, on the wall. He took it down when they repainted. I asked him to put it back up but he still hasn't done it. Will you ask him? The one with the courtyard and the staircase."

"I'll ask him." But *he* was my father and the picture was something I had never seen. She had mentioned it a few times lately and I assumed it was something from her life before I came along, possibly from her own childhood. I had thought of hunting down some picture that fit the bill – courtyard and staircase, how hard could that be? – to see if I could trick her into thinking my father had finally rehung it. But what was the point? If not this absent picture, then some other phantom item would dematerialize to justify her sense that something was missing. Something *was* missing: her memory. More of it was gone every time I came to see her and lately I struggled against the sense that I had already lost her. I had to remind myself that I hadn't, not quite. She was alive, right here next to me. I held her hand as she drifted off to sleep.

I remembered as a child studying this hand, thinking it perfect with its squarish palm and strong fingers. Her blunt fingernails painted red had reminded me of rosebuds as a little girl and I would gather them together into a bouquet. Then I would spread them out and place my small hand in her larger hand, press our fingers together and say, "See? Our hands are exactly the same size." She always agreed with me even though it was obviously untrue. I never questioned, until I got older, why she didn't remarry. We loved each other so powerfully that I didn't see why she would have a need to love anyone else. Later, a mother myself, I understood that this would be the fantasy of any child and asked her why she had never even dated after my father's death. Her answer: "I never met a man good enough to replace him." But she also never looked. I suspected that after my father's suicide she didn't want to do anything to diminish our bond. She recognized its importance to me and knew her abnegation allowed us to live for each other alone . . . until I grew up and left her.

I left her. Her hand in mine now felt weightless. Grey and veined, every bone revealed by fragile spotted skin. Seven years of college and work in Boston, then fifteen years living on the Vineyard. Twenty-two years I lived away from her with just occasional visits. *Well, now I'm back, Mom. We're back together.* But was it too late? I wanted so badly for her to tell me what was happening inside her mind so I could understand her journey. And I wanted to share my own challenges, to tell her about Abe Starkman and the bones, about Joe Coffin and how he'd been bothering me, about Nat and his glorious performance yesterday. I wanted to tell her I'd met a new man I liked and that his name was Rich. Everything. But I knew from experience that sharing details from my life only confused her. We could talk about events that were long past but lately she had lost whole decades of shared memory. She could not grasp that I had ever married much less that my husband had died or that I was a widow or that I had a son who was thirteen or that I now worked at what had been her daily newspaper. I had tried to tell her that I was a staff reporter for the *Times*, knowing that ten years ago she would have been very proud of me, but it slip-slid through her consciousness so fast it was as if I hadn't told her at all. Being with her, it was as if none of the past events that had shaped my life had ever happened. Sometimes it was liberating to pretend with her but I could never sustain the fantasy for long. I always crashed back to earth while she continued to float above it.

I couldn't tell how much of the past her failing memory had obliterated. For instance, did she remember the camps? She never mentioned them. I knew she remembered my father and their early marriage but she seemed to have forgotten his death. She had lost most of the last thirty years. It was a helpless, progressive form of memory loss much like a picture that fades from the top down.

As she slipped away, I found myself wishing that the eraser would reach deeper and wipe out not just her latest memories but the worst ones. If this was happening – and it was, undeniably – then why deposit her back in her childhood? It would be a cruel trick if her disease landed her in her earliest years when she was orphaned in one of the darkest nightmares humanity had ever suffered. Sitting beside her now, holding her frail hand, I prayed she would die before that happened. But if she didn't, if her illness forced her to return to that abysmal time, I would be right here with her, holding her hand, a connection to the present, in the hope that some part of her might realize that she not only survived but went on to find safety and love. Aside from caring for and loving Nat, staying present as a living reminder to my mother of her survival was the most important commitment of my life.

Seeing the bones today had touched the core of this fear: that my mother had also seen the bones. Different bones. That *the echoes*, as she called those memories, might have come back upon her like a tsunami and submerged what was left of her mind.

But sitting with her now as she slept, I felt reassured that it hadn't happened yet. She was still safe. I stayed another hour before kissing her forehead and quietly leaving.

Walking down the deep canyon of West End Avenue, I had a change of heart and decided that instead of going directly to the subway at 72nd Street I would turn around and detour to Zabar's on Broadway and 81st. Nat wouldn't begrudge me the extra half-hour and I would be able to pick us up a delicious dinner not to mention some treats from their bakery. I turned around – and there he was.

Joe. *Definitely* Joe. He was about half a block behind me and until I turned around he had been following me. I was sure of it. For a moment we were face to face. Mine must have registered the shock I felt. His also looked surprised: to have been caught. For a moment his expression appeared suspended between shame and the possibility of a quick-save greeting. The pupil of his gimpy right eye widened as if to drink me in, and then . . .

He turned and ran, *ran*, in the opposite direction.

"Joe!" I went after him. He couldn't follow me and pretend he wasn't. Following me was wrong but pretending he wasn't was even worse. And what was running? Cowardly. Idiotic.

He was a fast runner. Young. With my bag of laptop, books and other stuff weighing down one shoulder, I couldn't keep up.

"*Joe!*"

My voice trailed him as he disappeared around the corner in the direction of Riverside Drive. When I reached the corner, I couldn't see him anywhere. He might have ducked into the lobby of one of the buildings. Or sped up and made it into Riverside Park.

Panting, I ran partway down 74th Street in the direction of the park before giving up. "Joe!" I called again, and stood there, listening helplessly to my voice reverberating down the street. What did he want from me? Why was he following me? How could I make him stop?

CHAPTER 4

In January 1945 my father survived the infamous death march from Birkenau, Poland, by escaping into a forest so dense with snow – snow piled on the ground and snow relentlessly falling – he was able to hide in it. Because he was small and thin, a twelve-year-old boy weighing sixty pounds, he was able to conceal himself from sight behind the trunk of a tree. He waited all afternoon and through the night, his feet frozen in ice-socks that had formed inside the boots he had taken off a camp-mate "who was not so lucky" which was how he'd put it. My father felt lucky, and in the context of the moment he *was* lucky, to be hiding behind a tree trunk in the freezing snow for hours as tens of thousands of skeletons marched along the nearby road. These skeletons who were his comrades and whom he had abandoned with the certainty that at the end of the road would be more death.

Alone in the German countryside, with the last of the thunderous footsteps receding up the frozen road, he finally stepped away from the tree. "I was hot with fear," he said. The fear warmed him as he headed into the woods in the opposite direction from which they had just marched over three days. He ignored his frozen feet, hoping his fear would radiate into them and also warm them. The goal was to get back across the border into Poland and if he was *really* lucky meet up with the Russian liberators from whom they had fled at Gestapo-gunpoint.

He spent five more days alone in the snowy woods, avoiding the road, unsure what direction he'd pursued in reality or what country he was in. He might still have been in Germany or he might have crossed back into Poland; he had no way of knowing for sure. Without food or water, he lived on melted snow and the hope that his older sister – the last member of his family he had seen alive back at Auschwitz before she was transferred to a women's camp – had survived and they would reunite. She had not; they would not. But he didn't know that then. He trudged through the pillow-white frozen woods aware that the enemy could be anywhere and that if he was seen he would instantly be shot and killed. Which to a certain way of thinking would be a kind of luck. Because what he came to fear most was neither being killed nor failing to reach safety but suffering a slow demise alone in these woods.

To deal with this terrible fear he pretended he was already safe. He pretended there was no enemy. He pretended he had not been held captive and starved and degraded for three years, that he had not lost track of or possibly actually *lost* his entire family. He pretended he was simply walking through the woods. "The imagination," he always told me, "is a powerful friend." It was for him.

He did find his way back into Poland and he found the Russian army – or they found him: delirious at the edge of the forest. A couple of kind soldiers installed him in the home of a local farmer sympathetic to the Resistance. Thus my father found the end of the war in a feather bed and a plate of stuffed peppers. He never found his family – father, mother and two sisters – whom it turned out had all died, also alone, in various crematories. But he did, eventually, find Eva Gertlestein, my mother. They recognized each other across a crowded subway in Manhattan in 1952 and married soon after, joining forces in more ways than met the eye.

I had stopped needing my father out of necessity – he was gone – but I had never stopped needing his "powerful friend". I had employed imaginative escape many times, from the moment my father fled life. Had he deliberately taught me this skill to prepare me for his loss? All the hours he spent playing with me, lying stomach-down on the living room floor building castles and houses and amusement parks for my dolls. Later, I learned that reading was one way to escape. Writing, another. Love was an ideal escape in which imagination linked hopes and reality into a resilient web that could cradle you for years. You could escape into the eyes of your child and lose yourself in their needs. Or take up a cause and escape into that, believing your work important enough to give your life to. It was even possible to escape into every nook and cranny of your house, correcting its every imperfection. I had escaped all these ways. But one thing about escape was that you had to welcome the conduit that got you there. Work or love or children. To escape, you had to allow yourself to shift directions in a way that felt compelling.

My father had escaped life-threatening danger through a forest.

My mother was escaping old age by spooling herself back in, rewinding her life to the beginning.

I had escaped my husband's death by returning to my childhood city with the hope that I could help anchor my mother as she gradually departed into the past.

And now I had to escape a man who appeared to be pursuing me.

I had a problem: Joe Coffin. I no longer doubted that he was following me. He had a crush on me – or something – yet there was no one I knew whom I wanted less in my life. Escaping him would take ingenuity. We worked in the same office and soon he was moving to my borough in the general vicinity of my neighborhood. I lay on my bed that night thinking about how to handle it. Picturing myself alone in a snowy forest – an emotional forest, which is where Joe had left me, because that moment when I saw him on West End Avenue I *feared* him in a brand new way – I put myself to the test. What if, in a turnaround, I pretended he didn't exist? I would stop trying to convince him to keep a distance. I would stop talking to him, period. While there was no real comparison between my father's plight and mine, I would pretend, just as he had over sixty years ago, that there was nothing to escape from.

Lying on my bed with my laptop open on my stomach, I pulled up the instant message screen to see if Sara was online. She was; in fact, she had been looking for me.

"How's by you?" she asked.

"You first."

"Melanie had an abscess in her mouth today so

she skipped school so I could take her to the dentist. Which meant I had to miss my appointment with the washing machine repair guy which I've been waiting for for two weeks. Which means he can't come back for another two weeks. Which means the Laundromat in Sin City's gonna be seeing a lot more of me in the near future. Fun."

"Hasn't been brushing her teeth again?"

"Evidently."

"Don't you check for wet toothbrushes?"

"What am I, a spy?"

"If necessary."

"So that was the high point of my day. Now you."

"Joe Coffin is stalking me."

It was the first time I had thought of it in those terms and it shocked me as much as it probably shocked her. The screen dialogue froze for a minute before her response streamed onto the screen.

"Shit. Are you sure?"

"Positive."

"How bad is it? You mean stalking for real?"

"Probably not. I shouldn't have used that word. He followed me once definitely and maybe another time but I'm not so sure about that one because as you know I'm insane and I *see* things. And he keeps leaving breakfast on my desk. Stuff like that."

"You don't see things. If you think you saw him you probably did."

"Anyway I saw him after leaving my mom's tonight. So I've got a problem."

"Avoid him."

"How? We work together."

"Kind of, sweetie. He's in the mailroom, you're not. Ignore him if you pass him in the hall and stuff like that."

"That's what I was thinking. That he would get the message."

"Sure he'll get it. And he's got to be mortified that you saw him tonight."

"True. He was embarrassed after he called me all those times. This is worse."

"It really is. He'll feel like such a jerk. Maybe he'll even quit his job!"

"I can only wish. But you're right. I'll just ignore him and let his conscience do the rest for me."

"Meanwhile want me to check him out here on the Vineyard? I could stop at Copy Cats and ask what they know about him."

"Why not?"

"Will do then. I'll keep you posted. Meantime keep a low profile and get to sleep now because it's already past our bedtimes."

I drifted off to sleep that night calmed to have touched base with my dear friend and content with the solution we both agreed was best.

I decided not to tell Nat about having seen Joe last night; my son did not need this worry. So in the morning, after a quick breakfast together, we went about our usual business. He headed off to school, taking the city bus to Park Slope, and I made my way to the office.

Where I couldn't resist telling Courtney all about having seen Joe. I cornered her in the bathroom when she emerged from a stall as I was stationed at a mirror over the sink applying lipstick, a pale shade intended to appear invisible. Our mirrored faces suspended side by side in rectangular frames, we spoke to each other's reflections.

"He's not cute anymore," she declared after hearing the latest.

"For me he hasn't been cute since Monday, over lunch. And then he was only marginally cute, as in earnest-young-man cute."

"Four days later and he's gone from cute to creepy."

I echoed her final word: "*Creepy.*"

"I think your idea to ignore him is good. Pretend you don't see him. Don't return his calls if he calls. Don't say anything if he brings more of those bagels. Nada. Zippo." She drew a beautifully manicured fingertip across her neck. "He'll figure it out."

"I hope so. I'm still in my review period and the last thing I need is to bring a complaint to Human

Resources before I've been officially approved, you know?"

"Absolutely. And I'll tell you, the director of HR, Paul Assholedley?"

"No!"

"OK, Ardsley. I just can't stand him. He hit on me big time at last year's Christmas party."

Her expression in the mirror was wide-eyed with recalled outrage. I paused on her eyes a moment before asking:

"I thought you liked that kind of response. Gives you power, and all that."

"Not from guys in HR. That's just unethical, you know? It crosses a line."

I did know. Gender politics at work were tricky and could be dangerous and were best avoided if at all possible.

"So you think Paul Ardsley won't think Joe is a real problem, then?"

"I don't know, but my feeling last Christmas was that he thought there was a hands-on policy at work."

"I could tell Elliot."

She considered it. "Not yet. Wait. See if the silent treatment works. I really think it's better to handle this stuff on our own before we complain to a superior."

Complain being the key word. Every woman knew that men thought there was something wrong with us if we didn't like them enough or not in the

ways they wanted us to like them. If we asked them
to keep their distance it was a *complaint*. If we
insisted, we were *shrill*. If we raised our voices, we
were *hysterical*. My being offended by these close
encounters with Joe Coffin could be perceived as
oversensitivity or, worse, *frigidity*. I knew that.
Especially so soon on the job, when Elliot didn't
know me very well yet.

"You're right," I said. "Thanks. I appreciate it."

"Any time, sister." She flipped her long hair over
her right shoulder and faced me. "Bones, anyone?"

I laughed. "You need to call Anand for a delivery
receipt. Russet Cleanup doesn't have one."

"I'm on it."

We left the bathroom together and got to work at
our desks. From mine I could hear "Princess" talking
with Anand over the phone, chatting, zeroing in on
the purpose of her call. I eavesdropped, fascinated
with Courtney's flirtatious interview style, which
obviously she deployed selectively. I had heard her
interview other people and she could be tough as
nails. I still wasn't sure exactly what to make of this
young woman whom I was just getting to know.
From a distance she might have both intimidated and
repelled me for bringing cleavage into the office; but
up close complexities appeared, shades and textures
that belied the *Sex and the City* thing she did so well.

After the call she grinned at me across the space

that separated our desks. Then she did something that surprised and pleased me for its intimacy: she wheeled her chair out of the port of her desk until she was sitting facing me, our knees touching. She leaned in and kept her voice low.

"Here's why I love Anand," she said. "The guys who delivered the evidence bags that day didn't have a bill of lading. Anand knew they weren't regular city contractors and he refused to accept delivery without paperwork. So they made some up on the spot and guess what?"

Just at that moment the rattling sound of the mail-room cart materialized in the newsroom. Courtney and I turned our heads in a synchronized movement that caught the attention of the reporter two desks over. His attention glanced off the two-headed joined-at-the-knee creature that was Courtney and me before returning to his work.

Joe wheeled his cart through the newsroom, deposited mail on about half the desks – not mine – and then wheeled his cart out. For the duration of his presence, about two minutes, I ignored him as planned. I pretended to show Courtney an imaginary document on my laptop screen, pointing and gesturing as I scrolled through a web page I had randomly accessed. Joe also ignored me, which was definitely progress. When the newsroom door swung shut behind him, I breathed.

"That was good," Courtney whispered. "See? Now he's got the message."

"I'm not so sure."

"If he doesn't, he will soon. Just keep it up."

"What were you just about to say about the delivery receipt?"

"Right! Listen: the delivery guys weren't so smart. Wait – I'll show you."

Across the room the fax machine whirred and a new arrival began to thread its way out. Courtney strode over and held the top of the paper until the bottom end was released. Then she crossed back to me and put it on my desk so we could both examine it.

I immediately saw what she meant about the delivery guys being not so bright. One had scrawled both the pickup and delivery addresses, signed and dated it, and included their company name, Metro Trucking. Anand had neatly written the voucher number in the top right corner.

"Picked up at 'empty lot Pacific between 4 and 5 Aves'," I read aloud. "There are nine empty lots on that block right now. For the purposes of this story, does it matter which one?"

"I'm not sure. But this is pretty good, don't you think? Anand signed it and dated it, and he's a cop."

"Is he willing to go on record?"

"For me?" She grinned. "What about Russet?"

"Oh, I doubt it. But that doesn't stop me from reporting what they told me. Larry confirmed they received drums of chemicals. Bruce found no record of a delivery."

"But your source wants to stay anonymous – he'd be the deal-breaker if we could quote him."

"No. I promised. Courtney, it could be dangerous for him if we go public with him as the whistle-blower. He likes his job most of the time. I think he wants to retire in peace."

"Right." She stretched her long legs and crossed them at the ankle. Her strappy sandals revealed the pedicure she'd received yesterday: shimmery white.

"I'd really like to see the city analyze the bones," I said. "See where they came from. Whose they are. But they never will unless they admit they exist."

"Bones." Courtney rolled her eyes. "New York real estate's gotta be full of them. Bones and ghosts, you know?"

"I think we should go to Elliot with what we've got. You want to write it up or should I?"

"Me." She stood up and pushed her chair back to her own desk. "With a shared byline."

While she drafted the article I researched Metro Trucking and what I found only added to the cloud of mystery: Metro was a general hauling company registered in New Jersey and owned by a second cousin once removed of none other than Tony T. But if Tony had been involved in the removal of the bones, wouldn't he have had them disposed of? The fact that they ended up in forensics storage indicated city involvement in their transfer off the site. It just didn't make a lot of sense to me that either the developer or the city would hire the job out to Metro Trucking, an outfit so easily connectible back to Tony that I had just accomplished it quickly on the Internet. One thing, though, was clear: this strengthened Abe Starkman's hypothesis of corruption.

Courtney took the new information and wove it into her piece. Five hundred words later she had a good solid draft. We emailed it back and forth, editing and polishing together, until we both felt satisfied. Our short article would lead the reader to an uneasy conclusion that the city had gone out of its way to cover up the discovery of the bones. It was unnecessary to state the obvious question: Why?

We submitted the article to Elliot.

He was in his office. We knew this because we could see him through the glass wall. And we knew he checked his email every few minutes when he wasn't in a meeting. So we were fairly certain that we read our piece almost as soon as we sent it. But it wasn't until the end of the day that we heard back from him that it had been approved for tomorrow's paper.

He called us into his office and we stood across

from him as he prepared to go home: collating papers into a pocket in his briefcase, strapping in his laptop, paperclipping a stack of phone messages and leaving it in a conspicuous spot on his desk so he wouldn't forget to return the calls in the morning. While he did all this – daily movements mostly free of decision-making, performed with the ease of relative thoughtlessness – he spoke to us.

"I had to go all the way up with this one. Overly –" he was our publisher "– almost wouldn't do it without more confirmable sources. But the photos swayed him; you can't argue with an image. We don't like to make mistakes but worst-case scenario we print a correction later in the week and drop the story."

"Drop the story?" I regretted the question as soon as the words escaped me.

Elliot froze in the middle of sliding an arm into his jacket. "Yes, if necessary."

"Thanks, boss," Courtney said. "But I don't think we'll need a correction."

"I really hope we don't. Make any progress on the land purchase? Documents: who sold it, who bought it, how much, when?"

"Working on it," I said. "There's no confusion about who the buyer was, but so far there have been some contradictions about the seller."

Elliot nodded. "Contact your source."

I had been trying to avoid that so as not to unnecessarily expose Abe Starkman but Elliot was right – at this point I had no choice. If there had been a back-room negotiation resulting in the land deal, somewhere there was a trail of paperwork or money or something. My guess was that the real agreement that finally enticed Tony T to sell his lots was hidden behind dummy paperwork, since the lots were parts of a larger parcel of land and would have to be accounted for by many people over many years. I would call Abe and ask for help.

"OK," I said.

"Good. I'll see you two tomorrow." Elliot picked up his briefcase and walked around his desk to his office door. Courtney caught him with a question on his way out:

"What page?"

"Eight. Buried, like your bones. 'Night." And he was gone.

The day had passed in a flurry of putting our story to bed – though it felt like more of a start than an ending. Courtney and I both expected the story to grow after tomorrow and we were excited about delving deeper into it. We were aware that, if we were allowed to, it would mean peeling back one layer at a time, presenting elements as they were revealed to us, as opposed to pointing a finger at the government and crying, "Corruption!" You never did that because you'd only look crazy and what if you were wrong? We couldn't afford to be wrong. Which was why I had to call Abe Starkman; if he was as concerned as he'd said – and I believed he was – then he would be motivated to substantiate his claim about the developer buying land from the mob in a deal with the city for leniency. That, officially, would be the most explosive element of the story and we had to substantiate it before even an insinuation could go to print.

I left Abe a message on his voicemail, saying very little in case anyone else listened to his messages, using just my first name and asking for a call back on my cell phone. Then I went home.

I was too tired to cook so Nat and I shared a pizza and salad. He had finished his homework before dinner and to persuade me to let him watch some TV before bed, breaking a long-standing no-TV-on-school-nights rule, he did the dishes. I wasn't too hard to break down. We got into our pajamas, sat together on the living room couch and watched a random assortment of television that led us through a maze of laughter, disgust and boredom. At ten o'clock we said goodnight to the tube and each other. I kissed him on the cheek at the threshold of his room and reminded him to pack a bag for his sleepover at Henry's tomorrow night. They were going straight home to Henry's after school and in the evening The

Dad, as Nat called him, planned to take the boys to Yankees stadium. Nat had been looking forward to this for two weeks and it was why I had felt free to plan a meeting with Rich, who had custody of his five-year-old daughter on alternate weekends, this not being one of them. Such easily won freedom rarely occurred in my schedule and it had seemed a shame to waste it.

Before turning off the lights I sprawled on my bed beneath my laptop and checked in with Sara. She had already gone to bed so there would be no IMing but she had left me a goodnight email, which concluded:

"Stopped at Copy Cats this afternoon. Said Joe was born and bred on the island and they'd known him more or less his whole life. Said he was a hard worker. Said he worked there for two years. Said he didn't seem to have any friends. Said he tried to date their teenage daughter but they put an end to that and Joe backed off. No problem after that. Lived with his mother who sometimes brought him lunch. Said she was a 'strange cookie' and seemed lonely. Oh, but listen to this: Joe left a box of personal stuff behind and when they heard about you working with him in NYC they asked me to pass it along so I've got it in my car! Haven't had a chance to open it yet. Will keep you posted if anything juicy. Body parts etc. "

Joe. I didn't want to even think about him; if I did I wouldn't sleep and I wanted to be rested because tomorrow was a somewhat big day. The story would appear in the paper and there was always some backlash after anything remotely controversial came out – there would be emails and phone calls to field. Hopefully I would be able to make my regular Friday lunch with my mother. That I had visited her on Wednesday wouldn't alter her expectation of seeing me for lunch on Friday; she herself might forget but it was on her calendar and the attendants would remind her. Once, she waited for me all day in the common room when I had told her – but not written down – that I would stop by after work in the evening. So there was the article, there was lunch with my mother and at night there was my meeting . . . my *date* with Rich. And Abe Starkman still hadn't returned my call, which worried me. I took a sleeping pill, just to be sure I'd get some rest despite my churning mind, and the next thing I knew it was morning.

The *Times* hit the streets at about 6 a.m., earlier in some places. I didn't see it until nine, when I reached the office. By that time the story had gained some traction and my email inbox was brimming, more so than I'd expected. Elliot had forwarded some from home where he often began his workday before dawn.

The Buildings Department, the developer and the

contractor who had done the demolition on the Pacific Street lots denied knowing anything about the bones. The developer's spokeswoman also wrote in to say that Livingston & Sons would never have knowingly approved the use of any contractor she referred to as an "uncertified service provider", alluding to the bones' transit from Pacific Street to Pearson. So the players were nervous. Elliot was excited by the response and told us via an early morning email that we should "go with it". The emails themselves, and whatever else we came up with throughout the day, would be fodder for a follow-up piece.

Courtney came in shortly after I did, having been out on an early interview for a different story she was working on, and I told her to read her emails while I continued going through my own list of new mail. A list that would be longer than Courtney's, I discovered, as I had received some very special emails all my own.

From Joe.

I had taken the absence of a bagel on my desk the last two mornings to signify that he was backing off. I had really thought he'd be ashamed of himself for having followed me uptown on Wednesday. Instead, he had sent me . . . I counted . . . twenty-three emails. All kinds. Offering me no fewer than eight more writing samples. Giving me his new address in Red

Hook and inviting me and Nat to dinner at 6 p.m. next Saturday night. Supplying me with links to blogs I really had to check out. Chastising me for ignoring him like he was "just some guy from the mailroom". There were three identical emails with the nursery rhyme "Three Blind Mice". I didn't know what to make of *that* but I certainly didn't like it, any of it. Was he bona fide crazy? I set about deleting them until Courtney came up behind me, saw my screen and said, "Whoa!"

"Can you believe this guy?"

"Save them, Darcy. You might need to show them to someone."

I twisted around to look up at her. Her expression was dead serious.

"Just in case," she said.

I stopped deleting.

She leaned over me and commandeered my mouse. "Let's make a file where you can stash them. Here." She created a file called "Joke Coffin's Dead Ends" and one by one dragged his missives into it. I changed the name to just "Dead Ends", fearing Joe might see the file if he wheeled his cart too close one day.

He didn't appear in the newsroom all morning though I imagined him checking his email repeatedly, expecting – actually expecting – a reply. Realizing this was significant for me because I was beginning to comprehend that Joe was not an

ordinary man who had been rejected in an ordinary
way by an ordinary woman who didn't want to date
him. He was somewhere on a spectrum from totally
nuts to obstinately determined to get my attention in
a way I had never before experienced.

Before meeting Hugo I had known a guy or two to
turn up unexpectedly or call too frequently or not get
the hint long after he should have that I wasn't
interested. Every woman went through this and
knew that eventually the guy would back off. But
Joe wasn't backing off. By now I had stopped
blaming his youth and decided he had some kind of
personality disorder. "Asshole syndrome" Courtney
called it and continued to urge me to wait and watch
before deciding to go to Elliot or Human Resources
with my problem. I hoped that a weekend away from
the office, and me, might dampen his enthusiasm and
decided to stick with my plan not to alarm the
authorities at work by making a formal complaint,
especially when our bones story was gaining
momentum.

Abe Starkman finally called me back and though
he didn't say much, and what he said was practically
whispered, he made a definite promise to "get it to
you over the weekend". He didn't say what "it" was
or where he would deliver it but finding me was
fairly easy. He knew I lived in Brooklyn. He knew
where I worked. He had to have read our story,

which told him the *Times* was letting me run with it, and it didn't take a brain surgeon to figure out we could really break it open with substantiation of the land deal especially since we had already tracked down the bones. If he really wanted the whole thing exposed he would have to come up with evidence. And so I interpreted his cryptic assurance that "it" would be delivered as nearly a promise that he intended to produce some.

Courtney and I immediately set to work on a follow-up piece. Our publisher Matt Overly himself decided that it would run the next day. According to Elliot, Overly was receiving pressure from city officials – some of whom he socialized with – not to pursue the story. Overly was the thirty-five-year-old fourth-generation heir who had been appointed to run the *Times* when his father Sanford retired after himself having taken over from his father John who had taken over from *his* father Edmund who had founded the paper in the late 1800s. Matt Overly took seriously both his job and the claims that he was not up to it by dint of having had it handed down to him without ever having been a reporter or editor. And so when his social peers tried to exercise influence over his newspaper's considerable power, it was a test. Since he had taken over the paper three years ago, his erratic decision-making had demon-strated his struggle as inner and outer forces tried to sway his every move: the desire to please pushed constantly against a wish for independence. His decision to run with a follow-up about the bones – a story he had been wary about only yesterday – demonstrated that he had been pressured to bury it and was willfully resisting that pressure.

It was good news for me and Courtney. Elliot instructed us to keep our reports spare and factual. We wouldn't file until our 5 p.m. deadline in case there were new developments, a delay that allowed me to keep my regular lunch date with my mother.

She was waiting for me in the dining room where most of the other patients had already started their meal. It was a large, bright room with white-painted walls decorated with colorful framed museum prints, hanging plants in front of the wide windows, draperies pulled aside to let in the light and a shelf of pretty ceramics above the cupboards in the open kitchen. High-functioning patients shared a long table to the far left and a din of gentle chatter drifted across the room. My mother had long since graduated from that table to one of the small ones where I now found her sitting alone. She was surrounded by other small tables, islands of mostly silent patients concentrating on their food, chewing carefully, examining smells and textures as if cold cuts, cottage cheese and Jell-O were new culinary inventions. My entry created a pause in the clatter of utensils against plates as history-creased faces lifted to assess me. Who was I and why was I here? Eyes trailed me to my mother, watched me lean down to kiss her cheek and grasp her hands as they floated up to greet me.

"Hi, Mom." I sat in the nearest chair.

"I've been waiting."

"Not long. Lunch just started. I'm not late."

She smiled without answering. More and more, even the simplest statements confounded her.

"I'm hungry," I said. "Are you?"

"Yes. Lunch wasn't filling today."

"We haven't eaten yet." I turned to gesture to one of the attendants that we were ready for our food. The people who worked here could not have been more welcoming to family and always invited us to join meals and activities.

Sharing a meal with my mother was much like eating with a young child. Basic instructions were often necessary. Accidents happened. You couldn't expect much by way of conversation and yet startling exclamations often took you by surprise. "Jackie O had the smallest waist of any woman I ever tailored," my mother once blurted out over chicken salad. And I pictured the famous woman's slender waist beneath my mother's familiar hands and felt dual stabs of pride and jealousy. "Your father is the most tender lover I ever had," as a cube of red Jell-O wobbled off her spoon. *Is*. And I sank into a well of remorse at the thought of him and the affectionate gestures that had spun a protective layer of sugar lace around my young heart, while also thinking, *What other lovers?* And I thought of Hugo and nearly cried. These lunches could be emotionally treacherous or unbelievably dull. Today's was average, easy and fairly dull in a soothing way. Pleasant. There were no startling pronouncements or spills that made you jump out of your chair. We ate. Talked little. I walked her slowly back to her room. And then it was time for me to return to work.

On my way down the hall toward the elevator I was stopped by Nancy, the day manager. A tall woman with short blondish hair and a beautiful complexion like perfectly blended café au lait, she was one of those friendly and efficient people you were always pleased to see.

"Darcy – I didn't realize you were here. I was about to call you."

"Hi, Nancy."

"Someone tried to visit just now but he isn't on your list. I don't remember his name. He said he was a cousin."

"Cousin?" I had no cousins and neither did my parents; all their close relatives had been wiped out sixty years ago in the war and therefore we had no extended family whatsoever. It had always been just us three. Then just us two. "What did he say exactly?"

"He was downstairs, asking to be let up. He wanted to see Eva."

"You didn't let him up, did you?"

"No! Not without your permission."

"There are no cousins," I said. "Definitely don't let him up, OK? Don't let anyone up except me or Nat."

Nancy was directly in front of me now and she seemed to sense that I was upset. She put her hand on my shoulder and smiled. "Don't worry. We won't."

"Thank you."

I proceeded to the elevator and held my key in the lock until it arrived. My hand was shaking as I clumsily extracted the key. Alone in the elevator, gliding down toward the lobby, I took a few deep breaths. This couldn't be happening. Joe could *not* come near my mother.

When the elevator door opened, my heart jumped at the sight of a man standing directly in front, waiting to come in. I saw Joe for a split second before realizing that this man was about ninety years old, grey-haired and leaning on a walker. I held the door open for him while he hobbled in.

I expected to see Joe in the lobby. But didn't.

Outside on West End I walked down the wide avenue busy with traffic and looming on either side with tall, hulking buildings each of which housed thousands. So many people and everywhere I looked I saw him. But as soon as my mind focused on a face I saw that it wasn't him. I walked a ways and turned suddenly to catch him. No one. Walked some more, turned around. And again. Joe was everywhere now but I didn't see him. I felt him. *He was here*.

I was almost running by the time I reached the subway entrance. I had to swipe my Metrocard three times before it let me through the turnstile. Sitting on the train for the ten-minute ride down to 42nd Street, I struggled to breathe. I could not allow Joe Coffin to frighten my mother. Without meaning to, I had led him to her. He knew where to find her. And the more I went to see her, the more interested he would be in seeing her too, wouldn't he? Or would the building security dissuade him of his pathetic effort to get upstairs? I didn't know. But at that moment I felt unsafe in a way I hadn't all week since Joe had decided to pursue me. Worse was the sense that my mother could be unsafe as well. Joe was crossing boundaries, one after another after another. It had turned into a kind of pursuit the likes of which I had never quite experienced and my head spun from it all the way downtown. It confused me. What *exactly* should, or could, I do about it?

I talked with Courtney as soon I got back to work and we agreed that "freezing out the bastard" as she called it was no longer enough. It was time to ask for help.

"Maybe I should go to the police," I said.

"Listen, Darcy, there's something you should know about the *Times* if you haven't already noticed: it doesn't like the spotlight on itself. You're still in your hiring review period; they could let you go now without any real explanation. Start with Elliot. Let him guide you, OK?"

It sounded like good advice. "OK."

Elliot was not in his office so I lay in wait at my desk. As soon as he appeared in the newsroom and installed himself at his desk, I knocked on his open door.

"Come in!"

I did, closing the door behind me.

"How's the follow-up coming?" He assumed of course that I wanted to discuss the bones story.

"It's something else."

"Well, you're giving my door a workout this week, aren't you? OK. Shoot."

I told him about Joe Coffin. Elliot listened intently, tension appearing in horizontal ripples across his forehead. When I was through, he took a deep breath.

"Wow. That's not good. All this since Monday?"

"Yup. I didn't talk to you sooner because I honestly assumed he'd back off, but instead it seems to be getting worse. It really scared me that he tried to get up to my mother's floor."

"It would scare me, too. He's a new hire, you say?"

"Monday was his first day."

I could see Elliot's mind working. Something he didn't say, something that struck me for the first time and now seemed obvious, suggested a possibility that already made me feel some relief: if Joe was also in his new hire review period then he too could be let go without detailed explanation – if the *Times* chose to handle it that way.

"I'll think we'll take this to HR." He picked up the phone and dialed an extension he knew by heart, which implied a familiarity that was encouraging. As he waited for someone to answer he seemed to concentrate on what he'd say, but in the end all he did was leave a message for Paul Ardsley.

"We'll wait for Paul to call back," Elliot said. "In the meantime, try to get your mind off it and get back to work. But tell me if this Joe character bothers you again, OK? I'm in all afternoon. Any new leads on the bones?"

"No, but the racketeering trial for Tony T's guy starts on Monday."

"We've got a reporter on it. Anything interesting, I'll make sure you and Courtney know about it."

"Thanks.

"Get in touch with your source?"

"Yes. He didn't sound surprised we hit a wall. He promised me paperwork over the weekend."

"*Ex*cellent. Now get busy."

I returned to my desk. I took Elliot's advice and buried myself in work. By the end of the day we had our follow-up piece for the Saturday edition, basically explaining that both the developer and city officials denied any knowledge of or connection to the bones. It rang with the kind of overzealous protest you don't engage in unless you have something to hide.

We did not have a return call from Paul Ardsley in Human Resources. Elliot summoned me to his office to assure me that he had left another message before finally learning that Ardsley had been out at meetings all afternoon and wouldn't be in the office until Monday.

"Can we hold on until then?"

"No problem," I said with more confidence than I actually felt. Joe had my home phone number which meant he could easily find my address through a reverse directory. At this point I assumed he had already done so. The question was whether he would have the audacity to actually show up.

"OK. You've got my cell number, so if you need me, use it. And just to cover our bases, here's my home number, too." He wrote it neatly on a slip of paper and handed it to me with a smile. "This is top secret, so don't share it."

"I'm sure I won't need this, but thank you, Elliot."

"OK. So I'll see you Monday morning and we'll talk to Paul and see what we can do. Now go home and see your kid and forget about all this." He waved a hand toward the newsroom, meaning I should forget about bones and empty lots and anonymous sources and obsessive mailroom clerks – though how could I? Joe was *out there*. And Abe Starkman was coming to my house with copies of secret documents he was risking his career to share with me.

CHAPTER 5

I stood outside Rich's building – a wide double-door entrance to a converted carriage house on Verandah Place – and rang the doorbell again. I could hear the thrum of music coming from inside; it seemed reasonable to think that Rich might not be able to hear the bell. It made me wonder if he felt as ambivalent as I did about this possible *thing* that seemed to be developing between us. If he wanted to make sure to hear the bell, he wouldn't play loud music, right? And if I wanted to make sure not to discourage him, I wouldn't have arrived twenty minutes late. Right? But I had been on the phone with Sara, using the landline with its limited range, and lost track of time. I had wanted to talk to her about Joe and to find out what was in his box. She hadn't had a chance to look yet but promised she would.

"So what's the deal exactly?" Sara had said. "You can't go anywhere now without him following you?"

"I really don't know. I only saw him that one time near my mom's."

"Twice by your mom's," she corrected me.

"I didn't actually see him the second time, but you're right. Twice."

"It's not good, Darcy."

"No. But you know what? He's a jerk. I'm not going to let him scare me and I'm not going to stop living my life. My editor's going to talk to the *Times*' HR guy on Monday and hopefully that'll help."

"Maybe they'll can him. I mean, he's in the mailroom and you're a reporter."

"Exactly."

"Good for you. Just keep your eyes open, OK? And don't walk down any dark alleys!"

"I won't. Trust me."

On the way over to Rich's I had called him from my cell phone to apologize for being late and to say that I was on my way but his voicemail answered. I'd left a message. So as I stood there now, giving up on the bell and trying the old-fashioned knocker, banging the horseshoe handle against the oval brass plate three times, I was aware that he might have abandoned the idea of seeing me. He might have even felt relieved about it. I waited. He didn't come.

I crossed the narrow cobbled street and stood across from his house. There were two floors above the ground-floor carriage entrance, with wide windows whose shutters opened against a brick façade. I knew from walking the neighborhood and talking with people that the houses on Verandah Place were over a hundred years old and had all started out as carriage houses where horses rested and carriages were parked. Lowly carriage drivers and other domestic caretakers had slept in the apartments above. This narrow street free of traffic, across from which a small park offered a peaceful spot to read and play, had started its life as a kind of neighborhood garage and now boasted some of its most sought after real estate. I wondered how Rich had been lucky enough to land one of these houses, how long he'd lived here, if he owned or rented. But I was late and now he wasn't coming to the door so I wouldn't have the chance to ask him. It was my fault. The call to Sara could have waited. I had allowed my ambivalence to jeopardize my date – yes, *date* – with a man I actually kind of liked.

I stepped off the curb and onto the cobblestones and walked toward Clinton Street. Almost at the corner, I heard footsteps quicken behind me. *Joe*. He had hardly been out of my consciousness all day and I was determined not to let him scare me into hiding, yet it didn't surprise me that he had followed me here. I stopped in my tracks and took a deep breath, gathered my courage and spun around:

"Leave me alone!"

Rich looked stunned. His pale face went paler, accentuating the freckles that sprayed across his nose and cheeks. A few strands of his dark red hair had fallen into one of his eyes but he made no move to brush them away. His jeans were half-covered in paint and his black T-shirt was ripped above the pocket. He wasn't exactly dressed for a date; so he *hadn't* really expected me to come.

"OK." He opened his hands at his sides, revealing paint-splattered palms.

"Not *you*." My pulse was racing, hammering at my ears, introducing me to the sound of panic. A sound that proved how readily I feared Joe as soon as I sensed him (or thought I sensed him) enter my orbit. A sound as persuasive as it was unreal, like the ocean inside a shell. I forced a smile.

Rich matched the stilted smile, which made me feel like such an idiot. "You mean him?" He glanced right and left, indicating all the no ones surrounding us. "Him? Maybe *him*?"

"Enough," I said. "You scared me, that's all. I overreacted."

"Well, this is New York City, muggers every-where, got to stay on your toes." His eyes now twinkled with humor. Our neighborhood was known as one of the safest in the city.

"I rang your bell a few times and tried the knocker. And I left you a message saying I was running late."

"I just heard the message. Then I realized I might not have heard the bell. My neighbor blasts music every evening when he gets home from work. It's a real drag."

"I thought that was your music."

"No, I was listening for you. I was in my studio and I can usually hear the doorbell fine back there." We paused, looked at each other. This was quickly becoming an irresolute conversation that threatened real frustration – not an auspicious start to a third date – and then he said, "Let's start over."

Yes. I walked over and kissed his cheek, which was very soft. His skin had a nice scent I couldn't identify, something natural, not bought in a bottle. He moved his face to return the kiss and for the moment our cheeks pressed together I felt something inside me drop out – a barrier that had been there since after Hugo died, when I learned that men would now approach me. I was inapproachable, deep in my soul *unavailable* and couldn't understand why some men thought a new widow was fair game. Hugo's death was like a fortress crumbling, allowing wanderers to try to cross my borders. And so I threw up barriers around myself. This was the first time I had allowed one of them to falter.

Rich looked down at me, his entire face smiling warmly. Our eyes caught for a long moment. It amazed me that he could look at me this way after my harsh reaction to hearing him run up behind me, that he could take it in such stride and not ask for an explanation.

"Glass of wine before we go out to eat?" he asked.

"Sure."

"And I promised to show you my art."

"Your *real* art. I've been looking forward to it."

"I was touching up the piece I'm working on now, though I'm not sure I'll show it to you."

"OK."

"Don't make this so hard for me!" We both laughed.

We walked up the street and into his house. He pushed open one side of the double doors, standing back so I could walk in. When he touched my lower back as I passed him, I could feel the heat of his hand through my shirt.

He led me through a living/dining room with a couch piled with cushy pillows and a rough-hewn coffee table I guessed was an antique. A fireplace with an ornate marble mantle was fronted by a blackened screen and guarded by unpolished bronze pokers. Beside the fireplace was a basket of Barbies, pushed against the wall – and the moment I saw it I pictured his little girl, imagining her with burnt-red hair like his, crouched over the basket as she selected dolls for today's play. As quickly as I saw her, she transformed into a brown-haired girl, *me*, bent over my own doll box when I was little . . . my father emerging from the kitchen with an apron smeared with brownie batter . . . my mother in the living room armchair, her head thrown back against a crocheted lace doily, eyes closed. "Then I'll steal a nap," she had announced when Daddy said he intended to bake. He loved to make my favorite treats, reveled in it almost. I could practically smell sweet chocolate wafting through Rich's kitchen as we passed through a rear door and into a rectangular yard that was covered in autumn leaves. At the back of the yard was an old barn-like structure, two stories high.

"What's your daughter's name?"

"Clara."

I smiled. Clara. How lucky to have a daughter. But then I was lucky, too, to have a son.

"Do they live nearby?" *They* being his former wife and Clara.

"Closer to you, actually."

He opened the door and we stepped into his studio. It was not in fact two stories, but one high-ceilinged multi-windowed loft-like space filled with paintings. They were everywhere: hanging off walls, high and low, and from rafters twenty-five feet up.

They leaned against surfaces. One was covered with a dirty drop cloth – presumably his newest, the one he wasn't sure he wanted to show me. His canvases were mostly large and abstract, dense with color and energy. I loved them without knowing why. Painting was something I didn't understand but responded to (or didn't) and these had the impact on my brain of miniature explosions of energy. Or flavor on the tongue. Or feelings in the heart. They were alive, is what they were.

"They're beautiful," I said.

"They're full of rage." He breathed deeply in, then fully out. The air was sour with fresh paint but he had to be used to it.

"Rage?"

"I did all these after Lucy left me."

"Ah – she left you."

"Yup. For another guy."

"Who she lives with now?"

"They broke up, which I thought would make me feel better at the time, but it didn't. And I don't really want to see her unhappy; it's bad for Clara. That was three years ago and we're on an even keel now. We let Clara know that we're still a family."

"I actually tell Nat the same thing. That Hugo is still with us and we'll always be a family."

Rich's eyes settled on me. "I understand."

"Well." An awkward pause.

"So now you've seen my work. How about that glass of wine?" He stepped close to me and touched my elbow, to lead me out I guessed, but it was all I could do not to put my hand on his arm and draw him closer. Everything about him came at me as *right*. Which had to be, somehow, *wrong*. Didn't it?

"Actually, I'm starving." Staying here felt too tempting – dangerous. "Want to go straight out to eat?"

"Whatever you say. Let me change first."

I waited in his living room, looking at family photos on his mantle, while he went to a back bedroom to put on clean clothes. He rented the ground floor, which had two bedrooms, one very small which was Clara's on her alternate weekends with him.

Lucy and Clara looked alike, I saw: both trim and dark, Mediterranean. Both had long shiny hair parted in the middle and tucked behind their ears, only the mother wore hoop earrings and Clara, of course, did not. She was five now, which made her two when they split up. I wondered if it was better for a child of a broken family to have no memories of the time their parents were together, when the family was technically intact. Or was it better to have a conscious recollection of that time, if only as proof that it was somehow possible that these two had ever loved each other? These pictures would supply Clara's memory: frozen moments she couldn't actually recall. Nat's mind on the other hand was filled with an endless loop in surround sound of a father he had known very well. Which was better? I almost envied Rich his daughter's lack of consciousness when it came to the Family Pain. It distressed me to know that Nat's awareness of his father's loss would always haunt him and would probably even become a leitmotif for his life.

We went to a local Thai restaurant, a pretty, dimly lit space decorated with oversized lanterns, tall stalks of bamboo and orange lilies crafted from delicate paper. Nat had always refused to eat here; he called it "prissy" but I knew he was afraid to try what he deemed exotic food simply because he'd never had it before.

It was Rich's and my third dinner together and as usual there was a sense of furtiveness about it, as if we were grabbing time we shouldn't have been allowed. Tonight was a little different, though, because neither of us had a child to return home to, no babysitter to relieve or in my case marginally independent adolescent to check in on. Nat wasn't due home until tomorrow. Clara was with her mother for the entire weekend. This freedom began to feel like added pressure; I enjoyed this man too much. But was I ready? Would I ever be?

We kept the conversation light, typical early-date talk, touching up blank spots in the skeletal personal histories we'd already shared. I knew that Rich had grown up on a working ranch in Montana, had disappointed his father and thrilled his mother with his budding artistic talent, and devastated both of them when he moved east to study painting at Pratt Institute. And I knew that, ever since, he visited home twice a year, at Christmas and for a week in the summer. Now I learned that despite the distance that had grown and solidified between him and his childhood, he had found a way to keep a physical connection to it: on Wednesday afternoons and evenings, he worked as a horseback riding instructor at the Prospect Park stables. And it was no co-incidence that he'd chosen to live in a former stable.

"Have you thought of moving back to Montana?" I asked.

"Not as long as Clara's here."

"Of course not."

"Can I take you riding some time? The trails in Prospect Park can actually make you forget you're in the city."

"It would be my first time on a horse."

A glint in his eye, he grinned and said, "Giddy up!"

I burst out laughing. I *liked* this man – too much.

After dinner I tried to say goodnight outside the

restaurant on Smith Street but Rich insisted on walking me home, though it wasn't really necessary. It was a Friday night and the neighborhood hummed with activity. At ten o'clock it was still early for some, though not for us. Rich's day at school had begun at eight thirty and mine had gone full-speed since nine. We were both suppressing yawns as we turned the corner onto quiet, leafy Wyckoff Street – my block. Trees threw a gridwork of shadows over the middle of the street, which glowed with the ambient light that bathed the city at night, preventing it from ever being completely dark, except in the vestibules and alleyways you quickly learned to avoid. On these old brownstone blocks the menace was in the velvet darkness that soaked beneath stoop entries, like mine, with a deep shadow that fell off the stoop in a triangular slab.

We came to my house. I opened the half-gate, rusted iron squealing, and stepped into the blind spot.

Private entrance, the real estate ad had read. Duplex, two bedrooms, one full bathroom, one half-bathroom, clean kitchen, high ceilings on parlor floor, private garden, private entrance. The ad had failed to note that the arrangement of rooms was in fact awkward, with the kitchen, living and dining areas downstairs where the ceiling was lowest and there was less light and the bedrooms upstairs in a carved-up parlor floor which would have been a pretty place for a living room. But that was Brooklyn. It was because this was an old hatchet-job renovation and not a swanky new one that I had been able to afford this place and this neighborhood without digging into the principal – Hugo's life insurance policy – that was going to fund both Nat's college education and supplement my retirement. Renting this duplex suited me perfectly at the moment. I had decided not to buy right away, that moving to New York was an experiment to bring us closer to my mother and try a new life on for size.

Rich stayed right behind me, not hanging back to say goodnight on the sidewalk as I'd hoped he would. Hoped, because I yearned to invite him in.

I turned around to face him, my back to the outer gate of my door. In the darkness his eyes glowed and his hair looked chestnut brown. He was staring at me, trying to get up the nerve to kiss me, at least I was pretty sure of that. His hand tilted forwards to touch my arm and I felt it again: heat. My whole body seemed to flush with it. I couldn't help myself: I stepped forwards just slightly and lifted my face.

His lips were softer and thinner than Hugo's, more pliable. His tongue more elastic. Different. This close, I breathed deeply of that unidentifiable scent I liked so much. One of his hands came around my back and gently pulled me closer. I didn't resist, nor did I help, but allowed the pressure of his hand to sink into the curve of my lower back. Our tongues and our lips and our mouths joined deeply, lazily. *Dessert*, I thought. He was delicious. And I was a woman. And Hugo had been gone so long. Wasn't I allowed this?

But he was Nat's teacher. I pushed him away. "I think we should say goodnight."

His smile was forced but conciliatory, accepting. He didn't like it and neither did I but saying goodnight was what we were going to do.

"I'll watch you go in," he said, almost whispered, "and then I'll go."

We both breathed heavily. It was almost comical, embarrassing. I turned to put my key in the lock and that was when I noticed that a plastic bag was hanging off the knob.

It crinkled loudly when I removed it, saying, "What's this?" The first thing I thought of was Abe Starkman – had he been here? But he would never leave sensitive documents out in the open. And then I thought of Joe. Whatever was inside the bag was heavy and flat, like a book. I stepped out of the shadow and into the dim light. It was a gift, wrapped in green and gold striped paper.

"Don't tell me it's your birthday," Rich said.

"My birthday's in April."

Taped to the front of the gift was a card, no

envelope. A little brown bear smiled cutely and held a bouquet of red and blue flowers. It looked like a greeting card for a child. Maybe, hopefully, someone had mistakenly left it on my door, but I doubted it. I lifted the top of the card, which read: "Roses are red, violets are blue. When am I not, thinking of you?" Inside, a childlike hand had written in black pen: "For Darcy, Love Always, Joe."

My expression must have altered because Rich asked, "What's wrong?"

I looked into his face, warm and concerned, and asked him to please come inside.

My house was a mess but so what? Hugo had been the neat one and I had stopped caring about clutter around the time Nat was born. I paid a woman to come in weekly to deep clean; she also took it upon herself to stack up our messes. We had only been in this apartment for two months so it wasn't so bad. Now, with Rich walking in behind me, I gave the same explanation I offered everyone: "I'd say 'excuse the mess' but it's actually in pretty good shape for us."

He smiled. "Looks lived in."

"It is."

We settled on the living room couch, blue velvet, in front of which a glass coffee table was cluttered with books and magazines. A half-filled glass of water, Nat's from last night, tilted atop a paperback.

It was a miracle Mitzi and Ahab hadn't knocked it over, the way they darted around.

"So who left you a present?" Rich asked.

"This guy at work, *Joe Coffin*." I rolled my eyes. "He used to live on the Vineyard too and he's decided to take a shine to me. He's about twenty-two years old. It's ridiculous."

"Wow."

"Right."

"I guess he's persistent if he's leaving you gifts."

"Oh, persistent isn't the word. On Monday my editor and I are putting in an official complaint."

"So this guy knows where you live."

When he said that, a bolt of queasiness shot through my stomach. I ignored it. "You can find almost anyone's address on the Internet," I said, "and don't forget we work at the same place. He's called me here; I already figured he knew the address."

"He's called you?"

"Sixty times. I counted."

"Darcy, have you considered talking to the police? This doesn't sound good."

"It seems premature."

"Doesn't sound like it to me. It sounds like he's stalking you."

That was the second time that word had come up – stalking – only the first time I had said it to Sara in a fit of part-humor part-anxiety and this time it was being reflected back to me by an innocent bystander, so to speak. Each time I heard the term it raised the ante on my worry about how far Joe intended to go with all this. Every day this week I had promised myself he would back off *any minute now*. Then it was *any day now*. Soon, *any week now*. Was Rich right? Was this more serious than I allowed myself to think? It's just that – a stalker? Why assume the worst when patience (and a word from the director of Human Resources) might just do the trick?

"Joe and I work together, sort of. We work at the same place. I'm told the *Times* doesn't like publicity – ironic, isn't it? And right now I'm working on a story about something that's fairly sensitive, something my editor hesitated putting me on, and I don't want to blow it."

"Bones at the Atlantic Yards?"

"You read it?"

"It was intriguing. I could see that it might cause a stir."

"It did, and it's ongoing, and I don't want to blow it by overreacting to this thing with Joe. You can understand that, can't you? You must run into politics at school sometimes."

"All the time. I do understand. But this Joe guy—" He looked at the wrapped box. "Open it."

I ripped the paper straight down the middle. It was a plain box, which I opened at one end. I slid out a

frame made of a fine inlaid wood, highly polished.
Behind a sheet of glass was a photograph of Joe,
smiling sweetly, his eyes crinkling up at the corners.
It was a professional portrait, posed in front of a pale
blue backdrop. The queasy feeling returned, only
this time with a sharp edge.

"He must think you like him back." A stiff smile
appeared on Rich's face and I wanted to wipe it
off, to replace it with the tenderness with which he
had looked at me, and kissed me, a few minutes
ago.

"I can't tell you how hard I've tried to fend this
guy off. If he thinks I like him back, it's a fantasy. A
delusion. This is nuts."

"Well, the frame itself is really beautiful," Rich
said.

But I couldn't see the frame, just the image of Joe
inside it. I got up and took it to the kitchen trash,
stamping on the pedal so the top lifted with a clank.
I threw in the frame, box and photo all together and
let the metal lid slam down. Then on second thought,
I reached back in for the cardboard box and transferred it to our recycling bin. Rich was standing in
the doorway, watching me, his arms folded over his
chest. A little smile crooked up one side of his
mouth.

"Am I supposed to recycle the glass, too?" I asked
him.

He laughed at me, how I was mixing practicality with drama.

"Probably."

So I took the frame out of the garbage and laid it on its face on the kitchen counter. Rich came up beside me and took over the task of disassembling Joe's gift, removing the backing and the photo to get to the glass.

"Maybe you should keep the frame," he said. "There's really nothing wrong with it, in and of itself. It looks expensive."

"He probably stole it." I picked up the photograph of Joe and ripped him in half, straight down the middle. "Take *that*, and that and that and that," ripping again and again until a pile of torn paper littered the countertop. Rich helped me move the pieces into the trash. I realized there was a negotiation of sorts going on between us, that he had been bothered by the appearance of a gift from another man and I was going a little overboard to prove how little Joe meant to me.

"Maybe I *will* keep the frame," I said. "I just got Nat's school picture back and I've been meaning to buy something to put it in."

"Eight by ten?"

"Deluxe package. I've got every size print imaginable including eight wallet photos. You don't want one, by any chance?"

"It might not go over well at school if I carry a picture of a student in my wallet, you know?"

Of course it wouldn't and I laughed but the truth was I really didn't have anyone to give all those pictures too. I had ordered the deluxe set just to get the eight by ten, out of habit, because that was what a parent did. Hugo and I had once discussed not participating in the school photo racket – with our good digital camera we could take as many of our own pictures of Nat as we wanted – but it felt somehow like a parental requirement to shell out that annual fifty bucks for the bad photographer to pose your child in front of a stilted backdrop and transform him into a grinning mannequin. I no longer questioned it; I just filled in the order form and wrote out the check.

"But a picture of Nat's mother – *that's* something I might carry in my wallet."

That took me by surprise, jolting me out of the nervousness Joe's "gift" had returned me to and away from thoughts of refuse and recycling and parental habits and *this is a nice frame after all* and *where did I put that eight by ten of Nat anyway*. Rich walked over to me at the counter, where I had reassembled the frame, and took me in his arms.

The frame itself. Clear glass free of any image, just transparency. It was the simplest thought to keep it, not to waste something beautiful. My head tilted back as Rich lowered his face to kiss the front of my neck. His hands moved along my sides, tracing my ribs, waist and hips where they rested. Standing in the kitchen, our bodies aligned; mouth to knee, I felt every inch of him; and I was lost to a feeling that it was impossible for us not to make love. My own hands moved slowly down his back, which felt curved and strong as he held and discovered me, until my fingertips crept under his belt and found his skin. Tender, soft, alive, human skin. Our mouths found each other again and there was no turning back.

I didn't expect Nat home until 10 a.m. at the earliest so Rich and I slept late, naked and supple in each other's arms. We had alternately made love and talked until almost dawn, an experience I had thought was reserved for young lovers and I now learned belonged to lovers of any age. I was thirty-nine, Rich was thirty-seven. We had wrinkles and grey hairs and pouches and scars and yet we had had a night so romantic we might have been teenagers. We lay in bed, facing each other, actually gazing into each other's eyes.

Eventually we showered, dressed and shared a breakfast of toast and fried eggs which he cooked at my stove and cleaned up at my sink. I felt like saying, "You've got the job," but held my tongue. I didn't want to break the spell with flippancy, not yet.

What finally evaporated our lovely haze was the ringing phone. Nat. He was on his way home.

"Got a back door?" Rich asked.

"Yes, but you'd be trapped in the yard."

We kissed. He had brought nothing but himself and what he was wearing. I walked him to the front door where we said goodbye. He promised to call and then added, "Let me know if that guy bothers you any more, OK? Especially if he shows up here again. Don't suffer in silence."

That made me laugh. I hadn't exactly been silent about Joe; I had told Sara and Courtney and Elliot and now Rich.

"Thanks. I will."

"Promise?"

I kissed him. "Promise."

I resisted an urge to watch him as he walked away. What if the neighbors saw him leaving? What would they think? Would I become the neighborhood hussy? All that ran through my mind but then as I locked the door I reassured myself that in the city people didn't pay that much attention to each other. No one would care if their widowed neighbor had a lover.

A lover. *I had a lover*.

Nat brought me a Yankees cap. "Go ahead, Mom. Wear it."

I stuck it on my head and we cheered half-heartedly. It was an inside joke. Living on the Vineyard, in Massachusetts, it was all about the Red Sox and you learned quickly that wearing Yankees or Mets paraphernalia was considered a provocation. Ditto, in reverse, wearing Red Sox in New York. Hugo and I were never particularly into sports but Nat, strangely, was and so I became aware of the New York–Boston rivalry. Nat wore his Red Sox jersey around the Vineyard and only took out his Yankees shirt when visiting my mother in New York. Now that we lived here, it seemed he planned a transformation.

"We're here now, right?" he said. "I mean the Yankees aren't bad."

"You had fun last night?"

"Totally."

"How was it sleeping at Henry's?"

"I don't know how much we actually slept." He grinned, knowing that sleepover antics bugged me because next-day exhaustion made it almost impossible to concentrate on homework which Nat had a bad habit of putting off so it tended to pile up on the weekends. "Don't worry, Mom. I caught a few Zs. Bring on that science project and that English paper and those twenty math problems and studying for that social studies test on Monday morning." He collapsed, mockingly, on the floor. I willed myself to not get sucked into it, hung my Yankees cap on a hook by the front door and walked away.

And then, I couldn't help myself. Halfway up the stairs I turned around and asked, "Have you brushed your teeth at all since yesterday morning?"

He played dead, or sleeping, on the floor. He looked so big lying there, sprawled out in his jeans and sneakers and Yankees jersey like a giant toddler. His hair was a total mess. I loved him so much. He didn't answer. I'd give it an hour or so before making lunch; maybe then he'd be a little more tuned-in to being back home.

I lay on my bed and opened my laptop on my stomach. Could I really smell Rich on my sheets or was I imagining it? Breathing deeply, I tried to recall every sensation of last night. The silky feel of our skin together. His velvety tongue. The exhilaration of sex and the shock and pleasure of the first moment he entered me. The sense, as it was happening, that nothing about this was wrong, everything about this was right. The sheer pleasure of it. And afterwards his wide-open eyes unblinking as he gazed at me across a shared pillow.

Hickory. That was his smell. I closed my eyes and recalled it.

The sound of Nat's footsteps clomping up the stairs brought me back to the moment. As he passed my room he popped in to see what I was doing, and, finding me prone beneath my laptop as I often was, he turned around and left. A moment later I heard the shower running. Good. He was starting to tend to his personal hygiene without being asked and yet I was having trouble letting go of my role as his motivator even though it had gotten to the point that reminders not only didn't help but seemed to diminish his motivation. He was a teenager now and needed *space*. I would have to work on that.

I booted up my laptop and went straight to email. A bunch of messages streamed into my inbox, mostly junk which I systematically deleted. But there was one from Sara, sent right after we talked on the phone yesterday evening, so I opened it.

"Hi, Sweets, have fun on your date? Babysitter's on her way so I've gotta get moving. Don't want to be late for the movies on our annual night out! hahaha. Dinner too I hope if we can make it. Tomorrow is that wedding over on the Cape so we're out early and back late. Talk Sunday OK? Can't wait to hear *everything*. xoxoxoxox Sara"

I answered one more email, from Courtney, who asked, "Any contact yet?" She meant Abe Starkman. I sent her a quick answer that I hadn't heard from him. "But I did hear from Joe Coffin . . . he left a FRAMED PHOTO OF HIMSELF on my front door!!! I guess even after eight hours in the mail-room the guy can't stop delivering stuff . . ."

I almost hopped onto the Web to do a little preliminary research on something that had been bugging me about long-buried bones – I'd been wondering just how much information could be extracted from them in a lab – but decided not to let work suck up even an hour of the weekend, not when I could spend time with Nat instead.

Since Hugo died I had made a real effort not to spend so much time mentally and physically away from Nat, not to be so busy all the time, cherishing instead the connections we forged by spending time together even if just bodily in the same room. For me that meant not working on the weekends because once I stuck my head into a story there wasn't much anyone could do to distract me until I'd reached the end of a thought or sentence or paragraph or page or article. When he was younger, in our house on the Vineyard, Nat had complained about how my back was so often turned to him while I sat at the computer. I had thought that being home after school was enough. But it wasn't, quite. He needed my attention to be available and not be confronted with my back when he had a question or decided to tell me *really* how school had gone that day. I suspected that this was a big part of why I hadn't given myself a desk in our new home. I had intended to but hadn't gotten around to it, instead planting myself on my bed when I needed to use the laptop. This way he would never come looking for me and find my back instead. And really, lying down and typing wasn't so bad once you got used to it. I was beginning to feel a little bit like the writer Colette who was said to have written all her novels in bed. Ditto Edith Wharton. Who else, I wondered, lying beneath my laptop, had supplied the world with great art from the comfort of her mattress?

I closed the laptop and went rooting through my room in search of Nat's packet of school photos. My room, Nat's room . . . nothing. I finally found it on the kitchen counter in a pile of mail that had accumulated over the past two weeks. I was good about plucking out bills and important papers and putting them into a special drawer I'd reserved for things I couldn't afford to lose track of but the rest of the paperwork that flowed into the house could end up just about anywhere.

Nat looked so goofy in the photo, with his stiff school-picture smile and his hair frazzled out above his shoulders. A bright red pimple sat smack between his eyes where his bushy brows had started to grow together. The downy beginnings of a mustache looked like a shadow over his lip. It had darkened in the weeks since the photograph was taken. My beautiful boy. I kissed my fingertip and touched it to his cheek, then placed the photo face down atop the glass in the open frame. It really was quite a beauty and I was glad Rich had convinced me to keep it. So what if it came from Joe? It was just a frame, an object, and meant nothing in and of itself.

The photo installed, I propped the frame on the living room mantle. Ours wasn't as stately as Rich's but it served nicely as a place to put special things. We had made a nice display of family photos and a few choice knickknacks.

"What's that?" Nat asked, having run thumping down the stairs and emerging in a burst of energy into the living room.

"An elephant tusk. What do you think it is?"

"I look like such a dork!"

"You look adorable!"

It was our routine, every year: he pretended he didn't want his school picture on display and I argued in favor of it. But I knew that if I didn't put out the newest photo he'd feel I'd skirted a duty.

"Nice frame," he said.

"Isn't it?" No *way* would I tell him how I'd gotten it.

"I'm hungry."

And so we ate. Over lunch we made a plan for the day. He would do homework all afternoon while I chipped away at unpacking – we still had unopened boxes from the move stacked in one corner of the living room and in my bedroom – and later we'd go out to dinner and a movie.

Unpacking is no picnic when you're transferring stuff into an existing mess so I forced myself to clean and organize as I went. Despite gnawing fatigue from hardly sleeping last night I was happy, happier than I'd felt since before Hugo's death, and managed to enjoy the project. Or maybe happy wasn't the word. I felt *alive* for the first time in a year and a half.

The weekend flew by uneventfully: no dreaded contacts by Joe, nor any sign of Abe Starkman. I started to worry that the bones story would suffocate and die for lack of the kind of oxygenated information Abe could supply – if he came through as promised. I hoped he would; but it was beyond my control so I tried not to dwell on it. It was the weekend, I was home with my child, *I had a lover*. There were so many reasons not to worry about work.

Rich called my cell phone late Sunday morning. I'd been lying on the couch reading the magazine section of the newspaper and had to fly upstairs to my bedroom, where I'd left my purse, to answer it.

"I thought I couldn't call you," he said, "because I was worried about my name showing up on caller ID and what if Nat saw it and, you know. It shows my age that it took me this long to think of calling your cell phone." It was because he was a teacher and an artist, someone who focused only on what he was doing and could not afford to make himself constantly available to everyone else. I on the other hand would have thought of calling a cell phone in about thirty seconds. It didn't matter; he sounded as happy to hear my voice as I was to hear his.

"How's the rest of your weekend been?" I asked.

"Good. *Great*. I've been painting. You?"

"Hanging out with Nat. Unpacking. We saw a really good movie last night." I told him about it and we agreed, or hoped, we'd get out to the movies together soon. "Listen, Nat has an early rehearsal this Wednesday. He'll be leaving the house at about seven. Want to have breakfast?"

"Absolutely. I have to be at school at eight fifteen so it won't be a leisurely breakfast, but let's do it anyway. Where?"

I didn't hesitate: "Here."

He laughed because we both knew what we'd have for this *breakfast* and it wouldn't be food.

"So," he asked, "any more creepy guy?"

"You mean Joe."

"I remember his name; I just didn't want to say it."

"Nope. I guess he took a couple of days off. See? It's probably just an innocent crush."

"Darcy . . ."

"OK, it's stranger than that. But I haven't heard a peep from him since the photo, so don't worry."

"I am worried; it's partly why I called. Have you thought any more about talking to the police?"

"Yes, but I still think it's premature, and I still don't want to screw things up at work."

"I understand that, but please at least consider it."

"I will. If it gets worse, I'll call them."

We chatted a little more before saying goodbye. It felt funny having a boyfriend after having had a beloved husband from whom I'd never imagined parting. Now I knew how it happened: how you *moved on* after a tragedy. I had always wondered how my parents had managed to endure life after the Holocaust – though my father's survival had proved to be a drawn-out temporary solution to an inner death he could not ultimately overcome. A series of inner deaths; my mother's *echoes*. My mother, though, had truly survived and now I understood how she had done it.

You didn't forget anyone or anything. You remembered every moment, every feeling, every thought, every smell. You remembered details that would haunt you forever. But the conveyor belt of days and weeks and months and years moved you forward regardless of all that. You *moved on*, despite everything. And slowly, eventually, your senses and hungers reignited because that was what it meant to be alive. I understood that now and felt no sense of guilt toward Hugo, who was gone so completely it was hard to believe. But I did feel some guilt in regard to Nat, from whom I was keeping my affair with Rich a secret.

I didn't like to hide anything from my son. But on the other hand it seemed a worse option to flaunt a new relationship in front of a child who would have his own feelings and expectations, and possibly disappointments, about Mommy parsing out love to someone new. And then what if it didn't work out? How would that affect Nat? Luckily Rich had the same concerns and so it was implicit between us that our children would not be a part of this – not yet.

Nat and I took a long walk late Sunday afternoon, ending up in Dumbo where we ate brick-oven pizza for dinner followed by a dessert of homemade ice cream, which we ate slowly on a natch overlooking the East River as the sun descended behind us, casting the Manhattan skyline in a haze of lavender light. It was beautiful. I wanted to hold my son's hand but checked the urge. At thirteen, the only hand he'd want to hold would belong to some other lucky girl. After a long, slow walk home Nat read alone in his room and I did my thing on the bed with my laptop.

What I found waiting for me in my inbox would change everything.

PART TWO

PART TWO

CHAPTER 6

Sara had sent me another email:

"Hi, honey, hold on to your hat, because all that with Joe Coffin? It gets worse. I tried calling you but you weren't home and this I can't leave in a message. I called your cell but it isn't on. And now we're taking the kids to Jean and Larry's for dinner so I'm going to hit you with this in an email. Sorry."

I looked at the top of her message: written about an hour ago.

"I opened the box. I see why he didn't want to keep it at home in case his mother found it. There was stuff in there about different women going a few years back, things like fuzzy pictures taken from a distance and really obsessive love letters he wrote and never sent and also little objects, stuff like a dusty old box of little marzipan fruits and a pair of scuffed white high heels and a 1989 yearbook from a high school in Texas. Stuff that didn't make a lot of sense to me and here's the worst: two pairs of women's underpants that don't look clean . . . But I'm avoiding what I really need to tell you. He had a big fat scrapbook *all about you*. Everything. All your articles and the same kind of fuzzy distant photos of you and Hugo and Nat and even you and *me* and at least ten of those unsent love letters. There's also a framed photograph of him with his arm around a woman but he cut *your* face out of another picture and pasted it on the woman's head. Darcy, he's out of his mind. He *is* stalking you and has been for at least two years by the look of this box. He probably followed you to New York. HE IS CRAZY and probably DANGEROUS. *Go to the police NOW*. Call me first thing in the morning and tell me that you will. If you don't *I* will stalk you until you do!"

Stunned, I read the email through three more times. First time to get the gist of it. Second time to double-check that I hadn't imagined any of it. Third time to convince myself of what Sara already believed: that Joe was a bigger problem than I had realized or admitted to myself.

And then, as if he had been hovering and listening and watching and knew that now was the time to drive home the onerous reality of the box – the *contents* of the box – twenty minutes later the phone started to ring. And ring and ring and ring. After each set of ten rings the voicemail picked up. I listened to the first message: "Hi, Darcy, it's Joe. Hope you had a great weekend. Mine was quiet. Did you get the gift I left you? Give me a buzz when you have a minute."

As if we were friends! As if I would even consider calling him back! He *was* out of his mind. I no longer doubted Sara's or Rich's wisdom that it was time to call the police.

But first I called Rich. He wasn't home and he didn't answer his cell phone. He must have been painting. So I forwarded Sara's email to him and left a message on his voicemail: "It's Darcy. You were right. Check your email. I'm going to the police in the morning."

The phone rang seventy-three times before finally stopping. Nat came in and out of my room, asking what was going on and trying to accept my lame explanations about unsolicited salespeople not knowing when to give up. Finally, he threatened to answer it himself. I had to stop him.

"Sweetie, sit down."

It was late; we were both in our pajamas. He sat on the edge of my bed, turned to me and waited. I took his hand and he didn't flinch it away, maybe because we were not in public or maybe because he was scared. Weaving my fingers through his, I began.

"There's a guy at work who's been bothering me."

"Who?"

"I hardly know him, but he used to live on the Vineyard, and he saw me at work and was very friendly. I didn't think anything of it at first."

"So, like, he wants to go out with you?"

"If *you* wanted to go out with a girl, would you call her a zillion times like that?"

"No way." Without hesitation.

"Right. I'm not sure why he wants my attention so badly. It's a little unusual. I'm talking with the Human Resources guy at the office tomorrow so they can ask Joe to stop."

"His name is Joe?"

"Joe Coffin."

"*Nice name.*" It was what he had always said, growing up on the Vineyard, when he encountered the name *Coffin* on a street sign or mailbox or school roster or anywhere else. *Nice name.* "What's human resources?"

"The office that deals with employment related things, like making sure you get your benefits and stuff like that."

"And firing loser jerks who bother people at home."

"You got it."

He thought it over a moment. "So they'll fire him and he'll stop calling?"

"Hopefully. They might give him a warning first, you know, to give him a fair chance to improve his behavior before they do something as drastic as firing him." Though even as I said it I knew it was never going to be enough to deter Joe and I *knew* it was necessary that I summon real help. But I would not tell Nat about my decision to contact the police. I wouldn't even call them tonight, when he was home; I would wait until he left for school in the morning. I could not let him become any more concerned than he already was about the strangeness of the situation or the vague possibility that it might involve some kind of threat to his only remaining parent.

Soon after Hugo died, Nat asked me what would happen to him if for some reason I also died. "I'd be an orphan," he said. "Who would I live with?" The possibilities had fled through my mind at that awful thought and I understood how high the stakes were for him now that he was fatherless. We both knew that my mother was unfit for caretaking a child, and Hugo's parents were already gone. He had a brother in Florida, a man who lived alternately on welfare or as a transient farmhand; a man who was over forty yet hadn't "found himself" or anyone else who could tolerate his perpetual adolescence. He wasn't much of a grown-up and he would *not* do to raise my son. So who? "Sara," I told him. "Sara will always be there for you, Nat." That very day I asked her permission to list her in my will as Nat's guardian and she readily agreed.

"It's gonna be OK," I told him now. "Stuff like this happens sometimes."

"It does?"

"Sure. There are some pretty strange people out there, if you haven't noticed."

"Oh, I've noticed! Like Mr Strolene?" And he was off on a rant about his gym teacher, a man he had spoken of quite a bit lately and who either had a great sense of humor or was certifiably insane. I looked forward to meeting him and finding out.

After a while he went to bed. Mitzi curled up beside me, a purring ball of white fur, while Ahab, tabby investigator, sniffed around my room for the umpteenth time. I listened to the messages left on my voicemail: all from Joe and all pretending we were great friends. Later, as I lay awake in the dark, my cell phone rang and my heart jumped . . . but it was only Rich. I answered and we spoke briefly, in whispers; but not about our lovely time together on Friday. He was anxious for me and I repeated my intention to call the police.

In the morning, as Nat got ready to leave for school, I peppered him with reminders I knew would annoy him but I couldn't help myself.

"Do you have your cell phone with you?"

"Yes."

"Is it charged?"

"Yes."

"Is it turned on?"

"*Yes.*"

"And you have your house keys?"

"Mom – *yes*! I'm all set."

"I just need to know—"

Standing at the open front door, he leaned in to kiss my cheek. "I'll be fine. Don't worry so much." He didn't mention last night and neither did I. Was he thinking about Joe, now that he knew about him? Or had he already moved past it in his young, flexible mind?

"Call me when you get to school this morning and when you leave at three and when you get back to the house."

He stared at me, deadpan. "You're joking, right?"

Was I? Hadn't my mandate been to give him more freedom, not less?

"I'm not sure."

"Great. That's a big help. See ya, Mom." He stepped through the inner door, into the vestibule, through the iron gate and into a bright autumn morning. Standing in the hall in my nightgown, cool air flowed over me; but it didn't feel refreshing or good, as it normally did. Today the chilly air made my exposed skin feel raw and so I rubbed my hands up and down my arms, more to feel protected than to warm myself.

"I love you, honey," I called after him.

"Love you, too." He turned and smiled tenderly, just like when he was little. Then he headed off to school.

I sat down at the kitchen table with a cup of coffee and the phone. First I called Sara and we filled each other in, agreeing that Joe had stalked me from the Vineyard to New York. Then I called Elliot at home to let him know that my problem with Joe had escalated and I was contacting the police. He hesitated before responding but soon mustered encouragement.

"Do what you have to do, Darcy. Just keep me informed. First thing on my agenda this morning is to see Paul Ardsley in person. No more delays. This will be dealt with from our side, OK?"

"OK. Thanks, Elliot."

And then I called the police. I said very little before the officer who answered the phone told me to make my way to the local precinct. She told me something I hadn't known – that I lived in the jurisdiction of the 84th Precinct – and also that I was "lucky" because they had an in-house stalking expert there.

"Detective Jesus Ramirez," she said. "Ask for him specifically."

I fed Mitzi and Ahab, showered and dressed, packed up my laptop and was finally ready to leave when I had another surprise.

In the vestibule between the door and gate, the backside of a bulky envelope faced me from the ground. I stopped short, sucked in my breath; it was as if I had come upon a snake preparing to strike. Sun coming through the curlicue ironwork gate threw a shivering pattern of light on the tan skin of the envelope. Someone must have shoved it through the oversized mail slot after Nat left the house or he would have brought it into the foyer. I bent at the knee and carefully lifted it, turned it. *What had Joe left me now?*

But it was only the package of new jeans I'd ordered for Nat last week. The relief I felt was itself sickening, interwoven with a certainty that, if not now, the menace would find me later. *Joe would never leave me alone*; and just as I thought that, a clanking sound outside my front gate sent my pulse racing.

He was here. I knew it. I dropped the package and swung open the gate to confront him – a thoughtless move that might have cost me some unfathomable price . . . had it actually been Joe.

It wasn't. It was Abe Starkman, wearing his yellow helmet, his white bike leaning against my iron fence. He held a vertically bent manila envelope and was in the act of bending down to push it through my mail slot.

We stared at each other in shock for different reasons but with one thing in common on our faces: fear.

"I was just going to leave this." There was a tremor in his near-whisper. Perspiration from his forehead trickled down both temples and was absorbed by the black helmet straps that crossed his face, meeting tightly beneath his chin. His clean-shaven neck looked pinkish raw. Vulnerable. He had not wanted to encounter me. Didn't want to be seen here. Ached to get away as quickly as possible.

"Are you OK?" I whispered.

He nodded – a polite nod, a refusal to burden me with his personal conflicts, and an acknowledgment that he had made a choice and would take the heat no matter how blistering it became.

When I took the envelope from his hand, I noticed his wedding band, scuffed and time-worn, settled into the flesh of his fourth finger. His eyes, pale and bloodshot, reminded me how much this story meant to him, considering how much he had to lose.

"Thank you," he said.

"Thank *you*."

He turned, righted his bicycle and sped away.

I locked the gate behind me, ripped open the top of the envelope and pulled out a sheaf of loose papers. They were contracts and in a quick sweep of my eye I saw references to the Atlantic Yards. I almost forgot about Joe, about where I was going and why, in my relief to have this envelope tucked in my bag beneath my laptop. I would read it over carefully, later, as soon as I had the chance.

Walking over to the precinct on Gold Street, in the shadow of the Manhattan Bridge, I felt so angry at Joe for putting me through this. I wanted to get inside that envelope, not spend time complaining about some creep who wanted to date me. As I walked, my mind kept returning to the thought that this thing with Joe was nothing. And then I would remember the box and realize it was in fact *something*. I didn't want it to be, but it was. It was confusing and irritating and if Joe were here now I would have stopped in my tracks, spun at him and shouted, "LEAVE ME ALONE!"

Was he here? Wasn't he *always* here? How had I not noticed him for two whole years? Had my move to New York triggered an urgency for him to take action? He *had* taken action: he'd left his lifelong island, left his mother, and followed me to the city. Now I was the only person he knew among millions. Millions of strangers he had no interest in . . . and *me*, in whom his interest was wildly distorted.

I stopped walking halfway through MetroTech Plaza, almost at Gold Street, and looked around.

Office workers streamed in all directions; my standing still was completely out of synch with the fast rhythm of the morning rush. I didn't see him anywhere so continued on my way, thinking as I went that I was about to seek help from a man named Jesus . . . who woulda thunk it?

The 84th Precinct was a squat building sitting on the seam between the "reinvigorated" MetroTech Plaza complex and a grim stretch of housing projects which would qualify as urban blight if they hadn't been established by the city in the first place. The mid-century urban planner Robert Moses had left his mark on New York in many ways and this was one of them: affordable housing in the form of clusters of brick buildings that looked like stacks of blocks – or prisons. Demolishing them via eminent domain, as the neighborhoods surrounding the Atlantic Yards were being vanquished, would be admitting that the city's many housing projects had been a mistake. They segregated groups of people from each other and created insular communities where poverty consciousness ruled and despair was the standard atmosphere. It was economic segregation which on its surface looked like racial segregation. Hugo once told me he'd read a study that concluded that environmental activism routinely failed with people who felt hopeless. So it was no wonder that electric street lights shone in broad daylight and garbage was strewn all over the streets as far as I could see behind the precinct, as I approached its dirty glass doors.

The lobby was as grim as the outside of the building. Behind a scratched Plexiglas barrier sat a woman in uniform whose job appeared to be reception. I leaned down to the little semicircle opening and said, "I'm here to see Detective Jesus Ramirez."

"He know you're coming?"

"No."

It didn't seem to matter. She reached him on the intercom and in minutes he came down to greet me.

He was the ugliest man I'd ever seen. Though he was medium height, he managed to give the impression of being squat. He had tiny eyes, a prize-fighter's squashed nose and wide mouth whose fleshy lips came together in the appearance of a pinkish slab. His trimmed black beard covered the entire bottom half of his face and an attempt at hair plugs had failed glaringly, leaving red circles visible through the net of hair covering his scalp.

"I'm Darcy Mayhew." I offered a hand, which he shook. "I called and was told to ask for you."

In contrast to his face he had a lovely smile and the smooth, deep voice of a radio host. "Why don't we talk upstairs at my desk?" He led me to an elevator and when it came stepped aside so I could enter first. Riding up in the elevator with him I became aware of his cologne. Musky, reassuring, it triggered a memory: my father, singing "The Circle Game" in his German accent, driving me through an unexpected snowstorm on the way to a friend's party we would learn was canceled. How was it that this was the same cologne my father had worn decades ago? Two such different people in such different places in such different times.

Detective Ramirez's graciousness extended through a scuffed hallway and into the detectives unit – a busy room crowded with desks and people on phones or old boxy computers. It reminded me of a low-rent version of a newsroom and I liked it, felt at home here in a funny way. He found a stray chair, which he stationed at the side of his industrial metal desk, and motioned for me to sit down. I did. He then sat in his chair facing the desk whose prominent features were its neatness and a large family photo showing him shoulder to shoulder with a smiling wife with curly black hair, surrounded by five children.

I told him everything. He listened with an expression of growing concern. When I was finished he leaned forwards, clasped his hands on the desktop and said, "Congratulations. You have a stalker. Welcome to the club."

"Is that supposed to be funny?"

"Not at all. I'm sorry – maybe I'm jaded. I've

been doing this for twenty-five years. There's nothing funny about stalking."

"So how do I get him to stop?"

Ramirez pressed out a smile, but not a hopeful one. "You take precautions. I can tell you what to do and what not to do. You develop a low profile, you do nothing to encourage him, and we see if this has any effect."

I stared at him. "That's it?"

"That's what I advise. There are other options, like applying for a restraining order—"

"I want one."

"I know you do, but let me explain something. When it comes to stalkers, restraining orders have limited effect in reality. More often than not they can actually make things worse. Especially if there's not much going on in their lives and they don't have much to lose. The order's just one more door for them to break down to get to you, only if they're the type to get angry that you sought action against them, the rage . . . well, do you have any idea how many women we've found murdered with a restraining order in her purse?"

I felt the blood drain out of my face at that remark – out of my heart and my veins, out of my soul. Realizing he'd been insensitive, he tried to correct himself.

"What I mean is this. When you take out a

restraining order, the law is we have to inform your stalker about the order, and that's where we run into trouble. These guys are obsessive. They're determined. They hear restraining order and in their twisted brains two things typically happen: they're challenged, or they're enraged, or both. Sometimes, if the guy's not a career stalker, he might back off. But that's only sometimes."

"Career stalker?"

"Someone who's done this before."

"Joe has, I think."

Ramirez nodded wearily. "You could get yourself a restraining order. It's up to you. But you need to understand the possible consequences. Personally, at this point, I wouldn't recommend it."

I felt like a cancer patient being asked by my doctor if I wanted a treatment that might kill me. What I wanted was an authority to tell me what to do, to take over the Joe problem and use his expertise to make it go away. Apparently, that wasn't going to happen.

"One thing you should know," he said, "and here's the catch-22, is that without a restraining order in place, if things escalate, it's harder to prosecute. The courts are dicey when it comes to stalking – some judges take it seriously, some don't. Mostly it's a state by state thing. It wasn't even considered a crime until nineteen ninety."

"But it *is* a crime now?"

"Absolutely. The trick is feeling out if and when it's the right time to put an order in place. When these guys hear *Order of Restraint* and they read all that fine print, it's like the heavy hand coming down on them. You said you've got your personnel people at work dealing with it – that might be a more gentle solution, easier for him to swallow. It might shame him into pulling back. I'm telling you, some of these guys get scared of themselves and back off. Others don't. In your case, it's been, what – a week?"

"Two years, my friend said, based on the stuff in the box."

He considered that, leaning back and stroking his beard with a stout hand. "I'll get in touch with the Martha's Vineyard police, see if he has any priors, mental disorders, if anyone's had a restraining order on him before. And I wouldn't mind taking a look at the box. Can you ask your friend to send it?"

"I will."

"And you said you have a kid?"

"Nat's thirteen."

"Has he been bothered by this Joe guy?"

"No. Joe only seems interested in me."

"Good."

I half smiled and he matched my reaction with a small chuckle; there was nothing *good* about this.

"So what are the statistics?" I asked. "How bad *is* this?"

"Honestly? It's too soon to tell. If he keeps up what he's doing, he's a little leaguer, a bug in the room, basically. Here's how you find out what you're dealing with: you don't talk to him, you don't look at him, you don't smile at him, you don't give him the time of day. You do not answer the phone, ever, when he calls. You never respond to notes or emails or whatever. If he leaves you stuff, you act like you never got it. If he gets in your face and you can't avoid him, you tell him, point-blank, you're not interested. You don't give him a single loophole to think otherwise. If you see him following you again, you turn in the opposite direction."

"I've been doing most of that since the middle of last week," I said. "But he isn't stopping. And it terrifies me when I see him."

"I understand. But for now, it's what you've got to do. We watch and see if it escalates and then revisit the idea of an order – unless you decide you want one now."

It kept coming back to that. He would not tell me what to do; I had to decide on my own.

"So you recommend that I basically do nothing?"

"No, not nothing."

Bending down, he opened a low cabinet and pulled out a battered manila file folder. He withdrew a form titled "VICTIM STALKING WORK-SHEET". Together, we filled out all the information, which was a distillation of everything I'd told him, the bare facts without the irritation or the fear. Then – and this shook me – he led me to another room where he took my fingerprints and photographed me front, back and both my profiles. It was obvious why he wanted these records: to identify me, just in case . . . I couldn't even think it.

When he was finished, he shocked me again. "Bring your kid in as soon as you can, OK?"

"For this?"

"It's a formality, but better safe than sorry, right?"

"Right." But I didn't want to bring Nat here! It would terrify him. And then I remembered something. "He gave fingerprints at the agricultural fair on the Vineyard, at the police booth, just two summers ago. Can we use those?"

"Sure."

"And I can give you one of his recent school photos."

"Perfect."

He was humoring me now because he was a father and he understood. I liked this man.

"Another thing," he said as we walked back through the detectives unit and returned to his desk. "Get me copies of dental records, for both of you."

I nodded; at least I thought I did. My mind was reeling. I was basically to do nothing while simultaneously preparing for the worst possible outcome. How would I live with this? And then I thought of my mother – my sweet, strong, incoherent mother who had come through more than I could possibly imagine – and recognized the insignificance of my own problems.

"I'll call today."

He handed me his business card on which he had handwritten his cell number, and copies of a sheet entitled "STALKING LOG". I was to fill it out each and every time Joe made a move in my direction. The idea was to record events as they occurred, not to entrust to memory details that could prove crucial in the future. Clearly, our tactic was to prepare for the worst while hoping for the best. Not what I'd expected when I walked through the door.

"It's going to be OK," he said in a kind voice that was reassuring regardless of whether or not it was true – whether or not it *would* be OK. He walked me back down the hall and, in a gesture I now recognized as his signature gallantry, pushed the elevator button for me and waited for it to come. "If it makes you feel any better, you're not alone. Unfortunately I've had a lot of stalking victims ask for help over the years."

"Victim? But nothing's happened to me yet."

"Sure it has. It's happening to you right now; that's why you're here. It's ongoing. When it's finished – that's when you're a survivor of a crime. Until then, as long as you're experiencing it, you're a victim-in-progress. This is something I've said to cops and prosecutors and judges and everyone and I can't say it enough. It's a slow-drip crime, some people don't even notice until the consequences . . ." He stopped when he read the dismay on my face.

He smiled – a friendly smile – and touched my shoulder. "My wife Angela says I've been doing this too long. Says I don't understand how bad it sounds to people who aren't used to it. Honestly, it's a maze, but I'm here to guide you, OK?"

"OK." But could he guide me past dangers neither of us saw?

"Keep the faith. Jesus will show you the way." He smiled, revealing a wide gap between his two front teeth. "I hit everyone with that once."

Laughing, I stepped into the elevator. "Thanks, Detective—"

"Nickname's Jess." He winked.

"Jess. Thank you."

It was after eleven by the time I got into work. I stood in the elevator bank and waited five minutes until a door finally dinged open. And when it did, as if orchestrated to test me, Joe was alone inside. When he saw me a smile blossomed on his face and his eyes appeared to brighten.

"Hi!" He pressed his hand against the doorjamb to prevent the doors from closing.

I felt suddenly hot, confused, and hesitated. Stood there, remembering Jess's advice not to acknowledge him in any way. Certainly that had to include sharing elevators with him – and the last thing I wanted was to be stuck inside a tiny exitless room with the man. He pushed his mail cart into the far corner, as if that was what was deterring me.

"There's plenty of room. Sorry I missed you last night, by the way. Out having fun?"

I hated him. I believed he knew perfectly well I'd been home last night. He was probably outside, watching. I said nothing.

"You're getting back from an early interview, I bet. Morning meetings slow down the day, don't they? I've been here since nine on the dot. Left a little early Friday and didn't want to risk getting on Mac's nerves first thing Monday. Mac's my supervisor, nice guy. I think this job's really going to work out. I'll work on my writing, I *will*, and when the time's right I'll apply for the internship program. Maybe you can help me. Maybe—"

I walked five feet to stand in front of another elevator and stared at its tightly seamed doors. On the wall above, a light board showed that the next elevator was three flights away.

"I'm moving next week." Still holding his elevator open, he leaned out into the lobby to see me. "I hope you're still free Saturday night for dinner. Did I mention you can bring your son?"

I shifted so my back was to him. The lobby was empty except for a security guard, posted at a desk twenty feet away.

The elevator arrived. I stepped inside, feeling relieved to be away from him . . . until I heard the clatter of wheels on the lobby's marble floor. The mail cart entered first, followed by Joe, whose forehead was covered with beads of sweat.

How could I do this? I, pressed into one rear corner of the elevator, and he, his cart pressed into the opposite corner while he stood there effectively blocking the doorway. He emanated a sense of blind insistence and a strange rotten kind of misery. My instincts rose above my mind and everything Jess had told me flew out the window of this windowless elevator where I was now trapped with someone who frightened me more than anyone had ever frightened me in my life. Ignoring him wasn't working.

"Oh, so we do fit easily," I said, glancing at his mail cart.

"Sure. I ride up and down with people and the cart all day long." His tone was breezy in a forced way, incompatible with the tension in his expression. I wondered how I could ever have thought him *adorable* as I had just a week ago. Adorable and harmless and sweet. My antennae had never been more off.

"Joe." Seized by an inspiration, I looked at him straight on now, right into his weird off-balance granite-chipped eyes. "This has to stop, OK? No more following me. No more phone calls. No more gifts. It's become very . . . awkward, you know?"

"It doesn't have to be *awkward*," he said, adding a bitter twist in his mimicry of the word.

"But it is. We work together. There's some basic protocol to follow, isn't there?"

"I don't think so, Darcy." He was smiling now, basking in the attention I was giving him. The more of it he soaked up, the more satisfied and grotesque he looked. The mask of his face seemed to distort and magnify as if my words – any word from me, positive or negative – fed his inner monster. I saw I had made a mistake talking to him, had been making mistakes all along. "I know we could be really good friends. You'll see. And you're going to love the dinner I make for you on Saturday. I'm a pretty good cook. Is your kid a picky eater? I was."

We reached the fifth floor and the newsroom. I was shaking when I stepped off the elevator, shaking and praying he wouldn't follow me out. He didn't. I could feel his eyes burning on my back as I walked away.

The newsroom was buzzing and Courtney was deep into the bones story, phone pressed to ear and simultaneously typing. When she saw me, she angled the mouthpiece away from her face.

"I'm on hold. You OK?"

"I just rode up with our little friend and I did everything Jesus told me not to."

She was speechless so I saved her.

"My detective, Jesus Ramirez, goes by Jess. What's *your* detective's name?"

"I've got a hairdresser, not a detective."

"Touché, lucky woman."

"So?"

"A lot of advice, some protocol to follow. My stats are on record so if my body surfaces in the river they can identify me."

She put her call on speaker, lay the handset on her desk – tinny muzak now piping into our section of the room – and got up to hug me. It was a short but restorative hug, and then her caller came on the line and she jumped back to work.

I took a peek into Elliot's office but he wasn't there. Returning to my desk, I set up my laptop and emailed Sara: *Please send me the box*. I called our dentist on the Vineyard and asked his assistant to send me copies of Nat's and my dental X-rays; I gave her my credit card number so she could overnight them to my office. I phoned the Martha's Vineyard police and asked if they could dig up those fingerprints of Nat's – they impressed me with an immediate response that it was all computerized and they could email it by the end of the day. And then I took out one of the stalking logs Jess had supplied me with and made my first entry: *Monday, 11.00 a.m., followed me into the elevator, non-stop talk, repeated dinner invitation for Sat. night.* I stashed the log in the top drawer of my desk for future use; I had a feeling there would be plenty of opportunities.

Finally, I opened Abe Starkman's envelope.

I was just starting to look through it when Courtney finished her phone call, so I summoned her to join me. She rolled her chair to sit beside me and I handed her pages as I finished them. When we were through, we looked at each other, excited.

"Perlotti Industries, Song Song Direct Hauling – and Metro Trucking again," she said.

"Interesting." Metro Trucking, which we already knew was owned by a distant cousin of Tony T's, had been enlisted to transport the bones into storage – without proper paperwork. Finding them on the presumably *real* land sale documents strengthened Abe Starkman's claim that the actual seller of the lots was Tony T, hiding behind his cousin's company, an enterprise he very well may have bankrolled and controlled which was characteristic, after all, of how the mob operated. It also substantiated the idea that he may have bought influence when he undersold his land.

"Darcy, I'm heading over to Buildings in a few minutes to snag a hard copy of the official paperwork Livingston & Sons filed on the lot purchase, then I'm taking one of my Buildings contacts out for lunch. A good person for you to meet. Come."

"Love to. I just need to talk with Elliot when he gets in. Did you see him this morning?"

"He was here until a little while ago, then he went to see Paul Assholdley." She winced. "So you see? He's on the case for you. Elliot keeps his promises, which is only one of the things I like about working for him."

I liked Elliot too and felt he had my best interests at heart, much as he obviously didn't care for the direction it was taking. No one did – except maybe Joe himself. I was curious, and a little afraid, to find out how Paul Ardsley would react to the news that I'd taken the problem out of house before he'd even had a chance to contain it. I wondered if they would fire Joe, *hoped* they would, but wouldn't count on it.

Elliot still wasn't back by eleven forty-five. Courtney began to gather her things to leave for the Buildings Department.

"Go without me," I said. "It's kind of effort-overlap to go together, anyway."

"Well, yes, except that four eyes are better than two."

"I have to wait for Elliot."

"I know you do. Don't worry, I'll come back when I'm through and we'll compare notes. Anyway now you can talk to Elliot about your source's land sale docs; they'll give him a dose of confidence that he's doing the right thing."

"I will. Have fun."

"Oh, yes, I *love* the Buildings Department." She rolled her eyes, hiked her green leather purse to her shoulder and strutted out of the newsroom.

I worked alone for a while before Elliot finally appeared, trying to develop a plan to unravel the lot sale documents Abe Starkman had provided. We'd have to hit every nail on the head, visit every place mentioned in the chain of ownership, follow every lead to see where it originated. Bit by bit, we would lay out the puzzle pieces and see what picture materialized. Abe Starkman was making it easy for us, delivering a road map. First the bones. Now the documents. Meanwhile a hue and cry was rising among city activists to identify the bones.

Sitting at my laptop, I Googled key words and snagged threads of popular response to the two stories we'd published so far. Like a virus, it had already spread throughout the Internet. What I learned confirmed my own instinct that finding out who those people had been was precisely where the story lay. Most readers and bloggers were jaded enough to expect an unholy alliance between developers, government officials and to some extent even the mob, and while it inspired outrage they seemed prepared to leave it to the experts to resolve. But death and identity? Everyone felt a primal despair at the thought of dying alone and invisible. Already that was the drumbeat that was rising in reaction to our stories: people wanted to *know*. *I* wanted to know.

A remark my father once made to my mother, as I trailed them around our local mall, now surfaced from the depths of memory. I was six, maybe seven, and didn't understand what they were talking about but his tone caught my attention and vivified the moment. In his musical German accent, he turned a mall full of shoppers into ghosts in my young mind. "Eva – these faces! Strangers to us, all of them. But each has a unique soul and each lives life with purpose just as we do. *That* is what I saw in the half-dead skeletons I buried. So many of them. *Their faces*. I was just a boy and I didn't understand but now I understand perfectly. I didn't know them and yet I knew them all. Buried, some *alive*, without a marker! A heap of people. We failed them, we who survived. I can't help it, Eva; their faces haunt me."

She took his hand, squeezed it, cast him a concerned look. We kept walking, they ahead, I behind, as was our family pattern; a triad for just two more months before we were reduced to a solitary, resilient pair.

When Elliot returned he went straight to his office and immediately buzzed my extension, asking me to join him. I shut his door without asking and sat across from him.

"OK, I saw Paul Ardsley. He apologized for being unavailable on Friday. He was very concerned and I can tell you that he's already put things into motion to protect you."

I was encouraged by Elliot's decisive tone and his choice of words: *concern*, *motion*, *protect*. Never before had I worked for such a big corporation and the idea that they could enfold you this way, defend you, felt liberating as if now I could set down my burden and sigh.

"Thank you, Elliot."

"It's my job, and it's Paul's job. But I *am* concerned about you on a personal level. I don't like the sound of this at all. And I can tell you that I learned this morning that HR's been under some pressure lately for their less-than-scrupulous handling of certain personnel matters, so they're not hesitating on this one. What they're doing, what they've done already as a matter of fact, is issue something called a workplace restraining order – a

WRO. It limits contact at work, meaning he can't use work as an excuse to get close while in the building. Am I right to assume you asked for a broader restraining order from the police this morning?"

"No, I didn't get one. The detective said not to." I explained Jess's warnings about restraining orders sometimes backfiring, exacerbating instead of de-escalating a situation. "He's been doing this for twenty-five years. He seems to know what he's talking about."

"Oh, *great*." Elliot raised his hands to his face, shook his head, dropped his hands into his lap. "I had no idea. Ardsley didn't say anything about that. He said they print out an order that's like a contract, and they call the guy in to read it in front of him and sign it. They send him away with a photocopy. They've issued them in the past and he said they've always worked."

"*Always?*" That single word, infused with incredulity, ignited on Elliot's face an expression of unease the likes of which I had never seen on him. Normally he was upbeat, in control, and now for a split second I saw that he was worried about the ramifications of the ball he'd set to rolling by visiting Paul Ardsley. I had never met the man personally, having been taken through new-employee processing by a more junior member of Human Resources, but from what I gathered Ardsley was not known for his stellar judgment – hitting on Courtney at the holiday party alone demonstrated that. Elliot may have known that about him, and my response, my *always*, seemed to have plunged him into regret for taking Ardsley's advice in the first place. Elliot had been trying to help and protect me. I wanted him to know how much I appreciated that.

"Well," I said, keeping my voice cooler than I felt, "let's hope it does the trick. Maybe Joe will get the message and back off so we can all concentrate on our work." But even as I said it, I didn't believe it would make a difference to Joe if someone handed him a piece of paper to sign, a mere article of faith, like a homework contract given to a first-grader. Joe was in a different league than guys who paid female co-workers a little too much attention on the job. *He had followed me from the Vineyard to New York.* In a mere week, his stalking had bled into nearly every corner of my life. But Elliot was my boss and I liked my job a lot and it seemed important at that moment to let him know how much I appreciated his actions on my behalf and to give his judgment, even Paul Ardsley's judgment, the benefit of the doubt, despite powerful misgivings.

Elliot nodded, looking distracted, glancing at his phone. Then he picked up the receiver and dialed Paul Ardsley's extension. Someone answered, but not Paul – he had left for lunch. Elliot tried to find out if before leaving he had met with an employee from the mailroom, but whoever had answered the phone was not forthcoming.

He looked at me, smiled sheepishly. "*Do no harm*. That was my grandfather's motto. He refused to leave China to come live with us. He believed the world would be better off if one fewer person shifted positions."

"An interesting attitude."

"Isn't it? Well. We should listen to our elders. Sorry, Darcy."

"But no harm's been done, and maybe it *will* help. I don't think this kind of situation has any particular rules, just guidelines. Meanwhile, Elliot –" I recrossed my legs, leaned forwards, changed the subject "– we're moving forward on the bones story. I have more information from my source. Hard copies of what we think are unofficial land sale documents for the lot where the bones were found."

Shifting the conversation to pure work instantly lightened the room's atmosphere. Elliot seemed relieved to be shown the door out of my *situation*. So was I. Anything seemed easier and better than thinking about Joe.

"*Ex*cellent."

"Courtney's going after the official documents; she's at Buildings now. We've got a bunch more legwork to do before we can put this part of the story together."

He nodded, thinking.

"It could be explosive," I said.

"It already is."

"What do you make of the outcry to ID the bones?"

"Me, personally? I say ID 'em. Not doing it is nonsense."

I smiled. "And the paper? Is there an official stance?"

"Don't know yet. That ball's in Overly's court. Ultimately it's his decision to yay or nay an editorial position. He can pull the plug on the whole story if he wants to, but I don't think he will because it would show him to be a businessman more than a newsman and that would irk him. And I think the guy kind of *likes* getting backlash from the city's elder statesmen, you know? I think it's giving him the traction he's been looking for to really establish the Reign of Matthew."

We laughed. He glanced at his watch then flattened his hands on his desk to leverage himself up. "OK, Darcy. Are we square?"

"Totally. Thanks again, Elliot."

"I'm late for a lunch meeting. Keep me up on everything."

"Will do."

My stomach was rumbling with hunger as I left Elliot's office and started across the newsroom. I would just check my email before going outside to pick up my regulation takeout tuna sandwich and grapefruit juice.

But as I approached my desk, something seemed *off*. It took a moment to register what it was, and then I saw it; or, I saw its absence. My laptop was gone. I checked all around my desk, in my drawers, inside my bag – everywhere. It was definitely missing.

"Did you see anyone take my laptop?" I asked Stan, another Metro reporter who was my nearest neighbor other than Courtney.

Curved over his keyboard, Stan turned his head slowly, like a turtle roused from sleep, to look at me. His curly salt-and-pepper hair looked unbrushed and a bruised patina darkened the skin beneath his eyes. Two months ago his wife had given birth to twins, their first children, and he still looked stunned by the unanticipated changes new parenthood wrought on every couple. "Just got in," he said. "Can't find it?"

"Nope."

There were a few more reporters hunkered over their computers and phones, working, and I interrupted each one in turn. No one had noticed anyone at my desk.

Elliot had already left. So I picked up the phone, called Security and explained, giving only the bare facts: I had been away from my desk for about twenty minutes and upon returning discovered my laptop was gone. The response was interesting. It turned out that ever since the *Times* had issued a laptop to every reporter, loss and theft had been a common problem. They would issue me another one as soon as I filled out a form, which was available in the Security office on the second floor. I said I'd be there in about half an hour, deciding to pick up my sandwich first.

All the way to the deli, I fumed. *Joe!* I had no doubt that he had taken my laptop. Who else? I could just see him wheeling through the newsroom with his cart, finding himself alone at a unique moment when no one was at his or her desk, failing to resist (or not trying?) the temptation to plunder what he could of anything that belonged to me, sizing up the laptop as the richest opportunity, and then quickly hiding it among his boxes and letters. Yes, I had backed up my hard disk as recently as Friday afternoon – I was a stickler about that – but the information on it was *mine*, not his, and he had no right to it. And the computer itself belonged to the *Times*, so now he had added theft to stalking. Great first week on the job, kiddo. Of course I would have no way to prove that he had taken it and if I accused him he would only deny it. He might even claim sour grapes, that I had saddled him with a workplace restraining order and was disappointed that it hadn't even bothered him. Then *I* could look like the nut. No. I didn't want to go crazy accusing Joe of anything else. When Elliot got back, I would tell him my laptop was missing and he could draw his own conclusion.

I ordered my sandwich on automatic drive, hardly pausing my spinning thoughts to say hello to Brian behind the counter. After, walking down 43rd Street, I was only vaguely aware of the clamorous noises and smells that were lunchtime Midtown. It had been a grey morning and it was a grey afternoon, not sunny, not rainy, just plain dreary. Passing the hot-dog guy who was always parked near the *Times'* entrance, standing beneath his yellow and blue umbrella, I walked through a cloud of meaty steam. A dozen workers snaked in a curved line away from his cart as his metal tongs pressed a hot dog out into a splayed bun.

"Mustard and sauerkraut, please," said his nearest customer. Only then did I notice that it was Stan, my fellow reporter. Seeing him in line, I realized how tall he was, probably six feet. I paused to greet him, and that was when I saw, from the corner of my eye, the blur of what appeared to be a man racing in my direction.

CHAPTER 7

Joe ran at me, his arms pumping and those off-kilter eyes bright with rage. He wore an overloaded backpack that swayed behind him like a burden restraining him from flight. He was angrier than I had ever seen anyone: nostrils flared, teeth clenched, blood drained from his already pale face. Passers-by instinctively veered away from him.

"Darcy! *Darcy!*" His shrieking voice sounded like an adolescent's, lurching whole octaves in one word, in this case my *name*. It was like being hit with a bucket of ice water – and I froze. "*How could you do this to me? I never did anything to hurt you!*"

"Hey!" It was Stan, who, out of the corner of my eye, I saw turning away from the vendor, his mouth half-full of hot dog.

Joe came to a halt in front of me.

My heart, an echo chamber, beat so hard and fast I could hear the blood roil through my body. I grasped my lunch so close to my chest that the bag split open. Though he had stopped, in my mind he continued to propel forwards and his face, inches away, transformed into something truly monstrous. Grooves of deep distress ran down his waxy cheeks. His eyes, polluted marbles, threatened to pop out of their sockets. And his smell, it was awful: fumes of residual vomit emitted with each word.

Stan tossed his hot dog onto the sidewalk and stepped between us. "Leave her alone!" A damp stripe appeared down the back of his shirt behind which I huddled, immobilized by fear.

Joe's hands grabbed Stan's arms, his knuckles going white into the blue fabric of Stan's sleeves. This close, I could feel the vibrations of my colleague's effort to push Joe away. Joe was stronger than he looked; his physical determination took me by surprise. It was everything Jess had told me, this "bad reaction" to having been told to keep away. If Joe reacted this way to a workplace restraining order, how would he react to a real one issued by the police? Stan grunted and pushed forwards, blocking Joe from reaching me. Just then a woman's hand grabbed my arm and pulled me away. Two men tackled Joe from behind, pushing him to the ground, and it was over.

My lunch now broke free of the bag, wrapped sandwich and juice carton falling to the dirty sidewalk without apparent damage. The woman picked them up and handed them back to me.

"I think he works for the *Times*, in the mailroom," I heard Stan saying to the security guard who had run out of our building's lobby.

"Yeah, I recognize him. Anyone call the cops?"

The *real* cops, he meant. An admission that workplace measures – good behavior contracts and security guards – could only go so far to protect you.

"I called," a man from the hot-dog line said, receiving his foil-wrapped hot dog and standing off to the side to see what happened next.

Joe, pinned to the sidewalk now by four men all of whose faces were alert with purpose, had his eyes squeezed shut and his lips pressed together and he was taking deep breaths, calming himself. It was like watching a wild animal regroup, suddenly, for his own survival. I wondered if he had ever been institutionalized – medicated, strait-jacketed, therapied – because it seemed as if he knew what could come next if he didn't pull himself together fast. As if he was calculating the price he'd have to pay for his stunning transgression and figured he'd get a discount if the police, when they arrived, didn't see quite the same man *we* had seen charging at me. Standing there, surrounded by strangers who had taken the time to help and whose mere presence made me feel safer, fear sloughed off and left me with a stone of antipathy heavy in my stomach. The hunger that had sent me outside for lunch was gone, replaced by something I didn't recognize: a survivalist's determination to succeed against an overwhelming adversary. I had an enemy, a real one, and I would have to strategize against him.

The police came and took Joe away, shackling his hands behind his back. They had to remove his bulky pack to secure the handcuffs. They slid him into the back seat of the squad car then tossed the backpack in after him. Was my laptop in there? I felt like lunging in after him and demanding its return, but the laptop itself seemed inconsequential now. I would get another one and transfer my backup files onto it. The more I thought about it, standing there watching the car pull away with Joe slumped in the back, the more I didn't want anything near me that he had touched.

"Wow," Stan said. "That guy went seriously postal."

"Thank you for what you did."

"Anytime, babe." He winked, igniting a fan of wrinkles beside one eye.

I laughed at that; Stan was a fine writer, a respectful colleague. You just never knew what an emergency would draw out of a person: hero or damsel in distress.

"If we were cartoons, I'd squeeze your arm muscle," I said.

Now he laughed, and that was good, because neither of us really knew what to say. I wasn't sure what the protocol was. Did I announce that I'd had an in-house stalker or was that pretty much like telling a co-worker you had a venereal disease? *Too much information*.

I didn't realize until the crowd dispersed that Elliot had been among them. He joined me and Stan, asking questions, and we both reverted to reporters serving up information to our editor as objectively as possible. I spoke of Stan's heroism, he of my having been attacked. Elliot listened attentively, nodding as we took turns speaking. Outside in the natural light Elliot looked older, his skin more papery. Though still early in the day, a shadow of whiskers had started to form on his jawline.

"I think I'll go get a new lunch," I said. "It's still wrapped but it's been on the ground."

"I'll go with you," Stan offered.

"Darcy," Elliot said. "Go home."

"I've got a lot of work."

"Do it at home."

He was right. I couldn't just go back to work as if nothing had happened. I didn't know if Joe would be held or released – and as soon as I thought of Nat

I realized I'd feel safer meeting him when school let out.

I explained about my laptop. Elliot and Stan both accompanied me to Security where I filled out two sets of paperwork: the first, a theft report which allowed me to receive a replacement laptop; the second, an incident report which would be filed both on site and with the Midtown precinct.

"He'll be fired," Elliot promised.

"Funny how things happen," I said. "I'll actually feel safer at work now."

"Stan? Walk Darcy to the subway."

"My pleasure."

And so I gathered what I needed from my desk, remembering to take the stalking log I'd started from the top drawer. I filled in the new *event* while the backup of my hard disk transferred onto the new laptop. At the last minute I remembered to change my email password so that new messages would not be intercepted by my old laptop – and Joe. Then Stan walked me to the Sixth Avenue entrance of the F train. As we walked, he told me all about his twins, a boy and a girl, and how they were already developing differently.

"The nature/nurture thing takes on a whole new light when you have kids." He angled past a Dumpster protruding partway onto the sidewalk, a gesture that steered me away from a sharp corner he seemed to worry I hadn't seen.

"My husband used to say that, after we had Nat."

"I heard about your husband. I'm really sorry. It must be hard being a single mom."

"Not that hard." But tears formed in my eyes anyway, mostly because an image of Hugo cradling naked baby Nat had lodged in my mind. "He was born *whole*, Darcy," Hugo had said. Hugo: half-naked himself, his hair-flecked chest above the early bulge of a middle-aged paunch. "I never really got that about babies. They're born *who they are*." And then he gently kissed his son's face thirty-six times (I counted), saying, "A kiss for every inch," though there weren't that many inches on a baby's face.

I took the subway straight to Park Slope where I was forty-five minutes early to meet Nat. It was especially important to be on time since he wasn't expecting me. I bought a sandwich and a cup of coffee, parked myself on a stoop across from the school's entrance and called Jess.

"OK," he said, after I explained what had happened, "I'll make a call and find out where he is in the process, if they're holding him, all that. But my guess is they won't. He didn't actually touch you. And I talked to the police in Martha's Vineyard – they knew him, but they've got nothing on him, no restraining orders, no mental history, just some notes about complaints, all verbal. That makes it harder for you now. They'll probably give him a warning and let him go, but you should file an incident report as soon as you can."

"It's been done."

"Good."

"It was terrifying, the way he came at me."

"Sure it was."

"If I had filed a restraining order with the police, would he be arrested now?"

"Yes, but it doesn't mean they could hold him very long. You didn't like how angry you saw him? Picture that times ten. I still say it's best not to get an RO just yet. This guy, he's on our radar. We're watching him."

"Now what?"

"Keep safe. Be careful. Stick to routines. Go out, so long as you're around people. Keep your doors and windows locked. Everything I told you this morning."

"OK."

"Meantime let me get on the phone and find out where our guy is. I'll let you know."

Next I called Courtney, gave her the quick version of what had happened since she was in the middle of a lunch meeting, and told her I was working from home the rest of the day but would be in the office tomorrow.

Nat emerged just past three in a gawky crowd of eighth-graders whose bubble of noise moved with them until they reached the sidewalk and dispersed. The kids were so tall, I was lost among them, and Nat passed me right by, walking toward the corner with his friend Henry.

"Nat!"

He looked back and saw me. "Whoa! Mom! What's up?" Henry peeled away, joined up with another boy and turned onto Fifth Avenue.

"I had some business nearby," I said, "and thought I'd meet you."

"Business? Like an interview or something?"

"Research."

"In Park Slope?"

How did my child know to doubt me? Was I that bad at lying? Just as I was about to add lie to lie, Rich passed beside us.

"Hi, Mr Stuart."

"Hi, Nat. Hi, Nat's mom."

"Hi, Nat's teacher."

"Well, nice to see you." He smiled, glanced from me to Nat to me, and kept walking. As the distance between us grew, my eyes stayed on him: his paint-speckled jeans and orange shirt with the sleeves rolled just below his elbows, his moss-green suede sneakers, his thick brown hair cross-hatched after a day teaching art, the notches where back became neck and which I'd kissed just two nights ago, the skin I'd kissed and smelled and tasted. I had never noticed how graceful his body was in clothes.

"Earth to Mom. You like him. Admit it."

"That obvious?"

"Totally."

"I guess I do."

"So why don't you go out with him?"

"I did. Over the weekend." Sharing this with Nat seemed fair. And I couldn't bring myself to tell him two outright lies in a row.

"So, like, are you stalking him?"

"That's not funny."

"I get it." My son looked at me and said: "You're scared. *That's* why you're here."

I forced a smile. I couldn't let Nat share my fear. "Oh, sweetie, that's silly."

"You sure, Mom? Because you can tell me."

And I wanted to! In ten or fifteen years, I would. But he was still a child and my job was to protect him which included shielding him from worry.

"Positive. I just wanted to see you. Isn't that enough reason to show up?"

He smiled and nodded, his bushy hair bobbing around his beautiful face. "Totally."

We took the bus home together and after a snack he started homework. I lay on my bed with the new laptop, which wasn't exactly new and was identical to the other one except for a sticker of a blue Smurf on the lower corner of the frame. Checked email. Along with a new batch of junk from the usual unending flow, two caught my eye: one from myself – from my account; from Joe? – sent before he tried to attack me on the sidewalk, and the other from the Martha's Vineyard police with the subject line *Fingerprints Nat Mayhew*. I opened the one from myself first.

Bitch

it read, dead center, in a pretty font. Without thinking, I deleted it, sending it straight to the garbage can. Then I remembered the file Courtney had created on the other laptop, where I had gathered most of Joe's other crazy emails. I created another such file here, labeled it unapologetically *Joe Coffin Go to Hell* and dragged the new email into it. Dropping my head on my pillow, I stared up at a crack on the ceiling, following its ragged journey from the corner toward the center of the room. Thinking.

Joe would have seen that file. He would have read all the emails sitting in my inbox between me and Sara – how we'd discussed him, analyzed him, investigated him, belittled him. He would have all my work-related emails. Would he think to look into my Word files – my notes and reminders, where I detailed everything?

Of course he would. He wouldn't leave a single file unopened. He would see everything there was to see about me. All my thoughts and plans. Everything I had generated. Everything I had received.

I closed my eyes, banishing the crack, the ceiling, the house, the move, Hugo's death, my mother's Alzheimer's – *banishing Joe*.

From across the hall I heard Nat shuffling to the bathroom. Flushing the toilet. Running water in the sink.

I opened my eyes and called to him, "Don't forget to turn off the light."

"Got it."

Then shuffling back to his room. It was his *I hate homework* shuffle: lackadaisical, uninspired.

I opened the second email and thumbnails of Nat's ten fingerprints appeared on the screen. Each print was a perfect asymmetry of lines so beautiful it could only be found in nature; it was the kind of perfection art tried to imitate but rarely could. Each was unique – and yet I'd read somewhere that fingerprints were not as reliable a forensics tool as some had long assumed. Fingerprint analysis could be wrong. Dental records were better. DNA was better still. I pulled Jess's card out of my pocket to look up his email address, forwarded Nat's prints and shut the file.

I clicked *send/receive* again and found that Courtney had just emailed me about her visit earlier in the day to Buildings: a success. The official lot sale documents did not match the copies Abe Starkman had given me. *Abe Starkman* – I had saved his contact information in my computer address book – *Joe now had his name*. Queasiness bubbled from my stomach into my throat, arriving in my mouth as an acrid taste of vomit. I swallowed it, reminding myself that Joe didn't care about Abe Starkman or my work; he cared about *me*.

In the quiet of my bedroom, alone, thinking, I could hardly believe this was happening. That I was being stalked. I had heard about it on the news and read stories about women who had lived for years with stalkers in their shadows but I had never grasped the intractability of the situation. Stalked, like an animal; stalked for the kill. Why else would someone stalk you? In the hope that you'd cave in and love them? Absurd. Though I recalled once reading about a woman whose stalker had blinded her by throwing acid in her face when she opened her front door, served a long prison term, then come out and, yes, married her. If Joe blinded me, sentencing me to a life of darkness, would that make me lonely enough to love him?

Never.

And how had I not been aware he'd been stalking me on the Vineyard? It seemed impossible to believe I wouldn't have noticed on such a small island. He had been stalking me when Hugo was still alive. How would *he* have reacted to this now? Hugo would have known what to do.

I closed my eyes and breathed, loving Hugo, missing him, thinking of Rich and our Wednesday morning *breakfast*, hating Joe – feeling confused and exhausted. It was past five o'clock and I had a teenage boy in the next room; he would be hungry soon, ferociously hungry as only teenage boys can be and he would need dinner. We could go to the bistro on the corner of Smith and Dean Streets; Nat loved their burgers, which came with the world's best French fries and a side order of salad, a rounded meal. But as soon as I thought that, I thought of Joe. Had he been arrested? Or was he *out*?

I dialed Jess. He answered promptly: "Detective Ramirez."

"It's Darcy Mayhew."

"I just got word." He sounded glum. "They released him about an hour ago. Gave him a warning."

"Jess, maybe I should get a restraining order. I've been thinking—"

"Whatever you want, Darcy. It's up to you."

There he went again, like a doctor unwilling to advocate his own plan.

"But you still advise against it?"

"I do."

Silence. He really believed it was a bad idea. I really felt scared and wanted protection. But the workplace order hadn't protected me at all – so why would a police order? His experience-laced logic kept coming back at me. Every time I wanted to demand a restraining order, I heard his voice and saw his face – the ugliest face in the city on the kindest man – and acquiesced to his wisdom.

"OK. So he's out. Now what do I do?"

"Everything we discussed. And if anything happens, *anything*, Darcy, even if your phone starts ringing again – call me. Any time of the day or night. And don't worry about my wife; she's used to me getting calls from ladies at all hours." He chuckled.

"Thanks, Jess."

I hung up, feeling briefly fortified, but not enough to take Nat out for dinner. I wasn't sure exactly what we had in the cupboards, fridge and freezer but there had to be something I could whip up in a hurry.

Pasta and limp broccoli which, steamed, wasn't so bad. Ice cream for dessert. Then, later, I lay beside Nat in his bed like I used to when he was little. He rolled over to get his favorite backrub: two knuckles running up and down either side of his spine. When

I got up to leave, he surprised me by saying, "Don't be scared, Mom. I'm sure it's going to be OK."

"I'm not scared, sweetie," I lied.

"Can you put the bathroom light on?" Another old habit from earlier in his childhood: a distant light to glow reassurance from the hallway into his room. A bathroom in our Vineyard house had been similarly situated near his door. I shut his door partway, turned on the bathroom light and got myself ready for bed.

I was lying in bed in the dark, my mind battling what seemed the impossibility of sleep, when the phone rang. My pulse sped as I looked at the lit-up LED screen on the phone's handset. I was pretty sure Nat was asleep but even so I answered in a whisper.

"Sara!"

"He emailed me, Darcy." She wasn't whispering though I was sure her three little ones were all in bed. Her tone was heavy with some kind of resolution. "You wouldn't believe the stuff he wrote. It was *vile*."

"Oh, Sara, I'm so sorry. He stole my laptop at work today. But listen, they fired him, after he—"

"Kevin says I have to stop."

"Stop what?" But I as soon as she said it, I knew: her husband had told her to stop being my friend. As her familiar voice continued, as she explained, as the music of her words and tones and emphases filled my ear, I began to cry. Silently, though. I didn't want to burden her with guilt over her decision.

"He threatened my children. We already called the police. Everyone says I can't be in contact with you anymore – not for a while, anyway. Honey, they know him at the police department here. They were glad he left the island."

"So am I," I said, "if it keeps you and the kids safer."

"*Shit*, Darcy. Get out of there!"

"We're all settled now. Nat's happy at school. And Rich, I never had a chance to tell you about our date, but it went so well and I'm seeing him again. And I've got an amazing job, I'll never have another opportunity like this, and I'm in the middle of a really important story—"

"You and Hugo. *Work* – always so important. Isn't *this* more important?"

"Yes. It is. Absolutely. I went to the police today and I—"

"Kevin's telling me I have to get off the phone now. Darcy, I'm sorry. I'm going to miss you like you can't know."

"I do know. Bye, Sara. I love you."

"I love you, too."

She hung up the phone and I buried my face in my pillow and wept until the sun rose.

How could I live without Sara? She had been my

best friend for over eight years. Since Hugo's death, no one had done as much to anchor me.

Joe. I had never loathed another person as I now did Joe.

He had come into my life like a giant wave and the best I could do, short of running away, would be to hunker down and try to resist his antigravitational pull. Only once before tonight had I thought so much about the forces that seem to come from nowhere to displace you – the night of Hugo's accident when I floated between life and death in a terrifying freefall, thinking of my father's final moments, how one moment a person is alive and the next moment they're not – and now I thought of these forces again. One pushes, the other pulls; and hunkered between them all I could seem to do was hold myself in place. But without Sara, would I be able to?

Somehow I would have to. I was a mother with a child to love, raise, support and protect. I needed to keep Nat happy and safe. I needed to hold on to my job so I could keep a roof over our heads. And I needed to make sure Joe couldn't get to my son.

In the morning I accompanied Nat to school without trying to manufacture an excuse, and he didn't seem to need one. I watched him until he was inside the building, waited a few minutes to give him a chance to reach his homeroom, then went inside to the principal's office.

I knew that parents sometimes dropped in with questions, concerns and problems because Mrs Mazola, the principal, had once sent a memo home asking us not to try and see her without an appointment. She was standing next to a tall beige file cabinet when I walked in, trim in her purple suit. She neither came forward with a handshake nor settled behind her desk to hear me out; just stood there, looking interrupted, as if to discourage me from staying too long. I started by apologizing and quickly got to the point.

"I need to add something to the paperwork I filled out at the beginning of the school year," I said. "There's someone who can't have access to my son."

"Jan can help you with that." Her secretary, who sat in an adjacent office with two other administrative helpers.

"I just wanted to make sure you personally understood the importance of this."

She considered me a moment, her dark eyes settling on my face. I hadn't slept at all last night and if the way I felt inside – tired, terrified – surfaced at all in my expression, I knew she would take me seriously.

"Custody problems?"

"No, I'm a widow." I hesitated, then plunged in. "I have a stalker; his name's Joe Coffin. Young guy, white, brown hair, early twenties. He can't get near Nat, OK?"

Mrs Mazola stared at me a moment, reacting to the grim reality of a word – *stalker* – I'd come to detest almost as much as Joe himself.

"Nat's in what class?"

"Eight-oh-five."

"OK. You can do the paperwork with Jan and I'll mention it to the security guards myself. How's that?"

"Thank you."

I picked up some takeout coffee at the nearest café and walked to the subway. I had never been so happy to see a rush-hour crowd. I searched every face for Joe. If he was there, I didn't see him. How many times had he been near me when I hadn't seen him? But not seeing him now had little effect on my sense of safety; his invisibility was like toxic gas: I *breathed* him everywhere.

When I arrived at my desk, the overnight envelope with our dental X-rays was waiting. I didn't bother opening it. My eyes were raw with exhaustion. I would do some work, confer with Courtney, then drop the envelope at the 84th Precinct on my way to pick Nat up from school. It would be the most I could wrest out of the day.

Elliot confirmed that Joe had been fired and Security instructed not to let him into the building.

After yesterday's episode on the sidewalk, I didn't doubt that our security guards would take their instructions seriously. Elliot must have seen how wretched I was feeling – I was sure I looked as limp as I felt, especially after Mrs Mazola's accommodating response to my unannounced visit, even before she knew the reason – but he was kind enough not to mention it.

Courtney didn't hesitate. "You look like crap."

"Thanks."

"Good thing that jerk's out of here."

"The problem is he's still out *there*." I pointed to the window, half-believing Joe might swoop down from the sky.

"I did some research for you." She got up to bring me a printout. "Did you know you can hire a stalking consultant? There are whole companies devoted to it. A lot of celebrities hire them."

MacDonald, Tierney was the name of the firm she'd chosen for me.

"Is this the best one?" I asked.

"Yup. I'll go with you if you want."

That earned a smile – so I still had a friend.

"I think you should probably go home now," she said, leaning down to rub my back. "Get some sleep."

"But the story—"

"I'm on it. Don't worry. I'll get you up to speed tomorrow."

"I want to know now. What's happening?"

"OK. Perlotti Industries loops back to the Tarentino family, just like Metro Trucking. I'm still working on Song Song Hauling but it's kind of feeling like color by numbers now, you know?"

"I looked online but couldn't find anything unusual with the racketeering trial."

"Too soon. If there's any give there, we probably won't see it until sentencing."

"Right. Of course. And the bones—"

"Good news on that. Just found out this morning the city moved the barrel out of Pearson. Anand told me. He wasn't sure where they were taking them. I've got some calls in. Today that's what's at the top of my list."

"He's sure it was the city that took them?"

"Yeah – he knew the guy. And the paperwork was legit."

"You're closing in."

"*We're* closing in."

"You're really good at this, Courtney. Gutsy, focused. I'm thinking I should stick with reporting on the environment."

"Hey, I'd be the biggest wimp you ever saw if I had some nutcase stalking me. I think you're handling it really well."

Did she mean it? It was impossible to know. But it was nice of her to say it.

"All right. I'll go home. But tonight I'm taking a sleeping pill and tomorrow I'll be back."

"That a girl!"

"Woman." I eked out a smile. "I'm a woman. And so are you."

Stan, off to the side, laughed quietly to himself and Courtney took it as an invitation to stride over to him and box his ears.

I splurged on a taxi to Brooklyn. The FDR was mostly free of southbound traffic at this hour of the day and we flew beside the East River, a dull green-blue beneath a patchy sky. On brighter days the river sparkled, inspired; but today it was just a gloomy waterway separating two slabs of land. We crossed on the Manhattan Bridge and in moments I was dropped at the precinct door.

As before, the reception officer called up to Jess and I was asked to wait. This time, though, when he came down he was not alone.

"Darcy, this is Angela, my wife."

Angela was tiny, small-boned like a bird, with huge brown eyes and curly black hair to her shoulders. She held the hands of two small children, both boys, who looked to be about three and four years old. One had the ill fortune of having inherited his father's looks.

"And this is Ramón and Victor. Say hello to the lady, boys."

"Hi, lady!" one said, and both giggled.

Angela tugged their hands. "Be polite!" Then, to me, with a magnificent smile, "Five kids later and no one listens to me. What's with that?"

"I listen to you, *mi corazon*."

I knew a little Spanish from school; he had called her *my heart*.

"Five kids," I said. "That's impressive."

"You're married long enough, the kids, they just happen."

"How long have you two been married?"

"Nineteen years," she answered. "Together twenty-five."

"That's a long engagement."

"I never wanted to marry this man! But he's a good man, he works hard. He broke me down. What choice did I have?" She beamed at Jess and it seemed to me that she saw his face without the ugliness. Time did that: stripped away the mirage of a person's outer layer.

She released her sons' hands and came closer to me, raising one toughened manicured hand to angle my face so my ear was close to her mouth, and then she whispered: "I came to him just like you and he saved my life. The newspapers, they all wrote it up. You'll find it on the Google if you look. I was Angela Maria Cortez then."

"That for me?" Jess reached for the envelope with

the X-rays I held in my hand. He seemed uncomfortable with his wife's sociability toward me; I was a case, after all, not a friend. But Angela had taken our chance meeting to give me something she seemed to feel was important. Obviously Jess had told her about my situation and there was something she wanted me to know. I was curious now.

As soon as I got home I did as she'd said and looked her up on "the Google". Angela Maria Cortez brought up half a dozen links but paired with Detective Jesus Ramirez it brought up only one: a Wikipedia entry about New York City's most notorious stalking cases. I logged into LexisNexis and a list of the articles she'd mentioned filled the screen.

Angela Maria Cortez was eighteen years old when a family friend decided he had to have her. He wasn't a friend, exactly; he was a cousin of a neighbor who attended many of the Cortez family celebrations in Queens. The cousin, Raul, a thirty-year-old carpenter who also lived in Queens, tried the normal route and asked Angela out on a date. She had dinner with him once and decided he wasn't for her. "He was strange," she said later, when people became interested in writing about her, "kind of touchy-feely all the time and I didn't like it. He was a lot older than me and he wanted to move it along too fast."

After turning down Raul's invitations, Angela began to find things on the porch of her parents' home where she still lived. Bouquets of flowers, boxes of candy, books; the usual love tokens. He wouldn't stop giving her things, wouldn't stop calling, wouldn't stop waiting for her outside her job at a local dry cleaners. But then the gifts took on a threatening tone. Racy lingerie, pornographic videotapes, a pair of handcuffs, a package of raw beef. So she went to the police, where her case was assigned to Jesus Ramirez, a newly minted detective with no experience handling stalkers. Stalking, in those days, wasn't even counted as a crime.

Detective Ramirez followed a combination of procedure and common sense, and helped Angela file an Order of Restraint against Raul. A day later, arriving at the Cortez family home to bring Angela a copy of the order signed by a judge, Detective Ramirez, who was armed, came upon a surprise.

Waiting on the porch after the doorbell went unanswered, he heard what he thought were sobs inside the house. Coming up quietly to a front window, he found the curtains closed. Strange, since it was early afternoon. But there was a small opening between the edge of one curtain and the window frame through which he was able to catch a glimpse of what was happening inside. Enough of a glimpse to make his blood freeze.

Angela was tied to a chair, hands behind her, feet strapped to opposite chair legs. Raul stood in front of her with his pants lowered to his ankles. His back was convulsing and though Ramirez couldn't see exactly what was happening he was able to guess, and it sickened him. The handle of a hunting knife stuck out of one pocket of Raul's pants, collapsed on the floor by his feet.

In the time it took Ramirez to take a porch chair, smash it through the window and dive into the living room, Raul had his pants back on and the knife poised at Angela's throat.

"Get back!" Raul shouted.

"Drop the knife!"

"She's mine!"

"I said *drop the knife!*"

Instead, Raul turned, drove the knife into Angela's chest and pulled it out to drive it in again. She wept and screamed. Blood bubbled out of her wound. Blood dripped from the knife as it flashed through the air, back toward Angela.

Detective Jesus Ramirez, twenty-five years old, the newest and youngest detective in the New York City Police Department, drew his gun. He had shot it before in real-life situations but only to call attention to his authority; he had never, though, shot to kill.

He did now. Killing Raul with a single bullet to his heart.

Raul lay in a heap on the floor at Angela's feet, his eyes glazed, blood gurgling from his mouth onto the carpet, lifeless fingers relaxed around the handle of the knife.

After a moment of stunned silence, Detective Ramirez walked over and carefully freed Angela from the chair. Then he went to the phone and called an ambulance.

More police arrived within minutes and found a scene of almost church-like tranquility. An officer told the first reporter to arrive, "The girl might seem calm and collected to you but she's in shock." Detective Ramirez waited for the ambulance and was then ordered to report back to his precinct, where he was debriefed by his sergeant. He was later decorated by the city as a hero, a title he refused, saying, "I only did what any decent man would do."

Angela spent two weeks in the hospital, ultimately recovering from her wound, a deep one, which had required surgery to repair. Jess Ramirez visited her every day. He never asked for anything, just paid close attention to her needs. They became friends. Two years later, lovers. And eventually, more than six years after she first sought his help, they were married.

"And the rest," I could just hear Angela say in her colorful way of speaking, "is history, mister."

All the way to pick Nat up from school – in the

car, which I'd decided would be safer because I could lock myself inside and it was also essentially a two-ton weapon – I thought about Jess and Angela. What he did for her: killing a man to save her life. I saw that the rest of his life had blossomed out of that moment. And understood why he was adamant about the danger inherent in restraining orders. For a moment I wondered why Jess hadn't told me his and Angela's story himself; it was a perfect cautionary tale. But as soon as I thought that, I realized it just wasn't his style. He did not feel comfortable putting himself forward unless it was to respond to someone else's direct and immediate need. *That* was his talent. He knew in the moment exactly what was necessary. And he allowed himself to learn from history so that it wouldn't be repeated . . . by people like me.

Later, back home with Nat, I returned my attention to Google and LexisNexis. *Stalking*, I typed, and was astounded by what popped up. I clicked and read, clicked and read, for two solid hours. There were countless stories, each one exceptional for the terror it had caused someone – the *victim* – and yet they all shared common denominators. It was like the moment you see a stranger who looks almost exactly like yourself and you realize you're not as unique as you thought you were. You're one of many.

Every year in America, one out of twelve women, and one out of forty-five men, was stalked. While every stalker differed in his details, each fell into some category. Joe qualified as an *acquaintance stalker* with a *love obsession*, specifically *erotomanic-type disorder*. Meaning he really thought he loved me and, stranger still, believed I loved him back despite all my efforts to deflect, ignore, insult and reject him. And I had made so many mistakes. I never should have had lunch with him, because it had encouraged him in his deranged thinking about our so-called relationship. (But how was I supposed to have known what he was thinking? I'd had many lunches with colleagues and friends over the years and nothing like this had ever happened to me before.) I never should have called him in the mailroom to ask him to stop delivering breakfasts; paying him any attention, even negative, fueled his fantasy that I cared. I never should have stayed in the elevator the other day when he wheeled in; I should have hit the emergency button and screamed my lungs out.

Why didn't we, as women, scream our lungs out the minute some nutcase decided he had to date us? Why did we always stand back and make room? Chat with people we disliked? Feel obliged to be polite? Hope he would just go away? Why couldn't we learn when it was time to pull the trigger – and pull it?

And then I stopped myself. It wasn't women, generally. It was *me*. Why hadn't I followed my first instinct, two Mondays ago, and avoided lunch with Joe? That was really what it boiled down to. Not a failing on the part of post-feminist women. It had been a failing on the part of my*self*. That old need to please and a refusal to listen to my inner voice. Courtney, with her high heels and tight jeans and polished nails and highlighted hair, would have told Joe to take a hike from the get-go. *She*, post-postmodern femme fatale, would have immediately recognized that lunch invitation as a date and turned it down post-haste.

But was it really my fault Joe was stalking me? If I hadn't been nice to him at the beginning, would it have made a difference?

I shut the laptop and tossed it aside on my bed. Regardless of how long and deep I searched online, I would never find those answers.

For dinner I ordered Chinese food from the place Nat and I liked. They always sent the same delivery man, which was reassuring, but even so I peered through the window to make sure it was him before opening the door. It was.

Before we were finished with our meal, the doorbell rang again. Nat and I stopped eating and looked at each other.

"You're not expecting anyone, are you?" I asked him.

"Nope. You?"

"No." I got up and peeked out the window. It was the UPS man, all in brown, holding a big box. It took all of five seconds to realize that this would be Joe's treasure chest, sent by Sara before she bid me goodbye.

I waited until Nat went to bed before opening the box.

It smelled of dust and darkness and the contents were just as Sara had described. In my exhaustion each object felt unreal in my hands. Each *thing* was so ordinary and yet so telling my skin crawled when I touched them. A book. A stack of letters. The old marzipan: little colored fruits in bright, artificial hues. The shoes: scuffed white high heels that looked like something an unreal mother would wear to an unreal party in a long-past decade, the 1950s, when women and men strived to embody external perfection and internal life was wholly overlooked. Back when the news didn't report on presidential mistresses or lost children, when there wasn't even a word for stalkers. Back when dug-up bones would remain unidentifiable.

The bones. Courtney had called earlier to tell me they were in the NYPD's crime lab in Queens, under lock and key, slated for testing as soon as possible though "soon" in city parlance could mean a year, even two. So she planned to turn up the heat by reporting that fact.

I stayed up until midnight reading through the scrapbook Joe had kept on me. It was more extensive than any record-keeping I had ever done on myself. Sara's guess of two years looked about right: the first page showed the published photograph of me accepting the award for journalistic excellence that had ultimately propelled me past Hugo's death to a job at the *Times*. After that, he had collected every single column I'd written for the *Vineyard Gazette* and every article I'd published as a freelancer for a variety of other newspapers and magazines. Interspersed with this were photos of me with my family and friends. It was baffling and sickening to know that these images of myself, my loved ones and my life had been collected by someone whose existence I had barely registered.

If a tree falls in a forest and no one hears it, does it make a sound? Yes. It makes a sound. And Joe existed – he existed *in my shadow* – long before I knew he was there.

In the middle of all this, around eleven, Rich called. When I saw his name on caller ID I thought two things: *I hope he cancels our morning date because I'm not fit for him;* and then, *Don't cancel*. He didn't. He was keen on seeing me again in private, as was I him. Hearing his voice – one hand holding the phone to my ear and the other in Joe's box – was a weird counterpoint but I didn't want to tell him what I was doing and how things had escalated since we'd last spoken about it. Didn't want to ruin this new sweet spot in my life. I asked him to come fifteen minutes later, at a quarter past seven instead of seven o'clock as we'd originally planned; I'd be back by then from driving Nat to his early rehearsal. That would give us only forty-five minutes together, stolen minutes was how it felt, but neither of us argued that it would be too little time. We were hungry for each other. His voice on the phone those few minutes was enough to lull me back to his smell of hickory and the suppleness of his skin, giving to my every touch like well-worn beloved suede.

When I had looked through everything in the box I hid it in my closet and took a sleeping pill, which knocked me out, giving me six hours of something that felt more like oblivion than sleep but for which I was nonetheless grateful.

And then my bed was transformed. Shades drawn against a bright morning; seams of daylight outlining rectangular windows, empty frames, hovering on the opposite wall. Empty frames waiting for shades to be lifted, views to be filled. Limbs enfolded by dis-arranged sheets and blankets, pillows and shadows. Clothes heaped on the floor as with the rush of urgent teenagers into sex. Impatience. Yearning.

Balm to broken-hearted middle-agers. Reawakening of optimism. Too soon, too risky to call it *love* but certainly this was good. Very good.

And then, quiet. Stillness. Fingers entwined. A play of light and shadows on the ceiling. Attention glancing toward the clock.

"I have to go," Rich whispered.

"I know. Me too."

"How can we see each other more?"

"I could talk to Henry's mother, see if she'll encourage more sleepover invitations." We laughed. Silly though it sounded, it was actually not such a bad idea.

"It's complicated, my being one of Nat's teachers." Rich lay a gentle palm against my face. It was heavy and warm and welcome.

"When the time is right," I said, "we'll start spending some time all together. But it might have to wait until summer."

"I already thought of that. It's so far away."

I looked at him and smiled. Summer *was* far off and yet it wasn't, if only we could last that long in our strange state of limbo.

"So what's happening with that guy – Joe?"

"Don't ask."

His eyes turned from soupy to alert. "I'm asking. What's going on?"

"The short version is he got fired."

"Why?"

"Personnel put him on warning and he kind of flipped out, so they fired him."

"Flipped out how?" He was leaning on his elbow now, his face bright with concern.

"He didn't hurt me. It's OK. He ran at me outside our office building and he was stopped by a lot of people. New Yorkers are much nicer than they get credit for, you know?"

He didn't smile.

"The police took him away."

"So he's in custody now?"

"Not anymore. They let him out."

"I don't like it. How can we keep you safe?"

The *we* was heartening. Rich was to be my compatriot in this, I knew it now. I told him what Jess had advised me to do and about his wife, Angela, and their history. Rich agreed with me that if anyone had the right experience to guide me it was my detective.

"So you're actually going to work today?" he asked.

"Yes, I am."

"I wish I could go with you and make sure you get there safely. I *can* meet you at the end of the day."

"That's really sweet, Rich. Thank you. But it isn't necessary."

His eyes fled to the clock. He sat up on the edge

of the bed and twisted back to kiss me. "How can I leave you?"

"I'll be *fine*. It's broad daylight and there are people everywhere. What could possibly happen?"

CHAPTER 8

As soon as I walked into the newsroom Courtney jumped up and met me halfway to my desk.

"Abe Starkman. That name ring any bells?"

I had never told her, or anyone, the name of my source.

"Yes. Why?"

"He was a project manager for the Atlantic Yards."

Was? Had they found out he was the department leak? Had they fired him?

"What's going on, Courtney?"

"He was killed this morning, about six o'clock, riding his bike over the Brooklyn Bridge. Dressed for work."

"Killed? What do you mean?" Though in a heartbeat I knew what she meant or thought I did: killed for talking to me. By Joe. Or someone else.

"Shot three or four times. We're not sure yet; they've got him at the Medical Examiner. Stan's on it. They didn't even get him off his bike first; just shot him while he was riding."

"They?"

"They. He. No one knows yet. But here's the thing, Darcy." We were at her desk now, in a huddle in front of her computer screen. "Watch this."

She opened a YouTube window onto a dark, grainy shot and clicked the *play* arrow. It was a poor quality video, as if taken with a camera phone, of a man and a woman standing together talking although nothing they said was audible. As my eyes focused I saw that they were outside. In the city. On a street. And then I recognized Abe Starkman's yellow bike helmet dangling from the man's hand; and then I recognized Abe. And the woman, who was barely visible, as myself. And then I knew precisely what I was watching: last week, Tuesday morning, 6 a.m. It was the moment I'd taken out my pad and pen and jotted the voucher number for the bones before putting my pad back in my purse. We stood in front of the demolition site at the mouth of my lot. It was the beginning of the bones story. Someone had captured it on video.

The caption read: *Buildings Department project*

*manager Abe Starkman talking to a woman at Mafia
burial site.*

"Oh my God," I whispered.

"The caption names him, but not you."

"But it's obviously me. I'm on the byline of all
the stories."

"It could be *me*."

"You're taller than me, and your hair's much
lighter. It doesn't look like you at all."

She didn't argue because it was obviously true.

"Why would he do this? I mean really *why*?" We
both knew "he" meant Joe. Who else? And then I
answered my own question: "To spite me in every
way he possibly can."

"Because he loves you." She rolled her eyes.

"He *loves* me."

"But do you think that little wimp could actually
kill someone? I have a hard time picturing it."

"You didn't see his face yesterday."

"You're right, I didn't. But I still can't picture it."
Courtney leaned back in her chair and looked at me.
"It makes a lot more sense that the mob did this;
they've got so much riding on the trial. This video
names Starkman as the Department of Buildings leak
that might blow their deal with the city – so
Starkman has to die."

"You actually think the mob took this video?" It
made no sense.

"Nope. I think Joe took it and posted it to screw with you for yesterday, and someone tipped Tony T's people, and *voila*, they plug the leak lickety-split like the good plumbers they are."

"It's a good theory, Courtney, but we really don't know."

"You're right. I'm majorly jumping to a conclusion, big J-school no-no. But between us?" She smiled. "I'll bet you a hundred bucks I'm right."

"When will we know more?"

"When Stan calls in. Elliot's on his way. He said he wants to know immediately if Starkman was your source. Which, obviously, he was."

I nodded. Recalled flickers of Abe: pale eyes wavering between determination and apprehension; beads of perspiration gathering, dripping; yellow helmet radiating chin-cinching straps; wheels flashing; gold wedding ring. "Thank you," had been his last words to me. Abe had trusted me and now he was dead. It was unthinkable and yet it had happened. It was true. And if Courtney was right, it was all thanks to Joe Coffin. It was awful to realize that he had followed me that morning last week. I had walked to my meeting, in the dark, and felt safe. For two years I had inhabited that false sense of security. For two years I had been followed without realizing it. *Two years*.

"I'm sure the *Times* will throw you a lawyer. They

always do when the shit hits the fan with an anonymous source."

"Great." So now I would have a lawyer and a detective. When would I get a bodyguard? When would I start packing a gun?

I ran to the bathroom where I threw up in the toilet of the first open stall. The smell brought back Joe's breath yesterday, spewing stink and crazy words into my face. *Abe Starkman was dead*. Could Joe have really done this? *Did Joe have a gun*?

Courtney was waiting in the bathroom's common area when I came out. She had prepared a wet paper towel and like a mother she wiped my face to calm me. "I don't think he did it, Darcy. I really don't. I think he's just an obsessed kid. There's no real reason for you to think he's actually dangerous."

But she hadn't seen his face. I kept coming back to that. I might have agreed with her yesterday before that face came hurtling toward me without warning.

A little while later I walked into Elliot's office, girded to receive his reaction. He must have seen me coming because he was already standing behind his desk with his arms folded over his chest. No smile. No bounding around the desk to offer a high-five. No invitation to close the door.

"Come on in," he said. "Have a seat."

I sat. And waited. Feeling like I was in the

principal's office only I hadn't pulled anyone's pigtails . . . my homework partner was dead.

"This whole thing is a nightmare," he began. "I think we can agree on that. The fact that your source has been murdered, possibly in connection with your story. The fact that this fool has been stalking you and that he followed you here to New York and to the *Times*. So. Your work has been very good in the short time you've been here, Darcy. Very good. Promising. And I've really looked forward to seeing you develop, and you *wanted* to develop—"

"I still want to, Elliot. I can't tell you how devastated I am about this—"

The flat of his palm stopped me cold. I was to listen, not talk. But I had to speak because his tone, his direction, was adding pain to pain.

"You're going to fire me."

"Well, no. Not exactly."

"Because it sounds as if you are."

"Darcy, jumping to conclusions won't serve anyone. You of all people should know that."

"You're right."

"As I was saying . . . well, I've lost my train of thought. The point is, we think the smartest course of action right now is for you to do your work from home. Until we know who murdered your source – Abe Starkman, if I've got his name right."

"You do. He seemed like a good man; he talked to

me because he needed to tell someone."

Elliot's posture deflated as he sat in his chair. "That's always why they call us. If no one had any conscience, we wouldn't have any sources."

"But the thing with Joe," I said. "It seems so sudden. Out of nowhere – and now *this*."

"Everyone here's feeling stumped by it. But as an employer, we have to take the most conservative position. Let the police do their work, get the facts on the murder, and then we'll reassess."

"So I should work from home?"

"On your other stories. I'm putting Stan on the bones; he'll work with Courtney."

"But, Elliot—"

"It's not a punishment, Darcy. It's a tactical maneuver to keep people here safe. You understand that, of course."

"Yes."

"This is silly, but . . . here." He reached behind him into his briefcase and withdrew a child's drawing with a pink butterfly, a blue flower and my name spelled D-O-R-S-I cockeyed across the top of the page.

"Katherine –" one of his daughters "– must have overheard me and my wife talking this morning. She drew this. Well, I thought it was sweet."

"It's very sweet, Elliot. Thank you." I took the drawing and stood up to leave.

"The other stories you're working on are also important," he said, leaning up to half rise out of his chair as if he intended to see me out. Which he didn't. He hovered a moment before sitting back down.

"I know." Of course they were but the truth was I didn't care about them anymore. I only cared about Abe Starkman, the man who had given his life to meet with me and point me in the direction of buried bones in a questionable patch of land.

As I left his office, Elliot followed me with words meant to console: "Remember, Darcy, it's just a relocation until we have more information and things calm down. You're still on staff here. I expect daily updates on your work."

I turned to smile at him. "Tell your daughter thanks for the beautiful picture."

Things calm down. It was one of those wonderfully innocuous expressions, open-ended on both sides. If *things calmed down* I would be invited back to the newsroom. If they didn't, would I be cut loose? But how could I not understand Elliot's heightened sense of caution? If Joe *had* killed Abe Starkman, how could I and my shadow-stalker be allowed to endanger my colleagues? If I had been my editor, I would have made the same decision. So, Stan would be taking my place alongside Courtney on the bones story – a story that had grown from a small environmental piece to one on corruption and now murder. A story that had catapulted out of my hands and into my life.

Home. I arrived with a thwunk; at least that was how it felt walking in my door that morning. I set down my bag, heavy with laptop and files, on the hall floor. Marched to the kitchen and magneted Elliot's daughter's drawing onto the fridge.

Home. Where I hunkered down, fearful of over-exposure. Like a shade flower, I felt I might shrivel if I stayed too long in the light. I closed all the curtains and blinds and stopped answering the door. Periodically the phone burst into angry spasms of constant ringing. Thirty, forty, fifty times, and I could not figure out how to turn off the ringer.

I had already called Jess to tell him what had happened to Abe. Now the ringing phone reminded me that I'd forgotten to mention I had the box and planned to drop it off at the precinct on my way to pick Nat up from school later. I used my cell phone to call Jess for fear of accidentally answering one of Joe's calls if I lifted the landline receiver.

"Don't bother delivering the box," Jess said. "I'll have a patrol car swing by for it."

"Tell him to wait after he rings the bell. I'll have to get to the window and take a look before I open the door."

"Will do. And how about I send a car over to pick Nat up after school?"

"A police escort?" I could just see Nat's face: stunned, ashamed, angry. "No thanks. I'll get him myself."

"You sure?" His tone managed to express as much sympathy as doubt. But Jess was a parent and understood that dealing with Nat was something I had to do myself.

"Listen, Jess, if it gets to the point that I can't pick my kid up from school, then we're out of here." As soon as I said it, it occurred to me that maybe waiting was a bad idea. Maybe *now* was the time to leave. Leave the life we had started to build here and the people we had started to care about. Certainly we were capable of leaving; we had abandoned a whole life on the Vineyard. But where would we go?

"Don't," he said. "You're safer here, where we can watch you. And watch him."

A good point; but still, it was obvious that Joe's obsession could spill onto Nat sooner or later. The prospect of his following my son, watching him, documenting him, terrified me more than anything.

The cop came and went with the box.

Mid-afternoon I walked to my car, parked one block over, feeling and sensing and fearing and hating Joe every step of the way. I arrived early at the school and glued my eyes to the exit until Nat came out with his friends. When he saw me, he pulled away from the cluster of boys, waved and jumped into the back seat of our car.

"Hi, Mom."

"Hi, honey. How was school?"

"Good. Aren't you working today?"

"I wasn't feeling well so I came home early."

"If you're not feeling well, why'd you pick me up? I could have gotten home on my own."

"I know. I felt better so I hopped in the car."

In the rearview mirror, I saw his skeptical expression: the thick eyebrows pinching above his nose, the mind working behind his eyes.

Back in Boerum Hill, I parked as close to our house as I could and tried to act casual as we walked back home. But as soon as we entered the apartment, its eerie shade-pulled darkness contrasting with the bright afternoon outside, Nat froze, his bookbag slung over one shoulder. He looked at me with the same expression as when he was five years old and asked, "Why is the sky some color, Mommy?" I knew exactly what he'd meant: *any* color, as opposed to no color at all. *Why is the sky blue*?

This was something for which I now had an explanation, having researched it for an article, but at the time I had been unable to answer. The atmosphere of the earth is bathed in white sunlight. *Visible* light is made up of every color: red, orange, yellow, green, blue, violet, and all the other variations in the spectrum. Most colors are absorbed, passing right through molecules in the air, but not blue. Blue bounces off molecules, scattering, and so we see it. All the other colors are there, just invisible.

But as little Nat had looked at me and waited for an answer, I found myself at a loss. My own mother had told me, "The sky is blue because it *is*," a wholly unsatisfactory explanation. *Her* mother had told her that God had painted it with blueberry juice. My answer, automatic and absurd, fell somewhere in between: "The sky is blue so when we look up high there's something beautiful to see." A non-answer, but it had served the moment; Nat went back to blowing the fluffy white pollen off spent dandelions on our Vineyard lawn.

This time, the questioning expression on Nat's face would require a real explanation: *Our home is dark midday because* . . . But with all my heart and soul, I did not want to pollute my son's mind with one man's vile obsession, not if I didn't absolutely have to.

"I had a really bad headache. The sunlight was bothering me."

"Uh huh." He dropped his bookbag in the middle of the hall floor and went to the kitchen, which was the brightest room in the house as those windows were uncovered and faced the back yard. Opened the fridge door. Failed to find anything tempting. Closed it. Faced me.

"The test for specialized high schools is in two weeks, on a Saturday. I signed up to take it. Is that OK?"

"Of course."

"All the other moms are going on tours, looking for high schools."

"I plan to." Yet another lie: I had thought there was plenty of time for that. The New York public school calendar had struck me as overwrought. I had not only failed to master the instruction tome but had set it aside in one of my piles and completely forgotten about it until now. *Bad mother*, concentrating on work and survival instead of playing possum with the fact that my son did not possess the test scores necessary to apply to top city high schools because he had never taken the tests because we had lived elsewhere where tests weren't necessary where his father had died before which we had been happy and never planned to leave or even imagined we'd end up in New York City, pretending we – I – weren't being stalked by a madman. Back in the Vineyard where buried bones would have long ago been dug up by a wild animal and scattered, returning piecemeal, over time, to the earth. Where memories were not buried to be dug up and stirred but floated in a gentle, perpetual cloud. A suffocating cloud, which I had fled.

"Mr Stuart stopped me after art class today."

"He did?"

"Said any time I wanted to head back to the neighborhood together, it was fine by him."

"Oh. That was nice of him."

"I don't need a *bodyguard*, Mom."

"Who said you did?"

"You and your boyfriend are acting like I do."

"He's not exactly my boyfriend. And I know you don't need a bodyguard. People do care about you, you know, Nat."

"Then stop showing up at school, OK? It's embarrassing."

I stood there, frozen in his headlights.

"*OK*, Mom? Unless there's something you're not telling me, and I already know what it is, anyway. That freak from work's still bothering you, right?"

He knew. And he was right: it was time to stop pretending Joe would just go away.

"Nat, I've been thinking. What if we left? We could move someplace else. Someplace more peaceful, with good schools you don't need to test into. Someplace we both like, or maybe someplace we've never been. We could have an adventure, just the two of us – take off, go to northern California, live on a *real* vineyard."

He listened, or waited, with an uber-passive expression that said he thought I was rambling. And

I was! But staying here like a sitting duck suddenly felt insane.

"I don't want to leave," he said. "It's been hard enough getting used to it here, and I'm kind of liking it now. I've got friends and I can get around on my own. Anyway, Mom, face it: he'll follow you anywhere we go."

The wisdom in that was stark and terrible. If we ran, Joe *would* follow. He had done it once before. Why wouldn't he do it again?

Nat hinged a banana off the bunch in the fruit basket we kept on our table and refused to look at me when he walked out of the kitchen. I forgave him everything: his narcissism and the ease with which he squashed my plea. He was my child, poor kid, and deserved none of the bad stuff he was getting. I sat at the table for a few minutes, thinking. Then I walked through the house and opened all the curtains, letting in what remained of the afternoon. There were hours and hours left to the day, days and days left to the week, weeks and weeks left to the year. Nat was right: we couldn't spend them in hiding.

I went to my room and tried working on my other stories but had trouble concentrating on them. They no longer interested me. All I really cared about now were two things. No, three. *No*, four. First, purging Joe from my life. Second, safety, health and happiness for Nat. Third, peace of mind for my mother. Fourth, to know the provenance of the bones. The rest, as they said – anything that came my way – would be frosting on the cake.

I opened a new computer file and typed my wish list. Felt a little better. And decided not to even try to work today. Work, usually a good distraction for life's troubles, now felt irrelevant. Instead, I searched online for information about Abe Starkman's life.

There wasn't much, mostly it was in relation to Buildings Department work, huge Adobe files posted by bureaucrats in case someone might take an interest in their voluminous outpourings. But then I discovered that the *Times* had just posted an online obituary in which I learned that Abraham Starkman, age fifty-four, had been a senior project manager at the agency where he had spent his entire career; was known for his diligence; had been well respected; did not socialize much; had grown up in Midwood; had been long married to a woman named Ola with whom he had three grown children all of whom still lived in New York City; that he had been about to become a grandfather for the first time. I also learned that a memorial service would be held for Abe the following week and I wanted to go.

"You can't," Rich told me, over the phone. He had heard the news and put two and two together. "It could be dangerous for you and it could also be dangerous for the family. Shouldn't you think about them?" In the background I heard people talking, a child's voice. The *neigh* of a horse reminded me that Rich spent Wednesday after-school hours teaching riding at Prospect Park.

"You're right. It wouldn't be fair, especially since Joe might have—"

"Don't go there, Darcy. Let the cops figure that out. Your detective – I thought Jesus would show the way."

We shared a laugh. "I sure hope so. Meanwhile . . ."

"Meanwhile, if you're really worried, which you are and *should* be, let me take Nat back and forth to school for a few days, OK?"

"He mentioned you'd offered."

"It makes sense. I live so close. And I care about both of you."

How could that not melt my heart? My frozen-with-fear heart. "Thanks. That would be a big help. Just don't say anything to him about us."

"Don't worry about that. This is a teacher–student thing, purely. A neighborly gesture. OK?"

"OK."

"And I think you should get a restraining order."

"Rich, I explained it already. Go online and read about stalking. You'll see how not-simple it is. Please."

He paused, then promised, "I will."

"I loved this morning," I said to change the subject to a much, much better one.

"Me, too. I want to see you. How can I see you?"

"I don't know. We'll find a time; something will present itself. Right?"

"Right." Though he didn't sound convinced. Now that he'd be accompanying Nat back and forth to school, early morning visits were pretty much out. Maybe we'd have to resort to middle-of-the-night trysts while Nat was asleep in his bed. And if he woke? Heard a noise? Got scared? I knew what would happen: mother would leap from bed and run to child. Leaving lover alone, embarrassed, realizing he hadn't slept at all and had to appear at work the next day. Reality would infringe, spoiling things. But then again, it already had.

We said goodbye and I was back to where I was before he called: reading about Abe Starkman's life and assuming that Joe had caused his death. The more I thought this way, the more I realized I had to stop assuming that Joe had personally killed Abe Starkman. Maybe he hadn't; maybe Courtney was right about the mob's hand in this.

Two detectives from the 84th Precinct – Jess's unit – stopped by to see me late in the afternoon: Dee Solaris, a small African American woman who was all business, and Malek Rassood, an Egyptian giant with humor that flashed constantly in his black eyes. They sat in my living room, sharing the couch. Before joining them, I crooked an ear up the staircase: rock 'n' roll from behind Nat's closed bedroom door. To create another buffer so Nat wouldn't overhear, I shut the living room door then sat across from my visitors on a narrow wooden chair that had been one of Hugo's favorites.

They asked me all the obvious questions about my association with Abe Starkman. I answered; there was little to tell. And then Rassood floored me with this: "We hear you got a personal psycho, makes house calls. Want to tell us about that?"

"You've been talking to Jess Ramirez."

They nodded.

"Though *he* wouldn't phrase it as a joke."

"Don't be offended, ma'am," Detective Solaris said, casting a dark look her partner's way. "Rass here's got no tack." She meant tact and she was right; the remark just wasn't funny.

"He came to my house once, to leave me a photograph of himself." Then I told them about my encounters with Joe since a week ago Monday.

"So the warning at work escalated it," Solaris said, shaking her head.

"Yes."

"Since then?"

"Just the YouTube video . . . if he posted it. I guess we're all assuming he did."

Rassood's eyes flickered before forking over a line I suspected he'd delivered many times: "Assume makes an ass outta u and me."

"No," Solaris said to him, "just you." Then to me: "No one's assuming anything. The YouTube upload traced to Coffin's cell phone."

Of course; I hadn't doubted it would.

"Detectives –" I leaned forwards "– were there any witnesses to Abe's killing? Did anyone see Joe on the bridge?"

"We can't comment on that," Solaris said.

Then, with just the slightest delay, Rassood said, "Nah," contradicting her with startling directness. She looked at him with a killer glance, which he shrugged off. I got the feeling their good cop/bad cop routine was well worn and perfectly timed. It was as if they recognized the depth of my worry that my stalker might have actually killed someone, a man who had trusted me.

"Do you have any leads yet?" I asked. "About who might have done this to Abe?"

Ignoring my question, Rassood stood up, towering over me in my hard chair. Solaris also stood. They both handed me business cards, white with raised blue lettering and an NYPD shield logo.

"Call if anything comes to mind you maybe forgot to mention," Solaris said.

Rassood glanced around my living room like he was memorizing it, which made me uncomfortable, then he said, "Thanks for having us."

Just before six o'clock, I heard from a *Times* lawyer who told me she would be "handling any difficulties that might arise from your professional connection to Abe Starkman". In other words, if in the course of researching the bones story I had put my source in a position of undue risk, I was in big trouble. If not, I wasn't. But what about the fact that my stalker had caused the trouble by posting the video on YouTube? Was I to be held responsible for that? On this point I felt totally confused. One way or the other, I felt guilty for Abe's death. His brutal death. In the dark, on a bridge, alone.

Hour by hour, as I tunneled into myself, shining bright lights of blame, the focus of the unfolding story, as it was revealed via the keyboards and cameras of reporters, shifted away from Joe and thus me. I knew from talking to Courtney and following the story that the police investigation was gaining momentum. They had identified the four bullets that had shot Abe as having come from a gun known to have been stolen among others in a recent heist which investigators had already connected to the mob. Between that, and the fact that no one had seen

Joe anywhere near the Brooklyn Bridge early this morning, it did appear on the surface to have been a Mafia-style retaliation killing.

Courtney was running with that version of the story, reflected in her and Stan's piece the next day, Thursday, in which Abe Starkman was revealed as the source of our original information about the discovery of bones. She didn't spell out the fact that I was the woman in the video. It wasn't necessary; anyone who wanted to could easily make the connection.

Nat sat across from me, finishing a bowl of cereal and reading the Arts section of the *Times*. When the doorbell rang, his eyes flew to mine.

"It's OK. It's Mr Stuart. I thought it *was* a good idea for you to head over to school with him, since he lives around here. It makes sense, don't you think, sweetie?"

Nat stared at me, rubbing his cheek, leaving behind a ghost of newsprint ink. "Yeah, I guess so, considering." He had been down before me and must have read the front page of the first section. So he knew.

"And back home, later, too."

"Fine." He pushed the newspaper away and stood up. "I don't know, Mom. I mean, why didn't you just tell me?"

"There's not much to tell. Reporters have sources. Mine got . . ." *Killed* was still a bad word in the vocabulary I shared with my son.

"Guy got whacked by the mob, sounds like. I know about that stuff, Mom."

"You do?"

"*Yes*. And the mob knew about the guy who got killed because Joe Coffin put his video on YouTube and told his name. I watched the video and I saw you. I mean, I couldn't see you very well, but I recognized the way you stand."

"Maybe I should have explained yesterday."

"It doesn't take a brain surgeon to figure this out, you know. I mean, I got half of it online last night. I read all your stories, Mom. I know all about those bones and why the mob wanted to kill that guy."

He'd said it. The bad word. My baby.

"I think true crime is cool," he said.

The doorbell rang again.

Cool?

"Mr Stuart's waiting. Do you have your cell phone turned on?"

No answer. He cleared his bowl to the sink and left the kitchen. I heard him greeting Rich at the front door, and then they were gone.

"Turning the wheel," was what my mother used to call *getting through the day*. "Turn the wheel, Karl. Just turn it. Don't think so much."

"Not thinking is an *im-possib-ility*, Eva." Breaking up the syllables to make the word heavy and complex, so it would reflect the impact he wished it to have. "Our brains are filters. They hold things. Without them we could not live."

"Then *live*. That's all." Her emphasis bore equal but opposite weight, meant to reduce and simplify. She wanted him to stop remembering. He couldn't. It was a conflict they never overcame.

All day Thursday, I tried. *Turn the wheel*, I told myself, over and over, but the wheel instead seemed to turn me. By noon I found myself brain-dead in front of the television, desperately trying not to think. But I lacked my mother's focus and resolve. I couldn't not think. Thinking ruled me. It gave me satisfaction, release and exhilaration as much as it caused me grief, anxiety and fear. When the phone started up again – ringing and ringing in ten-ring spurts – I couldn't just sit in the echo chamber of what was essentially a voluntary confinement. I shot up off the couch, grabbed my purse and headed out the front door, my only real concession to common sense being that I locked it behind me.

I would walk the streets of my neighborhood, defying Joe. Or, my fear of Joe. Defying the idea that he had accumulated so much power over me. How had that happened in such a short period of time? But then I remembered the box and reminded myself that he had been working on me, like a project, for much longer than I had realized. Going outside for no reason, just to wander, was a stubborn test to find out if awareness of having a stalker made you more safe or less safe, if it changed anything at all about the fact that you were always being watched.

As I walked, I gathered courage by pretending Joe did not exist. Instead, I thought of Hugo, pretending he was alive, narrating (silently) everything I saw so he could see it too.

Pizzeria on the corner, three outdoor tables, mother and toddler having lunch.

Hardware store with displays spilling onto the sidewalk.

Dress boutique: window decorated with pointy-toed shoes and oversized plasticky bracelets.

Vietnamese sandwich shop; bubble tea.

"What's bubble tea?" Hugo – my inner-voice-Hugo – asked.

"Never heard of it until I came here."

"Where are you?"

"Went traveling but I'm home now. On the Vineyard. In our house. With you."

"Try not to travel without me again, unless you have to."

"Nothing can make me go without you again."

"I've missed you."

"And I you."

Bought myself some bubble tea to find out what it was: a sweet concoction with balls of tapioca on the bottom. Bubble tea. So now I knew.

"There is always something different to learn about," my mother used to tell my father. "Get your mind out of the past. It's an illusion. Get your mind into the present. Do something special. Learn something new." My mother the optimist, despite it all.

A hobby, she would urge; anything to get your mind off the past.

All my life, as a child of survivors, I knew I belonged to a special breed. We were neither here nor there, never allowed to be happy or allowed to be sad. Widowhood fit the same bill, I found, leaving you floating between two worlds: the one you had before and the one you still couldn't imagine having next. Darkness and light, black and white, good and evil. Memories and new experiences were polar opposites requiring the same host: you. Your consciousness must entertain every possibility.

I hated those hours, that Thursday, with Nat at school. I missed him. Wanted his company. And reminded myself not to show him how badly I wanted his company.

I walked and walked, ready to encounter Joe at any turn. Pretended to be ready. Realized, the longer I stayed out, exposed, how foolish it was to pretend.

I wanted to feel strong enough to face him, when my time came; and it would. I knew that with sudden clarity. My *time* could mean anything: indignity, capture, even death. I had to be ready.

The minute I was home, I called Courtney. "Will you still come with me to that stalking consultant?"

"Totally. Just tell me when."

"I'll call now and make an appointment, then I'll let you know."

"Great. Before you hang up . . ." I heard her shuffling papers, presumably on her desk, and pictured the newsroom with longing. "Got a rough preliminary on the bones: two males and a female. That's all we know right now."

"Ages?"

"Not yet. No ages, no time frame for how many years they've been there. That takes longer, they said."

"Keep me posted."

"Will do."

I called the offices of MacDonald, Tierney and was put through to Jed Stevens, who listened to my situation and gave me an appointment for the very next afternoon. "We don't like to postpone the initial consultation," he told me in a voice that sounded too young for this kind of work. Still, I appreciated his efficiency. Time was of the essence and he knew it. Maybe he would be able to help. I noted the appointment along with the address in my calendar, then called Courtney with the details. She wanted to meet me at my house and take me, like a child, but I refused.

"Meet me there. Friday's my day to have lunch with my mother."

"You really think you should go back there?"

"She waits for me on Fridays. It's on her schedule. The aides remind her all morning long."

"Call them and tell them not to. She won't know it's Friday."

"But I will. I've got to see her."

"Just do yourself a favor. When you're out there on your own, call Jesus first, tell him where you'll be and when, OK? Can't hurt to give him the particulars."

I promised I would. And I did: calling him Friday morning to give him my itinerary for the day.

A police officer was standing outside the building on West End Avenue, posted there like a guard, and I had to wonder if Jess had somehow finagled this for me. I tried to get a look at his badge when I passed but couldn't read his precinct number. His eyes flicked to me. I smiled. He nodded. And I decided I was safe, that the cop would wait right there until I came down and Joe would never get past him.

It was still a little early for lunch and I found my mother waiting in the common room where a game of bingo had just broken up. One man and four women crept and hobbled and caned their way past me when I came in, each eyeing me with interest as if I were a brand new face. I had met them all before and even knew most of their names but didn't let on. I greeted them one at a time, introducing myself as Eva's daughter.

"Eva has a daughter!" Hettie leaned her brown-speckled arm on the wall to support herself as she turned to look at my mother, seated across the room, staring out her favorite window. "How nice for Eva."

"I'm hungry," the man said. Bald and stooped, he wore a pressed yellow shirt and his belt was cinched nearer his ribs than his hips. "They didn't give us breakfast this morning."

"You had oatmeal, Frank," said Leah, who must have visited the hairdresser because her steel-hued hair had gone blue.

They left the room in a haze of confused chatter, one of them saying, "Who's that woman?" having already forgotten.

Mom wore black slacks, one of the elastic-waisted pairs I'd bought her so she would be comfortable. Over it she wore a pink eyelet blouse, buttoned crooked, one collar dipping low on the left side. And she had on her pearls, presumably at the suggestion of one of the aides, as she was having company today.

I pulled up a chair beside her, settled in and took her bony hand in mine. It lay atop my palm with a lightness I wasn't used to. Had she lost weight in the last week? It didn't seem possible. She continued to look out the window, apparently not registering my presence. In profile, she *did* look gaunter, the hills and valleys of her face more pronounced. The sun shone directly on her, making her skin transparent, revealing tangles of veins beneath her eyes and the skeletal tip of her nose off which cartilage seemed now to drop instead of flow. Her eyes looked watery and unfocused as if she were looking far beyond the Hudson River landscape seamed with apartment buildings across the water on the New Jersey side. A sailboat floated up the river but she didn't appear to see it. Was she asleep in her chair with her eyes open?

"Mom?"

Her fingers responded, thumb first – one two three four five – playing scales up and down my palm. She had studied piano as a child before . . .

"Marta, darling. We will practice *without* our instruments today."

"Mom, it's Darcy."

"That's it. We will keep our hands strong."

"Your daughter."

"We must pretend our clothing is clean."

"*Darcy*."

"Our shoes shined." She giggled like a young girl. "That we have shoes at all!"

And I knew: my mother wasn't here in this room with me. She wasn't even my mother anymore.

"Dancing barefoot is how we'll do it, when no one's watching. Isadora Duncan did it, so why can't we?" Her feet made small movements on the living room rug, shifting almost imperceptibly from side to side. And then she said in a voice so determined it took me by surprise: "We must keep ourselves moving, do you understand, Rose?"

Who were Marta and Rose?

"Those tears, no one can see them. So stop crying. It won't help. Lara, give me your hand."

In my mother's eyes I saw the girls dancing together in an unlit barracks – they'd called them "blocks", I recalled; my father had told me – during a rare moment when no one was watching. Eva, Marta, Rose and Lara forming a circle with held hands and moving their feet over a floor of hardened mud.

She began to hum a tune, one I recognized from my childhood. Once, when I'd asked her to tell me what it was called, she'd started to answer and then couldn't remember.

"What's the song called, Eva?" I asked her now.

"Dolly Bergheim, are you crazy?"

Eva, Marta, Rose, Lara and Dolly. I understood now: these were her friends at the camp. She had never told me much about them. She had talked a little about the resourcefulness of the prisoner-children in finding ways to play however they could, always in secret. But never before had she named them. I only knew about Bertha, her one friend from back then who had survived.

"Sing the song for me, Eva."

Her fingertips quickened on my palm. "I will *play* it for you."

I could almost hear my childhood piano resound with music under her slight touch. She was playing it, as she used to: the song whose name she had claimed not to remember but which she knew perfectly well.

"What's the song called, Eva?"

"Dolly, how can you not remember?"

"I do remember."

"'*Das Mädchen unter der Laterne*'."

"The Girl Under the Lantern". Easy enough for my rudimentary German to translate. The song Marlene Dietrich made famous as Lili Marlene – I recognized it now, knew why it had seemed so familiar. But my mother's song was different, more elemental than Dietrich's stylish rendition.

She played and hummed and finally sang, her frail

voice warbling in German until suddenly she broke her own spell:

"Dolly – quiet!"

Her eyes snapped shut and her face seemed to cave in. Head tilted down, chin lowered in submission, she bowed to a memory I couldn't fathom.

And she was gone. Alive, technically, but *gone*.

I sat with her for a while longer, her hand on mine, studying the dry softness of her skin. Sensing the remains of her meager presence beside me. Then I closed my eyes and concentrated, willing my love to cross the membrane of history that separated us. I wanted her to know that I existed, that I was living proof of her survival, that I was *right here*. But if she was aware of me at all, I couldn't tell.

"Mom," I whispered, hoping that somehow she could hear me. "I need you."

Silence.

Finally, I released her hand, lay it gently on her lap where it curled into a fist, and left early for my afternoon appointment with Jed Stevens.

CHAPTER 9

The threat assessment company Courtney had found for me operated out of a brownstone on East 83rd Street. On the outside it looked like an average Manhattan townhouse with its staid brown façade, tall windows under carved lintels and oversized Italianate flower pot planted with an autumn-bronze chrysanthemum. The firm's only signage, distinguishing it on an otherwise residential block, was a tiny plague by its door: MACDONALD, TIERNEY.

Courtney was waiting outside when I arrived. She must have had a meeting earlier in the day because she was smartly dressed in what appeared to be new fall clothes: a short skirt (matching jacket flung over her arm) of lightweight tweed that captured the reds, browns, oranges and yellows of a fading summer, a sheer peach-hued blouse over a brown camisole, and a pair of brown patent-leather high heels. No one else I knew could make a business suit so sexy. She wore large gold hoop earrings and her brilliant hair flowed down her back. When I got out of the taxi she walked over, kissed my cheek, took my arm and led me inside.

We both paused in awe when we stepped through the door into the reception area. The renovated interior was a cubist interpretation of bright, open spaces, startling at first encounter, then intensely pleasing. The standard twenty-five by forty foot brownstone layout had been reinvented with glass walls and interior balconies that carved the space into a series of light boxes.

We told the receptionist that we had an appointment with Jed Stevens, whom she buzzed to announce us before leading us up two flights of stairs. We were put into a small conference room whose walls of frosted glass created an intimate, private space beneath a flush of sun from a skylight. A white laptop sat neatly closed at the head of the table.

Jed Stevens appeared moments later, carrying a glossy blue folder emblazoned with the company name. My first thought was: *He's twelve*. Then I saw that he couldn't be twelve because his sculpted – and when you really looked at it *gorgeous* – face was sandpapery with fashionable stubble. He wore a well-cut crown of golden hair, and a fine web of crow's feet radiated from his baby-blue eyes. I gave him twenty-five, twenty-eight tops. If he was even thirty, he should market his genes. He looked far too dashing, in his designer suit and lilac tie, to be capable of tackling my kind of problem.

His voice had sounded young on the phone and in person it concerned me even more. But we were here and it seemed reasonable to give him the benefit of the doubt. Courtney, seated beside me at the narrow conference table, glued her eyes to the Adonis now at the head of the table, opening the laptop. She liked him, I could tell. I had only ever seen her work her wiles on men she pretended to like; this could be interesting.

Jed opened the introductions by sliding the blue folder across the table to Courtney, who sat with her back straight, legs crossed and pink-glossed lips smiling.

"It's nice to meet you, though I'm sorry it has to be under these circumstances." A greeting he had presumably spoken many times in this very conference room, but did he always deliver it to the wrong woman? And should I have been surprised that he would assume that Courtney, so irresistible-looking, was his new stalking client?

"*I'm* Darcy."

His eyes shifted and settled on me. He maintained

his smile though it stiffened into something vaguely pretentious and discomfiting, as if he was thinking: *you're* the woman some loser can't live without?

"I'm Darcy's friend," Courtney said. "I came to keep her company."

Courtney and Jed exchanged seductive smiles. The electricity between them was awkward, at least for me.

"We work together," I told Jed. "Courtney and I."

"Well, good to meet you both. Let me just pull up a new file for you, Darcy." He tapped away at the computer, squinted his eyes until the screen he wanted appeared, then leaned back and faced us. "So . . . you're being stalked."

"Yes."

"Tell me why you think you're being stalked."

"No," Courtney cut in, "she *is* being stalked. I know this guy. He's a total freak."

Jed typed a note. "How do you know him?"

"From work," she said.

"Actually I knew him before work." I went on to explain the whole thing despite a sense that Jed and I were making no connection whatsoever and he might not have even believed that *I* was being stalked when an eminently more desirable woman sat right there beside me. Unless I was imagining the disconnect. I plowed on anyway until I had laid the whole episode before him.

"OK." Leaning back, nodding soberly, fingertips steepled; boy playing businessman at work. "I've got to ask you some tough questions now, if you don't mind."

"Go right ahead."

He paused as if for dramatic effect. "Any prior sexual history?"

Courtney actually giggled.

"You mean with *Joe*?" I asked.

He nodded as soberly as a silly man could.

"Absolutely not!"

"My apologies, but I had to ask."

"Why? I just explained my history with him. I told you: I hardly know him at all."

"It's just one of our standard questions."

He was reading off a list on the computer. No, he wasn't twelve; he was nine.

He read the next checklist question aloud: "Does the stalker have a prior criminal history?" Then answered it himself: "You've told me that Mr Coffin had no prior criminal history on Martha's Vineyard, where he grew up, so let's call that a simple *no*." He clicked a box, then asked me: "Any issues of chemical abuse or dependence?"

"I have never been a drug user."

He grinned. "Not you. Mr Coffin."

"Look, I'm sorry, but I hate hearing you call him *Mr Coffin* like he's some kind of respectable grown-up."

"Call him Joke," Courtney said. "I do."

Jed's attention rested on her a moment, his eyes smiling. "We'll just call him Joe. It's simpler. So, let's see here." He clicked a few times, talking as he went and presumably entering my answers into little boxes. "No sexual history, no criminal priors, drug use unknown – is it fair to assume that?"

"Yes."

"Same workplace. You knew him for two years."

"*No*. He stalked me for two years. I only met him twelve days ago."

Jed nodded, thinking how to clarify that discrepancy on his form. Then he scrolled to another page and typed something. After scrolling some more, he hit *enter*, sat back and watched the screen.

"Good news, Darcy. Your threat assessment score is low. Just a two, on a scale of one to ten, ten being worst case scenario."

I couldn't believe it. He had summed up Joe's danger to me using a multiple choice computer program. This was proving to be a real waste of time. But there was more:

"You may not be aware of this, Darcy, but you're in pretty good company. Seventy-seven percent of female stalking victims are stalked by someone they know. But of that, a full fifty-nine percent are stalked by an intimate partner. Women who are stalked by a current or former husband or cohabitating partner report that they were physically assaulted eighty-one percent of the time and sexually assaulted thirty-one percent of the time. And a national femicide study found that seventy-six percent of the victims had been stalked before being attacked."

Finished, Jed smiled. I felt like giving him an A+ for memorization and a slap across his face for stupidity and insensitivity.

"Femicide?" I asked.

"Murdered women."

"Jed?" Courtney leaned forwards, pressing her arms against her ribs to accentuate her cleavage which was fully visible beneath the transparent fabric of her blouse. "Darcy's got a real problem here. I think you're *great*, but do you think we could talk to someone with a tad more experience?"

"I've been mentored by our founder, Alan Tierney, who has been doing this for twenty years and is recognized as one of the very best in the business of threat assessment."

"I know, that's why I gave Darcy this phone number to call. Where is Mr Tierney?"

"Unfortunately he's in the hospital at the moment, recovering from bypass surgery."

"And who's MacDonald?"

"Gerry MacDonald was a founder, but he's been gone seventeen years."

Courtney and I looked at each other. *Time to go.*

"One more question," Courtney asked. "How long have *you* been at this?"

"Ten, fifteen minutes."

"No, not with us. Your career."

"Six months." He smiled adorably and I wanted to puke.

As we stood to leave, Courtney took the blue folder with her, like a freebie she couldn't bring herself to pass up.

"Jed," she said, ratcheting up the charm, "thank you for your time." She reached into her purse and handed him her business card. "I don't think we'll be hiring you but I've got to be honest: I think you're sexy as hell. Call me?"

Strangely, he didn't look surprised. But *I* was, and nearly lurched out of the conference room. Courtney's sexuality was too, let's say, *evolved* for me to grasp. I waited in the hall outside until she emerged, smiling. One look at each other's faces – hers, glowing; mine, stupefied – and we burst out laughing.

"I don't want to know," I said.

"Never had a bimbo?"

"Nope."

"*Yum*."

"Just don't marry him, OK?"

"No threat of that. He'll be good for a week or two, though."

We went outside and stood together on the sidewalk. Her work days started at seven and for her it was almost quitting time, at least officially. I knew that she tended to continue working at home on her laptop, as did I.

"Heading back to the office?" I asked her.

"I already filed my story for tomorrow, so I'm good. Want to grab some coffee? We can read through this material." Meaning the material inside the blue folder she held in her hand.

I checked the time: nearly two thirty. "I want to be home when Nat gets there and I'm already pushing it."

"Doesn't he have keys?"

"Yes, but . . ."

I didn't have to finish the sentence before she nodded in agreement of the obvious: I couldn't leave Nat alone for too long, not with Joe *out there*. What if he rang our doorbell? What if Nat answered?

"Ever been to Brooklyn?" I asked.

"Used to date a guy there. Are you inviting me?"

And so we rode the subway to my borough, where I had promised to feed her coffee and scones from the bakery around the corner. All the way there, Courtney kept looking around – for Joe, I assumed – and I got the feeling she hoped to spot him. I almost wanted her to, wondering what she would do if she *did* discover him following us. Bite his head off, I guessed. I would have enjoyed watching it.

We didn't see Joe. Instead, in front of my house we found Rich with Nat, searching through his backpack for his house keys. He had the bad habit of tossing them into the middle section where they tended to settle on the bottom among pencils, pens, erasers, calculators, balled-up papers, you name it. It was a habit he would have to change; I didn't want to think of him out here, excavating for his keys, providing Joe with an opportunity to approach him. Luckily, Rich had the good sense to wait until he got inside.

"Hi, sweetie," I greeted my son.

Nat, kneeling, looked up and smiled. Rich, standing beside him, also smiled.

"This is Courtney, we work together."

"You went to work?" Rich asked – and everyone looked at him. The plainness of his reaction, the nakedness of his caring for me, put our relationship into sudden focus particularly for Nat, who had already guessed, and Courtney, whose antennae were always primed.

"No. Courtney and I went somewhere else."

Rich tried not to appear as interested as he was, but it was too late.

Courtney leaned forwards with an extended hand and a brilliant smile. "So *you're* Rich."

He turned crimson. The pink face and the dark orange hair were a beautiful combination and the very sweetness of his embarrassment deepened my desire for him. What was the point in hiding it anymore? It took too much effort away from what was most important: fending off Joe Coffin. I was surrounded by compatriots. They might as well know each other.

"Come on in," I said. "I've got scones."

We gathered around the kitchen table with a plateful of orange-peel and currant scones, coffee for the adults and a glass of milk for Nat. We chatted about things like school, the neighborhood, working at the *Times*. Only when Nat disappeared upstairs to play video games on my bedroom's TV did I allow Courtney to open the blue file.

As she did, we both told Rich about Jed Stevens, laughing as we ridiculed the poor guy. I was amazed at how freely Courtney participated, considering her plans to bed him.

"Ouch!" Courtney said, rifling through the folder's inserts and pulling one out titled "Our Fees". "That could have cost you five thousand bucks."

Rich reared his head; that was a significant portion of his teacher's salary. It was also a significant portion of my reporter's salary. Hiring MacDonald, Tierney would have been impossible regardless of their expertise (or lack thereof).

"Luckily," she said, "we've got all this good advice, right here. Check it out."

We passed papers among ourselves until we'd read them all. Jed had handed us, free of charge, safety checklists organized in varying degrees of urgency: "High Alert", "Staying Aware" and "Everyday Safety Plan".

"This one," Courtney said, handing me the stapled pages titled "High Alert". "Go with the gold, as they say."

"I agree," Rich said. "What's the point of not being as careful as you can?"

"Install an alarm system," I read aloud. "Install a camera to the front of your house with a video feed and monitor easily accessible inside the house. Install floodlights on the back and sides of your house. Get a postal box for mail delivery at a private company such as UPS; we do not recommend using the post office's similar service which has proven easy to infiltrate. Install an analog (tape recording, not digital) answering machine on your landline, dedicated to receiving and recording your stalker's calls. Redirect personal and other calls to a new cell phone number." I looked back and forth between Rich and Courtney. Both wore studious expressions; it was a lot to take in. I continued: "Consider buying a gun."

"A gun!" Rich was as shocked as I was.

"I think it's an excellent idea," Courtney said with an expression I recognized, both seductive and stalwart, her special brew of persistence.

"I have a child here, Courtney. I don't like guns in any way, shape or form."

"He doesn't have to know."

"He'll find out, trust me. He's a teenager – a kid in a man's body but without any common sense. Not to mention that I've raised him to be anti-gun. What kind of message would that send?"

"The message that you want to stay alive."

That quieted all of us. Right. Once you reduced all the talk and fear and second-guessing, *that* was what this huddle was all about.

"Maybe Courtney's right," Rich said. "What if you took a course in firearms so you'd know how to use a gun safely? And if you sat Nat down and had a serious talk with him . . ." He didn't finish that sentence because as a father he had to know how cynical it sounded. *My child, let me tell you why everything I've ever taught you to believe turns out to be wrong.*

But Courtney, being young herself and not a parent, missed the subtlety of that moment. "I *like* this man. He gets it. We'll start with gun training, then we'll find you the perfect gun. Something small and pretty that can fit right into your purse."

"Didn't I just read somewhere in there not to carry

a gun in a purse?" Rich found the page he was thinking of. "Right here: 'Weapons carried off-body can be grabbed and used against you. Strap your weapon under your shirt, on an ankle, or whatever keeps the weapon comfortably accessible so you can get to it quickly.'"

"You know what, guys? I can't think about guns right now. It's so extreme. I think I'll start with what I can handle, like getting an alarm system and all the rest of that stuff to turn this place into a fortress."

"I'll help you," Rich said.

Courtney smiled. "Are you *handy*, too?"

Rich flushed again. Courtney was playing him like a violin, as they say, and enjoying every minute of it. Since this man was my lover, I only partly enjoyed the show this time. But I was too old and too distracted to let it bother me. If Rich turned out to be seducible by a woman like Courtney – a terrific, powerful woman who knew how to use her appeal and thus was precisely the kind of woman a good man should intuitively know to distrust – let her have him.

Then and there, Courtney helped me compile a list of what I'd need to fortify our apartment, which amounted to the bottom two floors of a four-story house. (Another tenant, a married couple who worked regular hours and otherwise seemed to live quietly, occupied the two floors above us.) Once the list was made, we split it up.

I was to make calls: alarm company, electrician to wire the back of the house, cellular provider for a new number. Rich would go to Home Depot to buy the floodlights and the camera system, and sign up for a post office box, taking it in his name but listing me to receive mail and giving me the keys – his idea, and a smart one, both Courtney and I agreed.

"Here's something no one thought of," Courtney said. "Shouldn't you have a different email address? You can do with email what you're going to do with phone messages: collect Joe's at the address he has, but start another one for everyone else. You can get a free Yahoo account; it's easy."

Rich smiled a smile that lifted his whole face. "You should do their commercial."

"I'll take that as a compliment."

"Maybe you shouldn't," I said.

Courtney's glance was sharp but to the point: if I was going to be jealous of her natural charms, then we couldn't be friends. This new level of understanding came fast, like a drop down a well. Femininity came easily to her, she couldn't help herself, and she had been despised all her life by girls and women who couldn't stand what appeared to be a form of sexual deceit. I saw that very clearly now. Being that she was my only available friend (not counting Rich), I couldn't afford to lose her, nor did I want to.

"On second thought –" I smiled at her "– maybe Yahoo should hire you to do their whole campaign. You'd give them the best promotional boost they ever saw."

"Good girl." Courtney winked at me and me alone, leaving Rich out of the wordless conversation that had just sealed our friendship. "I'll check out firearms courses, so you'll have the info when you make up your mind. And I'll start shopping for guns – like I said, something pretty."

"Thanks, Courtney. I appreciate all of it."

"You better." She stood and gathered her purse to her shoulder. "I've got some things to do and later on I'm meeting someone." One side of her mouth crooked naughtily. The truth was, I was dying to know if she planned to meet Jed Stevens tonight but would have to reserve that question for another time, when we were alone.

I followed her to the front door. "I never asked you how it's working out with Stan. How the story's coming."

"Great. We've worked together before. He's a crime trooper like me so it's like an old dance."

"Any ID on the bones?"

"Darcy, I would have told you! But I'll make a prediction: they're from nineteen seventy-eight."

"I agree. But out of curiosity, what makes you think so?"

"A hunch. No, maybe it's more than that, if you take intuition seriously."

"I do."

"This morning, in the newsroom, we were talking about the Tony T trial and we all agreed the prosecutor's suddenly taking a lighter touch. Stan called it 'a set of nuances', you know, something in the ether, gestures, innuendoes of tone, stuff like that. Nothing concrete but everyone's aware it's happening. I mentioned it in tomorrow's piece: 'Abe Starkman's murder may have made the District Attorney's office nervous, which could account for a detectible laxity in yesterday's questioning of Sal Corarro on the witness stand,' which is pretty much what I wrote."

"That'll go over big with the powers that be."

"Elliot approved it and he even got Overly's OK, so . . ." She shrugged her shoulders with the mock innocence she was so good at, the glint never failing her eyes. "Our job is to keep our ears open and our pencils sharp, right?"

"Right. Except no one uses pencils anymore."

"Hal does." The newsroom politico who sat among us in his Lego sanctuary.

"Maybe *he* can give me some tips about how to hide from invading forces."

"Nah, he's just an eccentric. I'd stick with good old common sense if I were you."

Courtney and I kissed cheeks and she vanished

into the waning afternoon to pursue bones and killers and sex; a long-legged, fair-haired, elegant example of a workable contradiction.

Through the open door I felt that the air had grown sharply chilly as evening neared. It was the season's first hint that the darkness and cold of early winter would soon make its inevitable approach. I stood there for a minute, alone, drinking in an easy solitude – grateful for the reassurance of friendship the afternoon had brought – and, then, for a split second, I was certain I saw Joe across the street.

I stepped out in front of the house to get a better look. It was a man who looked like Joe: early twenties, pale skin, dark hair, red baseball cap, walking quickly with intense energy. And then I had the strangest thought: had the mask of outrage Joe wore last time I saw him up close replaced an accurate recollection of how his face looked? Had I forgotten what normal Joe (if he even existed) looked like? Would every man who resembled him seem to *be* him? It would be impossible to hold so many Joes in my mind.

I rubbed my arms to warm them against the chill and told myself not to be ridiculous because *of course* I would recognize Joe and *of course* there was only one of him. Then I went back inside the house to shoo Rich out on his safety-making errands so I could get started on mine.

But first, alone in the dark part of the hallway between the kitchen and the foot of the staircase, deep in that shadow of privacy, we kissed. Pings and ekes and bubbly tunes from Nat's video game whooshed down the stairs, reminding our hands not to wander too far under clothes. Still, for a minute, I found his skin and felt the tautness of his back, spreading my fingers across the long muscles that braced his spine. His fingertips followed the contours of my breasts, his mouth found my neck – and then footsteps above stopped us at the height of the moment when you might not be able to stop. When your body was charged, priming itself, preparing.

"Mr Stuart's on his way out," I told Nat as he came lumbering down the stairs and into the front hallway.

"See you, kid."

"Bye, Mr Stuart."

Nat stood and watched me walk his teacher to the front door. I kept my expression as placid as I could, bidding him goodbye with my friendly mom wave as he opened the iron gate and walked away down the sidewalk.

"He's cool, Mom." Nat was grinning.

"Don't you have homework or something?"

"It's Friday. What's for dinner?"

"Good question."

The fridge was basically empty. I discovered that

the local butcher delivered and ordered a variety of meats to stock the freezer. Fresh Direct could handle the rest of our weekly groceries from now on. The fact was, I could order in just about everything we needed, from food to clothes to you-name-it. With Rich bodyguarding Nat back and forth to school, and me now a work-at-home mom, I could redefine the meaning of reclusiveness. I could embody it, once all my systems were in place.

But when I was secure inside my home, cut off and lit up and alarmed to the hilt, what then? I would not be able to function indefinitely as a reporter or a mother, shut inside my house. I wondered if it was a better option to allow Joe to get to me, to prompt him to do whatever it would take for the police to lock him up for a long time. If he did something *really* bad . . . but that thought alone triggered a return to the pragmatic plan my advisers had cooked up for me: lay low and keep safe. After that, I really had no idea.

Friday night, as Nat and I sat together in the living room watching a movie, the phone started up, ringing and ringing and ringing. We tried to ignore it, putting the TV's volume as loud as we could stand. Even Mitzi and Ahab had grown used to the noise, no longer hiding under furniture or running around nervously but lounging right out in the open where we could hold them on our laps or tickle them with our feet.

Nat's threshold for the incessant noise proved lower than mine or the cats'. He paused the movie and one by one figured out how to turn off the ringers of all three phones. It took some time as each was different and none had a simple switch. One required removal of its back with a Phillips head screwdriver, for which I searched before finding it in one of our unpacked boxes in my bedroom. Finally, in the calm of silence, we finished our movie and our night.

Turning off the ringing phones did a lot to turn off the ringing in our minds, too. In the morning, without consciousness of whether or not Joe was strugging to get through, it was almost as if he wasn't trying. It freed us to go about our business. We had a quiet breakfast together, sharing the early half of the weekend *Times*. I read Stan and Courtney's story with great interest, of course; she had quoted herself verbatim yesterday and the article was much as she'd described: implication without accusation. They had also, for the first time, made reference to the conflicting land sale documents. In the three days since we'd obtained them – the days I'd been out of the office – Courtney and Stan must have vetted those documents, otherwise Elliot would not have allowed their mention in print. It didn't take a genius to predict that this would prompt the city to step up its defensiveness against the idea that it may have made a kind of devil's deal in their brokering of the developer's land purchase. It was already well known that the city's current administration was over-friendly with real estate developers and it didn't need to be pointed out that the mob played ball for a price, but there was friendly and there was *friendly* – effectively it was the difference between a handshake and extramarital sex. Perhaps this time the city had gone too far in its flirtation with power. If Abe Starkman hadn't called me, or some other reporter, the bones would still be hidden in the wrong place in the Pearson warehouse, buried in a different grave, and the corruption would have died another death right along with them.

Whenever I thought of Abe – realizing again and again that the man was actually dead – my heart sank, inevitably returning me to a parallel resonance: the deeper, colder, rougher ocean of Hugo's death. And whenever I thought of Hugo's death, my body brimmed with misery. Nat must have noticed my eyes watering because he had his usual reaction, rising suddenly from the breakfast table and leaving the room, leaving me alone in the kitchen of the home we had still not fully inhabited. The quiet kitchen. Outside, birds sang, a child shouted, an electric saw buzzed; and thus, after days of ringing phones, I was reminded that the quiet was not actually *quiet*, after all.

Later that morning, Nat had a few schoolmates – Henry, whom I knew, along with two new faces, Charlie and Maura – over to rehearse for a play they were in at school, while I continued down my To Do list. I scheduled an electrician to come on Monday to wire a video camera above the front door and floodlights in the back yard. The soonest the alarm company could come was Wednesday. Meanwhile I checked my email to see if Courtney had sent me any of the promised information about a firearms course – an idea I continued to resist and yet did not fully reject – but she hadn't sent anything. Probably still in bed with Jed Stevens, a thought I found both amusing and revolting.

It was a little awkward when Rich showed up later that afternoon in full view of three of his eighth-graders, who were gathered at the kitchen table devouring a pizza, but we managed to act as if it was nothing unusual. He had brought with him three large bags from Home Depot and Radio Shack, and one adorable little girl, his five-year-old daughter Clara who wore a pink princess costume fully equipped with a faux tiara and magic wand. It was all I could do not to scoop her up in my arms.

Rich cut up some pizza into little squares and set her on a kitchen chair, elevated on a phone book. She sat erect so her tiara wouldn't fall off. Nat and the other boys seemed to think nothing of it but Maura doted on Clara, asking her questions about kinder-garten and whether or not her art-teacher dad did art projects with her at home.

"Watch out, Maura," Rich said, "or I might enlist you as a babysitter."

"Oh, I would *love* to babysit her, Mr Stuart! I started babysitting last year. I'm really good at it."

"I can see that." Rich smiled, watching Clara and Maura beam at each other. "You can start right now, if you want. I've got a few things to do to help out Mrs Mayhew around the house."

"OK, Mr Stuart." Maura inched her chair closer to Clara's and proceeded to help the princess sever a too-long strand of pizza cheese.

As we left the kitchen we overheard one of the boys saying, "Whoa, Mr Stuart moonlights. My mom said lots of teachers can't live on what they earn."

I listened for Nat to add something – *moon-lighting's one word for it! heh heh* – but fortunately my son was discreet enough to not to turn it into a joke. He wouldn't have wanted to be embarrassed, either, by the impropriety of his mother dating one of his teachers. Instead, he changed the subject.

"Hey, anyone want to go see the new Spiderman movie tomorrow?"

"Saw it," Charlie said. "It's great."

"Can't, I still have that lab report to finish," Maura said with an unmistakable note of frustration.

"I'll go." Henry. "But not until late afternoon, OK? My parents have some people coming for lunch and they said I have to be there. Maybe after the movie you could hang out at my house for a while. My mom won't let me have sleepovers on a school night but she'd probably be cool with dinner."

"I'll ask my mom," Nat said.

Rich and I looked at each other. I leaned toward his ear and whispered, "When does Clara go back to her mom's?"

"Tomorrow at five."

"Dinner?"

"I'll come over here and cook."

"No. I've got to get out of this house. Let's eat at your place."

"OK," he whispered.

Their conversation faded to distant voices as we got settled in the living room. Rich handed me two mailbox keys for a post box at the UPS store on Court Street along with the receipt showing the box number. Then he emptied the bags and showed me the purchases he'd made. It was everything we'd discussed: floodlights and bulbs, surveillance camera and tape deck, and an analog answering machine that could store messages on a small, removable tape. I wrote him a check to reimburse him for the cost, whispering, "So you won't have to moonlight," and furtively kissed the edge of his ear.

On the front page of Sunday's *Times*, a weekend
Metro reporter I didn't know announced that a minor
league Mafia soldier from the Tarentino family had
been arrested late Saturday night at a social club in
Bay Ridge, Brooklyn. Specifically, he was charged
with participating in grand felony theft for stealing a
cache of guns in New Jersey and moving them into
New York, the crossing of state lines making it a
federal charge. More significantly, he was also
charged with the murder of Abe Starkman with one
of those guns. And the district attorney had real
evidence with which to prosecute: fingerprints,
bullet grooves matching the interior of the gun – and
an eyewitness. Apparently the FBI had agreed to
pass along a prized informant, a Tarentino minion
who was willing to come forward to testify against
his colleague. That handily sealed the deal. The killer
would go to jail for Abe's murder and the city would
look tough on racketeering.

So it was done, that fast. Abe's murder was
solved. You could almost feel the reverberations of
the city machine clicking over the past few days,
pulling strings and favors to steer attention in an
acceptable direction. See? They were not soft on the
mob when it suited them. See? They were fully
prepared to send a Tarentino soldier to prison.

What land deal? Whose bones?

Maybe they did have the real killer, maybe they

didn't, but it was such an obvious maneuver. I wondered what Courtney thought about it and dialed her cell phone to find out. It went straight to voicemail so I left a message: "I just read the front page. Start pedaling, Courtney; looks like you've got some ground to make up. What *do* you think about this? Call me."

Sunday afternoon I walked Nat over to the movie theater where Henry and The Dad, Bill, were waiting with tickets in hand. When I asked what time I should pick Nat up after dinner, Bill said not to worry, that he would personally bring him home. He said it in a tone that insisted that this was how it would be and I knew in that moment that Nat had told Henry about Joe and that Henry in turn had told his parents. I thought it was kind of them to help this way when they might have forbidden their son from being involved with us at all.

"Expect us around nine o'clock," Bill said. "Come on, boys, let's get in there and find some seats."

I had told Rich that I'd meet him at his place right after dropping Nat off at the movies but wasn't surprised when he appeared around the corner from the theater.

"So now *you're* stalking me." I kissed him right on the lips – boldly, in public. We turned away from Court Street and walked up State, a leafy block of brownstones bathed in century-old shadows.

"I saw Joe a few minutes ago," Rich said as we neared Clinton Street, where we turned in the direction of Verandah Place, his home, a meal, our bodies. "He must have followed you here. I'm glad I didn't listen to you and let you meet me at my place."

"I'm glad you didn't, either. What was he doing?"

"He crossed the street a ways behind you, then crossed back. I think he saw me. I think he knows who I am."

"Really?" But why wouldn't he? He was always, always there whether I saw him or not.

"So we have to figure out how we pick Nat up later without Henry's parents cottoning on."

"Taken care of. The Dad's bringing him home at nine."

"Then I'll get you home before that."

Plans, evasions, strategies. I could no longer live without them. It was a leap of faith that I was out of the house at all yet I was grateful for the break from my four walls.

Although it was only my second visit to Rich's apartment, I felt at home there. This sensation of comfort struck me as I moved through his spaces and among his things. I felt at home with Rich; that was it. It was a fresh branch, a first budding, of something new in our relationship, this sense that I belonged in his home. I remembered feeling a similar kind of camaraderie with Hugo right off the bat though being young there had been no pretense that a protocol of separation needed to be adhered to. Hugo and I had fallen in love and bed and life with remarkable haste, satisfaction and ultimately success. It was like an undertow, this sensation with which I surprised myself by feeling it for a brand new man. I wouldn't have thought it was possible – yet here we were.

He had mostly prepared an elaborate meal, which he must have gotten started before returning Clara to her mother's. He had made a complicated rice-and-nut dish and a fresh salad, and had a tray of salmon ready to cook on the grill in his yard. He poured us glasses of white wine, which I carried outside. While we waited for the grill to heat, he said, "Come here, I want to show you something."

He led me into his studio, the old building at the far end of the yard. The waning autumn sun cast the space in dust-hovering amber light. It was beautiful. Paintings hung everywhere, just as before. But there was one change: the canvas that had previously been covered by a paint-spattered drop cloth now sat naked on the floor, leaning against the wall.

"Is it me?" I walked closer to it. "Or maybe not. Who are they?"

Though the painting was an abstract swirl of color, two entwined figures were clearly represented among the vibrant chaos: a man and a woman, embracing.

"But you were painting this before we even—"

He walked up behind me and set both his hands on my waist. "It wasn't you, at first."

"Someone else?" I turned to grin at him, pretending jealousy just to tease him, though I felt nothing but affection for this man.

"It was a wish, I guess, or a memory – I'm not sure. I just started painting it one day. In my mind, I was thinking of Lucy at the beginning of our relationship. It was the first non-angry image about her I've painted in three years."

"But you gave her my hair and my skin tone. Lucy's darker."

"I changed that after the first time we . . . "

He kissed me and this time there was no reason to stop. I felt vaguely nervous about the grill out there heating up in the yard, but *our* heat was irresistible. We didn't bother with the niceties of gently removing each other's clothing and quickly stripped off our own, leaving them scattered over his studio's dirty floor. I didn't care about the cleanliness of this place; I cared about *him*. But he, concerned about my comfort, simultaneously drew me to the floor and maneuvered himself beneath me. We were both bursting and couldn't wait and once he entered me my mind flew away. I was lost to this man: his body, his mind, his heart, his soul. I had fallen off the cliff of my past, dropped away from all my certainty that I would never be able to fall in love again.

And then, like kismet – just as he had read my mind before moving down onto the floor – he said it first:

"I love you, Darcy."

And I echoed him, naturally:

"I love *you*."

It was too soon to speak these words to each other but there it was: they had been said. Everything about this defied common sense. As had so much of my life with Hugo – moving to a remote island, focusing on work then considered obscure, eventually making a difference – until the passage of time revealed an inherent logic. That was inspiration. That was love.

Dinner was delicious and though anything might have tasted good to me in my state of mind this really *was* good. I could almost hear Courtney's commentary: *So you're handy* and *you can cook, too*? Courtney. I hadn't heard a thing from her all weekend despite two messages and an email.

At eight thirty, Rich took me home. We walked arm in arm from genteel Cobble Hill, with its whispery nineteenth-century quiet, crossing Court Street where traffic zigzagged even on a Sunday night, bearing right onto Smith Street which as always was hectic with restaurants and the ambitious diners who ventured here from all over to enjoy the creations of some of the city's best renegade chefs.

The intersecting neighborhoods seemed magical to me tonight. It was hard to believe how much life could change in a year and a half, and yet it had, and here I was in the warm scope of a man I hadn't even known existed. *Yes, you could love two men at once*, was the answer. A widow's answer to a young woman's question. An answer anyone would be better off never needing to know.

In the dark shadow of my stoop, I found the keyhole of my front gate by moving my fingertip over the face of the steel lock. The gate squealed, as always.

"I'll oil that for you," Rich said, and I loved him.

We kissed goodnight. I slid my second house key into the lock of the interior door, and pushed it open.

The stink hit me immediately: something noxious I couldn't name. And then I saw Mitzi and Ahab . . .

PART THREE

PART THREE

CHAPTER 10

Ahab had gotten partway up the stairs but Mitzi hadn't made it that far: she was curled on the floor in front of the bottom step as if she had suddenly decided to take a nap. Her white fur was bloodied at both ends, mouth and rear. The blood didn't show on Ahab's tabby-brown fur, which looked wet, soaked at either end.

"What happened to them?" I kneeled above Mitzi and lifted her side; she felt heavy and a little stiff. "They're dead."

Rich turned at the arched entrance to the living room, turned and stared at something and said, "What's that?"

I followed him to a whitish lumpy spill of something on the floor by the fireplace, its gooey mess seeping into the fibers of Hugo's family's heirloom Oriental carpet. It looked like chicken stew in the kind of béchamel sauce I hated; but instead of being smoothly creamy, this sauce was pimply with something granular. A square plastic container lay overturned on the floor near the mess.

Rich reached for something on the mantle.

And my mind did a flip: *The eight by ten photo of Joe was back in the frame.* It couldn't be. I had ripped it up and thrown it away; the garbage men had long since scattered it to the fetid winds of some landfill somewhere.

Rich picked up an envelope propped against the frame. "It's for you," he said. "What's your detective's number? I'm going to call him."

"His card's on the fridge."

Rich went to the kitchen while I read the note from Joe.

Dear Darcy,

All day yesterday I shopped and cooked for you and your son. Dinner at six o'clock, remember? YOU FORGOT. Or . . . you remembered . . . but you didn't show up. I don't know what's worse. I thought maybe you forgot my new address. You see? I can still give you the benefit of the doubt. But you didn't answer any of my calls or return any of the messages I left. Sometimes I feel like you're trying to pretend I don't exist.

But I'm going to give you another chance because I care about you and because I believe you will care about me once you get to know me better. I am a good person, Darcy, which is something you will find out sooner or later.

Love, Joe

"How did he get in here?" I asked Rich.

"Detective Ramirez is on his way."

"The door didn't look broken into."

"I'm going to check the windows." Rich went from window to window, downstairs and up, avoiding poor Mitzi and Ahab on the stairs. *My sweet kitties*. They were sister and brother. Hugo and I had gotten them for Nat on his sixth birthday.

Nat. He would be home any minute. He would have to be told about his cats but did he have to see them like this? And this scene; the police coming; the smell . . .

In the kitchen I found the school directory and phoned Henry's house. His mother Karen answered. Luckily, Bill hadn't left yet to bring Nat home. Without explaining the details – I didn't want Karen to feel too disturbed – I asked her if she minded if Nat stayed the night. She readily agreed, assuring me she had an extra toothbrush and plenty of clean clothes of Henry's which Nat was welcome to borrow. So that was a relief: Nat would be spared the blunt shock of this.

The police arrived first, Jess about forty-five minutes later as he had come in from his home on Long Island. The first thing the police did was order Rich and me to stay in the living room while they searched the house. I don't know why it hadn't occurred to me that Joe could still be here – it just seemed that staying would have been a really stupid thing to do. And then, as they searched in every nook and cranny of my home, I realized how logical it was that he *would* stay. Logical with the kind of illogic that drove everything he did. Joe wanted to be close to me, at any cost.

He wasn't there. By the time Jess arrived, that had been established. A forensics specialist appeared to retrieve a sample of the chicken stew and search for evidence of Joe's presence in the apartment. She found nothing. There was also no sign of forced entry.

Jess sat beside me and Rich on the couch and handed me some paperwork he'd brought with him. The top read "APPLICATION FOR AN ORDER OF RESTRAINT".

"The wait's over," he said.

"It's about time." Rich's tone was tense, almost angry. "It's ridiculous that it took *this* to make it happen."

"Rich, I explained all that to you." I laid a hand

on his knee, pressed into mine, and he covered it with his own hand.

"I know. I'm sorry. But this is getting scary."

"I'm going to put the application in tonight, as soon as I leave here," Jess said. "And I called a locksmith to come and change all the locks. He said about twenty minutes."

"Thanks, Jess."

He didn't say "Jesus saves" like he did sometimes to lighten the mood, but I wanted him to. The atmosphere in the room felt heavy as wet cement. It was almost unbearable, this feeling of helpless slow suffocation, this onslaught of *love* Joe wouldn't stop shoveling my way.

"And if it doesn't stop him?" Rich asked.

"It won't." Jess looked tired, with purple swaths beneath his eyes. "But he's accelerating and we'll need it to lock him up next time he makes some kind of sicko move like this."

"*Next* time?" That astounded me. "What about *this* time? This is pretty bad, Jess, you've got to admit it. He obviously meant for *me* to eat that stew. My cats must have smelled it and knocked it over . . ."

"I've got no doubt it was for you, Darcy. But the letter – it doesn't say so. It doesn't even say he made it. It doesn't say he spiked it with poison."

"It doesn't have to," Rich said. "Obviously it was him."

"You're right." Jess nodded. "Agreed. But I'm reading it like the DA's going to read it when they look to build a case. Sharon, forensics – she didn't find anything, no prints or fibers or hairs in or around the stew, just cat hairs. It's like he wasn't even here."

"He was here," I said. "Who else put his picture back in this frame?"

Jess looked at it, closely, for the first time. "Nice frame."

"It's the one he left me before. I tore his picture into a zillion pieces and threw it out. This is a new copy."

Jess overturned the frame on the coffee table, pinched back the clips and lifted off the back. Nat's school picture was still there, behind Joe's new print. Jess picked up Nat's photo and turned it over.

It had been slashed, sliced and punctured. What did it mean that Joe had savaged my son's picture? Look what he had done to our cats. Did it mean that he could . . .? *Don't even think it.* I could shake the thought but not the chill because I *felt* it. This image of Nat, defaced, buckled me over and I wept into my hands.

"I bet he used a key," I heard Jess say to Rich. "See how thick and jagged some of the cuts are? Probably got a copy of Darcy's house key some-where, used it to get in, slashed the picture with it, covered it with his own picture. Psychos like this, they're into metaphor, believe it or not."

"That's one heavy-handed metaphor," Rich said.

"Yeah, well, he's no poet."

"How would he have gotten Darcy's key?"

"He got the laptop. Maybe she left her purse unattended at work sometimes."

I sat up, wiping tears off my face with the palms of my hands. "Of course I left it unattended. I didn't carry it around the office with me. I left it in one of my desk drawers."

"Locked?"

I shook my head no.

Jess helped me fill out the paperwork while the locksmith changed all the locks on my front and back doors. He waited while Sharon tagged and bagged Mitzi's and Ahab's bodies to be autopsied at Forensics; they had to verify the cause of death, obvious assumptions not being enough in the hyperrational world where creeps who killed pets in a fit of terror-love might be thrown in prison – or not. Then he gave us a ride over to Rich's house, where I would spend the night. I called Karen and Bill to let them know that I was staying with a friend in the neighborhood and asked them not to tell Nat that I wasn't home. He knew my new cell number by heart and my phone was charged; he could reach me anytime. Before saying goodnight, I gently asked them to be careful answering their door, should someone ring the bell.

"Don't worry," Bill said. "We've got that figured out."

Nat called me at seven in the morning after a night of restless sleep in Rich's bed. Green sheets, very soft. We had not made love because the mood was so wrong, but he had comforted me and I him. While I talked with Nat, Rich hurried into the shower to get ready so he wouldn't be late for school.

"How was the movie?"

"Great."

"What did you have for dinner?"

"Spaghetti and meatballs. Why did you want me to stay over? You never let me have sleepovers on school nights."

"Long story. I'll tell you later."

"Are you OK, Mom?" The warble of worry in his voice: I hated it.

"*Yes*, absolutely fine. I'll be home when you get there after school."

"Speaking of school, Mom – I need my bookbag."

Of course he did; I hadn't thought of that. "I'll ask Mr Stuart if he can swing by and pick it up."

Nat went to school with Henry, so Rich didn't need to drive him. Instead, he took the time to chaperone me back to the house of doom and gloom where I now dreaded spending the day watching handymen install things I didn't want to need as badly as I did. But I *did* need them – all of them. After locking the doors and double-checking all the windows, I sat at the kitchen table and started to call Courtney again; this time I would try her at work.

Out of habit I reached for the landline phone before remembering that this line was now reserved to receive Joe's calls and record his messages. *His messages*. How many more times had he called after Friday night, when Nat had figured out how to silence the phones? How many times had he called since yesterday afternoon when this new machine had been installed?

Thirty. That was the magic number after which my new answering machine was too full to hold any more messages. Plus *twenty-one*, the number of messages picked up by voicemail before the machine was installed. I listened to them all, listened to the steady escalation in Joe's desperation as his messages went from quasi-casual pretend-friend missives, small hellos, to reminders, to enticements, to pleas. He had left me his address and directions to his building in four separate messages over the course of Saturday night. He had waited for us, for Nat and me, to grace his table. One message described candlelight. Another, betrayal. By Sunday the messages had degraded to raw shame; and then by afternoon he had regained some of his chirpy tone as if he was ready to reconcile after a lover's quarrel. He was ready to "give you another chance" he said in a syrupy voice that made my skin crawl. But not once did he say he was coming over. Not once did he say he had my key, or that he was bringing me a specially toxified leftover of the meal I had so heartlessly missed. The messages offered heaps of lunacy but no actual evidence that he had been the one to come in here last night and crazy up my life and home some more.

I called the alarm company with renewed conviction that Wednesday was too long to wait for their best alarm system, all the bells and whistles, whatever technology had to offer. When begging didn't work, I flat-out told the customer service agent that I had a stalker who had infiltrated my home last night and killed my cats. That got her attention; she set me up with an appointment for an installation that afternoon.

Then I called Jess; and now the bad news: just as he'd predicted, Joe had been released for lack of evidence.

"If I'd had a restraining order—" My old saw.

"Right, we'd be able to hold him. But maybe it wouldn't be for killing your *pets*. Do you hear me?"

"Loud and clear."

"I've asked for a warrant to get into his apartment and search for traces of the poison that killed your cats. It'll take a day, maybe two. Meantime, we wait and watch."

And what then? What to do with yourself when you're watching your hole grow deeper and deeper, darker and darker, when you're burrowing with all your might, trying to hide from an enemy who manages to keep invisible most of the time? Lethal gas, that was Joe, following you, weakening you, poisoning your life by degrees. What do you do when nothing you do seems to stop him?

You reconsider leaving.

And in the meantime, you decide to buy a gun.

I left a voicemail for Courtney on her work line, then spoke with Stan, who told me she hadn't come in to the newsroom yet. It was ten o'clock and she was always there by seven so that worried me.

"I asked around and she hasn't called," Stan said. "I gotta admit it's not like her."

"I think I know who she was with on Friday night. I'll give him a buzz and see how long they hung out."

Stan snickered at that: *hung out*. He had known her longer than I had. Courtney didn't hang out; she came, she saw, she conquered.

Jed Stevens seemed embarrassed by my questions about his social itinerary Friday night, until I told him that I was starting to worry about Courtney since it wasn't like her to hold a silence this steadily, over days, nor was it like her to not show up for work without a call. Finally, he told me, "Yes, she was with me Friday night. My place. Left about eight in the morning. Said she had to get home." He sounded like he hadn't known what to make of her early-morning disappearing act.

I pretty much knew what *she* would have said: "How many men would even spend the night? It's not like I owed him anything." The more I heard her voice in my mind, the more her silence worried me. Courtney was brave and bold. In some ways, she acted like a man, using every tool in her arsenal to get what she wanted. But when it came to staying in touch with her friends she was all woman, a master communicator. I knew she would not have dropped my cause without an explanation. Plus, she owed me information that I now badly wanted: she had promised to find me a firearms training class and a gun, something pretty. But more than anything I wanted what she most had to offer: herself. I wanted my new and currently best friend. Courtney's silence was like throwing stones into the echoey well that was missing Hugo, missing Sara, missing my mother, the distant echo of missing my father. Missing everyone I had loved and lost.

I went outside into the back yard to see how far the electrician had come in wiring the outside for floodlights, telling myself to snap out of it and stop casting Courtney in reflected dread. So she'd gone AWOL all weekend. So she was late for work. It didn't have to mean anything more than that.

But ten minutes later I couldn't help myself: I called Jess. He asked for some information about her but our friendship had only just started to blossom outside work so I didn't know much. I knew where she lived – in a doorman building on the Upper West Side of Manhattan – and gave him her address. I also told him about Jed Stevens.

While my home was wired – an apt word for what was happening here as I was now bound ever closer to my home, picturing myself literally wired to it, a female Gulliver hog-tied to the beams of her house, actually *homebound*, not unwilling but unable to go out – as my home and I were wired, I traveled the Internet. Weapons; I wanted *weapons*. Going against the grain of everything I had ever believed, I wanted a gun.

Immediately, I discovered that Courtney had been wrong about something: the pretty guns might not be what you needed to protect yourself. Most were dark, ugly mechanisms made by and for men to extend the hand of violence and *I hated them* and it irked me to be doing this and I thought of Hugo standing behind me, peering over my shoulder, his face twisted in disgust. The more I looked the closer I came to knowing what I wanted. Not wanted:

needed. Though it was a skewed need. According to statistics, for every hundred women who bought a gun, only one successfully used it for self-protection; the rest were killed with it by someone else.

A compact gun seemed to be the ticket, and soon I found the one: a three-inch-barreled micro-compact .45 caliber pistol that had been voted the *perfect carry gun for women*. Not a pretty gun but a good gun. I so wanted to share my discovery with Courtney.

Courtney, who, had she been around and done what she'd promised, would have already known what I learned next: that to have a handgun in New York City you needed a permit to purchase the gun and a permit to carry it. The permit applications could take months, yet, strangely, no gun training was required. Other than the permits, all you needed was a background check and fingerprinting. All well and good for the so-called hobbyist, but for me? I didn't have a month or a week or possibly a day. For all I knew, I didn't have an hour. I didn't know how much time I had.

So I called Jesus, the man with the answers, to see if he could expedite things, given my situation.

"You don't want a gun," he told me.

"Actually, I think I do."

"No, you don't. Trust me." And he spewed off the same statistics I had already found on the Internet.

"I know, but Jess, the threat assessment firm recommends it. You know as well as I do – no, you know *better* than I do – that this situation is out of my control. I'm a sitting duck."

"The alarm system installed?"

"He just finished."

"Lights in the back, camera on the front?"

"Yes, but—"

"I'm thinking you might also consider calling an ironwork outfit, get bars on the windows."

"Then I'll be the one in prison. Why should I be locked up when *he's* the criminal?"

That silenced him. I knew what he would have said, had he spoken, which he didn't dare: *He needs to commit a crime before he's a criminal*. A verifiable crime.

"Listen," he said, "as soon as he violates the order, he's locked up."

"For how long?"

"A day or two."

"Much good that'll do me."

"It's better than nothing."

"No, Jess, it *is* nothing, for all practical purposes."

"You're in a shitty situation, Darcy, I know that. I am here to help you. I just want you—"

"I'm thinking Nat and I might leave. I'm going to talk to him about it this afternoon. The problem is Joe will follow us. I know that. So I want a gun.

Please, Jess, can't you help me expedite the permits?"

In the brief pause that followed I felt a trickle of hope he would agree. But instead he gave me the professional, disciplined answer: "Can't do it, Darcy. And I strongly suggest you don't do it on your own, either." But I heard the hesitation in his voice, that fissure of doubt, because he knew *all* the statistics, especially the ones about how impossible it can be to get free of your stalker once he sets his sights on you.

I would have to go through the regular channels, then, which meant appearing in person at the NYPD's License Division at One Police Plaza in downtown Manhattan. I would go tomorrow, plead my case, beg if necessary for an emergency permit. To hell with it: Joe could follow me there if he wanted to, in fact I hoped he would. I'd like to see what would happen if he attacked me at Police Headquarters.

Before hanging up I asked Jess if he'd found out where Courtney was.

"Since she lives in Manhattan," he said, "she's out of my jurisdiction. I passed it on to her local precinct – they'll look into it."

The first thing Nat did when he got home from school was wave hello to our new electronic eye, the camera that now hovered conspicuously above our front door. I watched him through the monitor on the kitchen counter. He entered with his own key, then I heard Nat and Rich talking in the front hall.

"Whoa, what's this?"

"A keypad for an alarm system."

"Mr Stuart, maybe *you'll* tell me what's going on because my mom's not talking."

"I think you should ask her."

"What's the point? She treats me like a kid. She won't tell me anything."

"Because you *are* a kid," I said, emerging from the hallway's shadow to join my two favorite (living) men.

I kissed Nat's cheek, though he tried to avert it. Some days he let me kiss him and some days he didn't but I always tried.

"Thanks, Rich.

"No problem. I'll see you in the morning, kid."

"Aren't you coming in?" Nat turned to me: "That's another thing. Like, you and Mr Stuart – so what? I know you're dating. So like what's the point of pretending you're not?"

"You're right, sweetie. We're dating. But right now I have to talk to you alone."

Nat's eyes shifted between me and Rich. He had heard that tone in my voice, that *Mom's got to have a word now* tone, and he didn't like it.

"Mom, do you know how much homework I've

got?"

"Thanks again, Rich," I said. "I'll talk to you later."

Before turning out the door, Rich's eyes rested on me a moment in gentle and appreciated acknowledgement of what I now had to do: tell my son that his beloved cats were dead.

"Henry's clothes fit you pretty well." Though the jeans were an inch too short and the T-shirt bore the legend of a band that was *not* Nat's ultimate favorite, he looked pretty good for a boy who had gone to the movies then stayed out all night and most of the next day.

"What's up, Mom?"

"Let's sit down."

"Uh oh."

In the living room, I patted the spot on the couch next to me but he chose to sit in a separate chair.

"Nat, I have some bad news."

He took his eyes off me and settled them on the surface of the coffee table: three magazines, a hand-held portable fan with one missing blade, a purple guitar pick, the coffee mug I'd been using all day, a book I had tried and failed to lose myself in. *Took his eyes off me* – eyes, attention, focus, heart – because we both knew that the last time I had spoken those words to him, about needing to talk, his father was dead.

"Grandma's gone," Nat said.

"No."

Now his eyes flickered back, considered me a moment, fled again.

"Where's Mitzi?" His favorite of the two. "She always comes running when I get home."

"Sweetie . . . Mitzi and Ahab passed away."

Lame words, is what they were. A useless explanation. As if they had dematerialized, evaporated, *passed away* out of the physical world, just like that.

Nat said nothing, just sat there, pretending not to have heard. But a shadow passed over his expression, a brief muscular contraction of pure grief. It came and went quickly, like the stab of an invisible blade that leaves no scar to map a deep wound. I *felt* his wound inside the muscle of my own heart, which was my soul, a mother's soul housing all the echoing facets of both our lives. It all lived right there inside me and that brief contraction of agony that flitted across my son's face opened a door to the darkest vault in my heart. He was hurt, and so I was hurt. Trying to be brave, he mustered stoicism; and so I cried for him. In a wavering voice, I tried to explain.

"It happened last night. That's why I wanted you to stay at Henry's. I didn't want you to see them. It was . . ." I wished I hadn't gone anywhere near a description of what it had been like.

"Why is my school picture gone, Mom?"

"What?"

"It's not there. And there's a big stain on the rug. And something kind of smells."

"Nat—"

"I get it, OK? Joe fucking Coffin. *I get it.*"

A thousand explanations fled through my mind but nothing was the right thing to say to Nat. So finally I just said, "Yup."

"How'd he do it? I mean, he killed them, right?"

I nodded and his face rose to mine, the beautiful tender face of this beloved man-boy who shared every element of my being and yet sat on the fine line between loving me back and refuting everything about me. He was that age and I'd always expected he'd rebel like every other kid – *but not now*.

"Poison. He fed them something with poison."

"What kind?"

"They haven't told me yet."

"They? You mean, like, the cops were here last night and everything?"

"Yes. They've got the cats at a lab so they can find out exactly what it was."

Nat's face flushed and he stood, infuriated as the news of his pets' deaths sank in. He paced, back and forth and back and forth, just as Hugo used to when he felt restless. Hugo had always paced when he talked on the phone, a habit that annoyed me but never seemed worth complaining about. I was glad

I hadn't. Now, as Nat paced with the same wiry lurches forwards and nervously angled redirections, propelling his legs from wall to wall, I kept still and waited. After a couple of minutes he came to a standstill and faced me.

"We have to bury them, Mom." I heard the tears form in his voice before they arrived in his eyes.

"Yes, we do. But it's going to have to wait."

Nat crumpled into my arms, sobbing, and I held him. He cried for a long time, releasing long-held agonies scraped open by these new losses. I knew that this trembling boy flung against my body sometimes cried alone in his bed at night. I'd heard him. If he hadn't cried, I would have worried. I knew how important it was because I myself had been that child, alone in a bed whose warmth had turned cold, whose gravity had transformed into freefall, in a room whose shifting nighttime ceiling-shadows had gone from soothing to perilous: more change in the alignment of elements outside your control, portents of more dreaded loss. A child *must* mourn a lost loved one, must pass through the intolerable pain until it becomes bearable. I welcomed Nat's tears as much as I detested the reasons for his pain. Held him. After he breathed a deep, long sigh, I spoke.

"We can go away."

He nodded. "Can we go back home?"

"Probably not a good idea. Joe's from there, too."

His face screwed up and I soothed him by running a fingertip along his forehead like I used to when he was a baby.

"Where?" he asked.

"Someplace really far, but someplace where you can go to school."

"So it has to be this country?"

"No. Some countries have American schools. We've never been to Paris."

"How about England?" His favorite band was British; good enough incentive in a thirteen-year-old mind. "I mean, they speak English there. I could go to any school."

"Maybe. I'll look into it. It'll take a few days to figure out, OK? Can you hold tight and not tell anyone about this conversation?"

He nodded. A successful escape would depend on total secrecy.

"What about Mr Stuart? Maybe he could come with us?"

"That's sweet, but he's got his daughter here and he has his job."

"So what? I can tell you guys are really into each other. It's kind of obvious."

"Clara's kind of into him too, don't you think?"

He considered that. Nodded.

"Rich will understand," I said, as if I really believed it. He *would* understand. But it would break his heart, and mine, when I left. Then I thought about my mother. How could I leave her just when she was slipping away? I would have to visit her before we left, explain, and hope she somehow understood.

On Tuesday morning, as I got ready to leave for the License Division, the phone rang. It was Elliot, his frazzled voice conjuring an image of his face: round, earnest, thin lips not uplifted in their usual smile.

"Please tell me you heard from Courtney," he said.

"I haven't. She didn't come in again?"

"No one knows where she is. A pair of detectives was here this morning, asking questions. Her parents filed a missing persons. No one's seen her since Saturday morning after her last story came out. This story has gotten way out of hand."

"Which is exactly why it's important."

"I agree, and Overly's more gung-ho about this than I've ever seen him. We're staying with it, I just don't want to see—" *Anyone else go missing or dead?* "How's your situation, Darcy? Any chance you can come back to work?"

"Joe Coffin got in here two nights ago and killed my cats."

"Oh. I'm sorry."

"I've turned my apartment into a fortress."

"Wow. OK, so it's worse."

"I'd say so." *If my tone sounds flippant*, I wanted to say but didn't, couldn't, *it's because I've made some decisions: I'm getting a gun and getting out of Dodge. Courtney would be proud.*

"Darcy, we're staying behind you. When all this blows over, you're back in the newsroom. OK?"

"Thanks, Elliot." I was crying now, just a little, but sucked it back in the hope of maintaining some professionalism – an impulse that almost made me laugh as I cried.

"I've got three reporters working the bones story with Stan now."

"Is Courtney's disappearance being connected to Abe Starkman's murder?"

"Not yet. But we all expect to see it head in that direction. Don't you?"

"I hope not – but yes."

But not until this conversation had that awful possibility really hit home: that Courtney had gotten caught up in a power struggle between the city and the mob, just as Abe had, fatally. All because he had blown the whistle about the bones. And because I couldn't let it go. Because Courtney got dragged into it. Because we just had to know who the bones belonged to in some self-righteous crusade to rescue the dead from obscurity.

Because we were all terrified of death.

Was that it? Were we that afraid of the inevitable

oblivion of death? Would assigning names and histories to the bones strengthen us? These people would never be brought back to life, no matter what we did or how many government bureaucrats and ambitious reporters were lost in the effort.

Hugo would never be brought back to life.

Nor would my father. Nor would the millions of others whose cruel deaths had preceded his in spirit and in bodies upon bodies, piles and piles and piles of bones. *What was one more?* he must have thought as he jumped, flew, into that beckoning void that promised the relief of total amnesia.

Why hadn't I been smart enough to thank Abe for the information and advise him to leave the dead buried? How could I – the widow of a car-smashed husband, the child of Holocaust survivors – not have recognized violent death for the snake pit it was? Why hadn't I run as fast as I could away from it? Why had I assumed that the bones belonged to people whose families needed to know what happened and who would welcome the reopening of that wound?

"You're *idealists*," my mother had said when I announced that Hugo and I were moving to the Vineyard, that he planned to open a law practice specializing in environmental protection. *Idealists* – spoken by a true cynic like it was a dirty word.

At the age of thirty-nine, hadn't I learned anything?

But then again . . . then again . . . if Joe hadn't posted that fifteen-second video clip of Abe talking to me at the empty lot, he would not have been identified as the leak. He would not have died. The gun thief would not have been assigned a murder. And possibly, probably, Courtney would be sitting at her desk right now pounding out a follow-up with her perfectly manicured fingertips.

I set the alarm and locked up behind me. It would be the first time I'd walked outside alone since going to work Wednesday morning, the day Joe attacked me in front of the *Times*. *Joe*. How I loathed him. Walking swiftly up Wyckoff Street, turning onto Smith in the direction of the F train, I turned around three times hoping to find him trotting right behind me like a little dog. *Joe*. This time I wouldn't run. I'd face him, I'd scream bloody murder, but I wouldn't run.

CHAPTER 11

Nearly at the subway entrance, a red minivan swerved to a stop and honked its horn. I kept moving. It honked again and I turned around. A woman with bouncy black hair and a bright smile was waving me toward her window.

It was Angela, Jess's wife. Angela Maria Cortez Ramirez. I turned on a dime and went to talk to her.

"Angela – nice to see you."

"Get in," she said.

I must have stared at her. *Get in?*

Seeing that she'd need to convince me, she leaned closer and whispered, "I've got a gun for you. Cancel wherever you're going because I'm taking you to the West Side Range."

I got in and as soon as I'd slammed shut the passenger door she zoomed off, turning and turning again to redirect us toward the Brooklyn Bridge.

"What's the West Side Range?"

"This morning at ten they got their 'New to Shooting' class. It's just once a week and I don't want you to miss it. Firearms training, it's what you gotta have to use the thing. I'm loaning you my own personal weapon until you don't need it anymore." We entered the bridge ramp and then drove onto the bridge itself, traveling between the swooping cables that defined the New York skyline. "Jess told me about your problem."

"He said I shouldn't have a gun."

"Said the same to me but the thing is you gotta think for yourself. You're the one who's in it, not him. My husband's *the best* but he never had to get followed day and night by some freak who wanted to . . . Never mind. Open my purse and take a look. It's a .45 handgun, fits right in your palm."

I unsnapped her large brown leather purse and there, along with a checkbook, a bulging wallet, at least three pens, a hairbrush, a cell phone and a crumb-encrusted pacifier . . . was a little black gun.

"Don't take it out. That you can do after we get there. I already called and signed you up. Just one thing: today you're me, OK? See that envelope?"

White, unlabeled, on the bottom of her purse beneath the gun.

"That's my permit. You gotta show that and

borrow my ID and stuff or they'll only let you shoot with a rifle. But you don't wanna rifle. Trust me. You want this baby."

"Have you ever used it?"

"Threatened Jess with it a coupla times!" She winked. "No, never had to. But I like to know I'm ready just in case."

"Angela, we don't look alike. They won't believe I'm you."

"Open my wallet. See? That driver's license? My old hair, back when I had it straightened and used to color it brown. This style's better for me, no?" She shook her black curls so they bounced around her shoulders.

"Yes. It makes you look young."

"*Thank you*. So. Slide out that license, okay? When we get there, I'll park and won't need it to drive until after you're all done."

"How long is the class?"

"Three hours."

"You're going to wait in the city all that time? Angela—"

"Don't worry about me; I got plans. My mother-in-law's got the kids until dinner and I'm going to have my day on the town. *Alone*."

Right: she had five kids. Spending a few hours wandering around Manhattan by herself was a vacation for a mother of small children.

"After, if you want, we can go out to lunch."

"I thought I wasn't allowed to do stuff like that."

"You can go back to your jail when I'm through with you. Meantime, trust me, I know how to shoot this thing, and soon so will you. Good enough, anyway, to get you through a pinch. By the way – do *not* mention this to my husband."

"I won't."

She dropped me off on 20th Street between Fifth and Sixth Avenues in front of a narrow eleven-story limestone building. The front was ornamented with the kind of elegant detail common on the city's old buildings and unheard of on the new ones.

"Pick you up here at one, OK? Wait in the lobby until you see me pull up. There's a doorman."

And so, instead of applying for a permit, I sort-of had one along with a fake ID and a gun. Angela had the confidence of a warrior. But what if they arrested me for false possession?

They didn't. Once I'd stepped off the elevator into the basement shooting range – a gritty space that was host to the grittiest intentions – I was signed into the class with only the most cursory look at my (Angela's) ID and permit. I put them back in my purse, making a small show of sliding her license into my wallet, and proceeded as directed to Range D.

Doors along the bright hallway were lettered from A–F. Six shooting galleries, holding ten shooters apiece. This morning Range D was devoted to the "New to Shooting" class: myself, four other women of varying ages and races, and two youngish gayish men who seemed to be friends.

Our instructor was Gary, who introduced himself as "an NRA certified instructor". He looked like one, too: pot-bellied and beefy-faced – I hadn't known this kind of man existed in Manhattan. He explained the mechanics of guns, what the magazine was, how the safety worked, all the physical elements of the weapons we held shakily, each of us, in our hands. Then he pointed to the wall where a poster listed the three most important rules about guns and told us that this was our new religion.

RULES OF GUN SAFETY
ALWAYS keep the gun pointed in a safe direction.
ALWAYS keep your finger off the trigger until ready to shoot.
ALWAYS keep the gun unloaded until ready to use.

It was printed in a dated font that was yellowed and curled at the edges.

Gary handed us each a pair of safety glasses and ear protectors that looked like bulky headphones. Then we were separated in booths with individual targets twenty-five feet ahead. I had wondered if we'd be shooting at human silhouettes, like in the movies, on the assumption that none of us were here with the intention of weekend deer hunting in the woods of Maine. But for us crowd-addled city folk some wise manager had chosen a simple shape, a circle, in layered rings that passed through descending shades of grey until they contracted into a black dead-center bull's-eye. It was a good, plain, crisp piece of graphic design, not too evocative, which I imagined was the point.

The moment the red light turned on above the row of targets, we all started shooting. Silenced by the headphones, the shots sounded like thuds. Each time I shot Angela's gun my arm jerked back convulsively and the impact sent reverberations throughout my body. The muscles in my shooting arm soon ached. But three hours later I had not only grown used to the smell of burning metal but was hitting near enough the bull's-eye to feel confident that I could use the thing if I had to. My shooting was rough but I essentially understood how to handle the gun.

Angela was waiting in the van when I emerged into the lobby just after one o'clock. I got into the passenger's side, feeling elated.

"That was *great*."

"You see? It's easy once you get the hang of it."

I handed her back her license and permit but kept the gun in my purse.

"Lunch in Brooklyn or do you feel better staying in the city?"

"Angela, could we take a detour? I need to say goodbye to my mother. She's in a nursing home uptown. She's got Alzheimer's."

Her black eyes steadied on me. She nodded. "You bet. My dad? Alzheimer's took him a little bit at a time. We finally lost him last year. You need this like a hole in the head right now, don't you." It wasn't a question so she didn't phrase it as one. "West side or east?"

"West Seventy-fourth Street and West End."

She got us there in fifteen minutes and maneuvered into a parking spot around the corner after another car slipped out. I realized that she intended to come up with me and decided not to argue her out of it; it would have been wasted breath, anyway. Angela didn't prevaricate or doubt herself; she made up her mind and took action. I liked that about her.

Lunchtime had just ended and I looked for my mother in the common room, expecting to find her by her favorite window. She wasn't there. In the hall on my way to her room I ran into Nancy, the home's day manager.

"Darcy! Nice to see you. Actually, I wanted to talk to you."

"He didn't—"

"No. Don't worry about that. Security here is very good."

"Things OK with Mom?"

"When did you last see her?"

"Friday; my usual visit. She was pretty out of it."

"That's what I wanted to discuss with you. She's been in and out these past weeks, as you know, but the last few days she's gone farther out. I just wanted you to be prepared."

"Thanks, Nancy. I appreciate it."

"It was inevitable."

"I know."

"It's just that sometimes families don't really believe that it's not a matter of *if*."

When she said that, Angela put her hand on my shoulder. The warmth of her touch startled me into an unexpected thought: I had not, in fact, been as prepared as I thought I'd been. Deep down I *had* thought it was if, not when, my mother's mind relinquished all ties to the life we had shared. But Nancy understood this and so did Angela. I felt heartsick as I entered my mother's room and found her sitting in the armchair in the corner, staring into the middle space of something I couldn't see.

"Hi, Mom."

She had no reaction.

"This is Angela; she's a friend of mine."

The corners of my mother's mouth curled. "Friends are like gold but they don't fit in your pocket."

Angela and I glanced at each other and smiled.

"Mom." I pulled a chair close to her and reached to take her hand. "I'm Darcy, your daughter."

"Darcy was the name of my favorite doll."

"I didn't know that."

"I had to leave her."

"Mom. Listen: I have to go away for a while."

"Alone in the doll crib Mama had bought me."

"Just for a while, until . . . well, until . . ."

"She has to take care of some important business," Angela said. "Then she'll be back."

"That's right, Mom. I'll be back, definitely."

"If we go together, it may be dangerous. But better to stay together, yes?"

"Mom? Where are you?"

"We *must* leave before the transfer. Are you coming, Rose?"

OK: I would be Rose. "Yes."

"Marta?"

And Angela would be Marta. "Yes."

"Wait until sunrise," my mother whispered, "and go to the latrine one at a time. We'll meet by Block Fourteen, where the dog gave birth last week. I noticed a dip in the ground where the mud was soft."

"OK, Eva," I said.

"Be careful, girls."

"We will," Angela said, moving closer.

We sat before my mother, taking the journey with her. She had always refused to talk to me about her escape from the camp. Now, she had forgotten, or forsaken, that level-headed resistance. She was back there, preparing to leave.

"Me first. I'm oldest. I'll dig a tunnel in the mud and make a passage. Rose follows. Then Marta. *As quietly as you can.*"

She took a series of deep breaths, clenching her fists, squeezing her eyes, her supple lids fanning into long folds of loose skin. Then she held her breath and she was burrowing in the mud beneath a fence. She concentrated so hard I could see her, eleven years old, determined to get to the other side.

And then her entire body startled as if she had heard a loud sound. "No, Rose! Do not go back for her! *Come.*"

Her eyes fell shut again and her breathing accelerated. "Faster, Rosie. Not so slow!" They were running. Running away from the camp. Marta was no longer with them. And their feet were cold; my mother was curling her toes inside her fleece slippers, rubbing her feet together. Remembering.

"Don't stay so close to me!" she whispered savagely. "Run until you get into the woods. I'll meet you there."

She seemed to pause but I could see her: moving, hitting her stride on the frozen ground. And then, again, she startled. It was the same way a baby startled, suddenly, flinging her arms out, eyes snapping open.

Now as she ran she cried and the tears streamed down her face. She didn't wipe them because they froze right away. I could see her girl's face glistening with crystals of ice as she ran and ran toward the woods, alone, for now both Rose and Marta were dead.

"No going back, *no going back*." She spoke the words mechanically, like a mantra. "Get away. Faster. *No going back*."

"Mom," I cried. "I can't leave you."

"Save yourself; leave them behind."

"I'll be back. I promise."

"No going back."

"How did you survive that, Mom? How did you survive? Tell me!"

"Forget them. They're gone. Save yourself."

She leaned her head against the soft cushion of the chair and fell asleep. And I saw her: a flying angel, sprawled in the snow in the woods. She had made it; I knew that much about her, because she was here to tell the story. But would she ever tell me the rest of the story? (Would I be back in time?) What happened between that day and the day she saw my father seven years later in Manhattan? The way she always told it, her life began the moment they recognized each other across a crowded subway in 1952. But now there was also this: a frantic run through the snow, shots fired, a trail of dead friends. She had carried them in her mind all this time, never speaking of them until now: Marta and Rose. And what had become of Lara and Dolly? That question infused the goodbye kiss I settled on the yielding skin of my mother's sunken, sleeping cheek.

Marta, Rose, Lara, Dolly. Four little girls whose lives had been interrupted by history and yet were vividly alive today in my mother's distant memory.

Angela and I left my mother asleep in the snow in the woods in Poland in the winter of 1945. We didn't speak on our way back to the van. She drove us onto the West Side Highway, heading downtown toward Brooklyn. I didn't have to ask if she planned on taking me all the way home; she had come this far for me, why wouldn't she complete the journey?

Only when we were all the way at the southern tip of Manhattan did we break the silence – passing the gaping hole, now a construction site, where the Twin Towers had once stood.

"Angela, do you think it's easier to get lost in a crowd or someplace remote and hard to reach?"

"If he finds you on a desert island, honey, you're cooked. I say it's easier to hide in a crowd."

"I think you're right. We should go to a city."

But which one? I'd liked the idea of going overseas, really far away, but I'd never get across an international border with a gun. We would have to stay in this country and travel with cash so Joe couldn't find a way to track us down. We would lay low, living the old-fashioned way, *unplugged* from any and all cyber connections he might use to trace us. Cash, pay phones, no set plans. Like fugitives. I would try to convince Nat we were embarking on an adventure, not running for our lives.

Tomorrow morning at nine, as soon as the bank opened and I could withdraw a significant amount of cash in traveler's checks, we would leave. Tonight I would pack – and say goodbye to Rich.

The van pulled to a stop in front of my house. It was almost four o'clock; Nat would already be home.

"I hope you don't hit traffic on your way back to Long Island." I leaned over to kiss her cheek. "Thanks for today. I can't tell you how much it meant to me."

"You don't have to. Send us a postcard, OK?"

"Promise."

She waited until I was inside the house. As I turned off the alarm, locked myself in and rearmed the alarm, I heard the van roar away. And then something occurred to me: if Nat was home, why had the alarm been on? Had he actually remembered to rearm it when he came in, as I'd asked? I hadn't expected him to fall so quickly into step with the new vigilance plan I had laid out before school that morning.

"New rules, Nat," I'd said over breakfast. "Listen up."

His milk-dripping spoon of cereal stopped midway to his mouth. He lifted his eyes from the article he was reading in the Arts section of the newspaper and looked at me grudgingly. I had interrupted him *again*.

"Sorry, sweetie, but this is really important. Are you listening?"

He nodded. Ate the spoonful of cereal. Kept his eyes on me because he knew I would not relent until he heard me out.

"Always have your cell phone charged and turned on and always carry it with you."

Nod.

"Never travel alone."

Nod.

"Don't walk down empty streets; keep among people even if it means going out of your way."

Nod.

"Do not answer the landline."

Nod.

"Do not answer the door."

Nod.

"Make sure the alarm system is always armed. Do you remember the code?"

Nod.

"OK?"

"Are you finished, Mom?"

I'd had to refrain from asking if he'd really heard any of it and later, after he'd left for school with Rich, the thought crossed my mind that he could get so fed up with all this that he might run away. He was that age. He wanted new freedoms, not new restrictions.

"Nat? Sweetie! I'm home."

The house was eerily quiet without Mitzi and Ahab darting around whenever someone came in. I wished I had been here to make some noise when Nat got home from school so he didn't have to hear this lonely silence. The stillness.

"Nat?"

He wasn't anywhere downstairs in the living room, kitchen, bathroom or yard. Nor was he anywhere upstairs.

"Nat!"

I went back downstairs. As I took my cell phone out of my purse my hand bumped into the gun: hard, cold metal. Immediately I worried that I might not have properly engaged the safety so I took it out and looked it over. It felt heavy in my hand though it was light compared with other guns; Gary had had us pick up a rifle, a shotgun and two other models of handguns so we could feel the difference. Mine – Angela's – was the lightest by far and I had felt a certain borrowed pride in that.

The safety was on. I put the gun back in my purse.

I speed-dialled Nat's cell phone and listened to it ring as I walked into the kitchen, filled a glass with ice and poured over it the leftover coffee from that morning's pot. The ice made cracking noises when the lukewarm coffee spilled onto it. I stirred in some milk as Nat's voicemail picked up. Left a message. Dialed again. Listened to more unanswered ringing.

Carrying my iced coffee in the hallway connecting the kitchen with the front hall, nearing the foot of the stairs that led upstairs to our bedrooms, I began to hear an echo. Another phone was ringing somewhere else in the house. I stood still and listened a moment before realizing that the other rings exactly matched the ones at my ear.

I let it ring. Followed the sound into Nat's bedroom. There, on the corner of his messy desk, was his cell phone . . . ringing with my call.

My first reaction was anger: he had forgotten it again, after I'd practically begged him not to. And on top of that the battery was about to run out. Why couldn't he take responsibility for a simple phone?

Then worry sank in. *Where was he?*

Maybe he'd forgotten the alarm code. Maybe, seeing that I wasn't home yet, Rich had taken him somewhere to wait. Of course that was it. They were bonding and had gone out for some special treat.

Or maybe Joe had gotten in again. Maybe he had taken Nat knowing that *would get my attention like nothing else*.

No: the alarm had been on when I came home. You didn't kidnap a child and rearm the alarm system on your way out. Did you? Would *Joe*? To prove that he had already learned our code?

I tried to stop my hand from shaking as I dialed Rich's cell and left a message asking him to call me. Then I called the school to find out if anyone knew if Nat Mayhew had made alternate after-school plans, but it was a large school with almost a thousand students and none of the office ladies even knew who he was, and his teacher had left for the day. Next, I called Karen, Henry's mother.

"Nat and Henry just got here. They're making sundaes . . . I hope that's OK."

"It's fine." I tried but failed to soften the edge in my voice.

"Darcy, do you want him to come home?"

"No, it's OK. He just didn't tell me he was going

with Henry today so I was a little worried." *A little worried;* it was the understatement of the year.

"I'm sorry. They've had it planned since yesterday."

"He must have forgotten to mention it. Really, it's OK, Karen. I'm just glad to know he's there."

"We'll drop him off at about five thirty on our way to Park Slope. We're taking Bill's cousin out for dinner for her birthday, to Belleville. Have you tried it?"

"Not yet, but I hear it's good."

"I'll let you know. See you at five thirty."

"Thanks, I appreciate it. Tell him I called, OK?"

His expression that morning over breakfast: weary, annoyed. Had he deliberately not told me about his plans? Or had he told me, either yesterday or this morning, and was I too preoccupied to hear him?

But he was safe. That was what mattered. I took three extended breaths, drawing the air deep into my lungs, holding it, letting it go. Felt calmer. Took my iced coffee into my bedroom, set it on the dresser and opened my closet. It was deep, built both for clothing and storage; the closet was an unusual and welcome feature in these typically closet-less brownstones. Our suitcases, a large one with a smaller one nested inside, were at the far back. I had to weed through a chaos of shoes, boots and fallen hangers to get to them. After dragging them out, I kicked all the stuff back into the closet and splayed both suitcases open atop my bed.

I decided to pack Nat's things first but had hardly gotten started before the phone rang with the kind of call no one would expect to receive twice in a lifetime.

CHAPTER 12

"Hello?" A woman. For a split second I thought: *Courtney*. But soon realized that I didn't recognize the voice.

"Yes?"

"Did you just try to reach Richard Stuart on his cell phone?"

"Who is this?"

"Teresa. I'm a nurse at Long Island College Hospital. The message sounded like you were close to him so I thought I should call."

"Is Rich in the *hospital*?"

"He's been injured. Are you his wife?"

"No. He's divorced. I'm a close friend. Injured how?"

"Do you know if he has any family I could call?"

"They all live in Montana. What happened?"

She hesitated but finally told me: "There must have been a gas leak in his home. The EMS guys said it blew up when he opened the door."

"Blew up?"

"Any movement triggers it. He's pretty badly burned."

"But he's alive?"

"Yes. He's still in the ER but they're transferring him to the ICU in a few minutes. They'll be sending him over to the Burn Unit at Kings County as soon as a bed frees up."

I flew the five blocks to the hospital.

They were still working on him when I arrived so I sat in the fourth-floor waiting room until a nurse appeared, a young woman with dyed-blonde hair pulled into a tight ponytail, lithe and sprite in her white pantsuit and rubber-soled shoes. She took a guess that I was the friend Teresa from ER must have said would be coming, asked my name, introduced herself as Sally and led me down the hall to Rich's room.

They had mummified him, covered almost all of him in white gauze, elevated both his legs and both his arms, covered him in a bubble of plastic into which oxygen was pumped through a tube. About half his face – a lopsided area revealing both eyes and most of his nose – was the only uncovered part of him, and if not for that I wouldn't have believed it was him. I didn't *want* to believe it was him. My beautiful man, his tender skin. My fingertips retained a sensory memory of it: the suede-like quality of him as I ran my hands over his body. What was beneath the bandages? In my imagination I could see and feel and smell the raw melted skin. I had seen burn victims after recovery, surgery and healing: the hard casing of skin, its lumps and rivulets and discolorations as if water had dripped over sand. The skin lost flexibility and sensitivity and became something people either winced at or studiously ignored. And I remembered now – as I walked over to Rich, my eyes filling with tears, wiping them away – I remembered one night after Hugo died when I drank too much wine and indulged myself in the kind of wishful thinking that only left you more depressed afterwards. I allowed myself to imagine what he would have looked like had he survived the crash. The police had described it as a fireball. "Instant death," the cop had said, as if to reassure me that Hugo hadn't suffered, or suffered too much, or for very long. I remembered wishing he had survived that fireball and had pictured his face a melted orb of skin whose eyes I recognized as my beloved's. I had wanted him back, even like that. I had *wanted* him. How, I wondered, looking at Rich now, had a small area of his face been spared? What other parts of him were whole beneath the wrapping? Or had he been otherwise incinerated except for this small window into what he used to be?

"Can he see us?" I asked.

"He's heavily sedated."

"Is he sleeping with his eyes open?"

"Possibly. He's in shock. He was burned over about forty percent of his body, which believe it or not isn't too bad, considering the blast he took. His arms and legs are elevated to keep pressure off his skin."

"How was he when they brought him in?"

"I wasn't in the ER but usually they're unconscious when they take that kind of burn."

"So it was a real explosion."

"I heard the whole house was incinerated. Gas leaks are like that – they're bad. I heard the gas company and fire department are already over there investigating."

"Do they think arson?"

"I'm not sure what they call it when it's a gas explosion. Tampering, I think. Something like that."

Joe. Had he done this? Had he tried to actually kill Rich? Eliminate a rival? The thought ripped through me in a twisted, jagged braid of helplessness and rage.

"Can I use my cell phone out in the hall?"

"Sure, but you've got to walk all the way to the end by the window to get a signal. And please remember to turn it off if you come back to see him again."

"I will."

"Try to keep the visit to fifteen minutes, tops, and keep it low key, OK?"

It was a strange thing to say. Rich was unconscious, wrapped like he'd been prepared for burial in an ancient sarcophagus. Did she think I'd throw a party?

At the far end of the hall I stood by a window overlooking the rooftops and church spires of Cobble Hill and phoned Jess.

"This is good," he said.

"No, Jess, it's not."

An embarrassed pause, and then: "I don't know what I was thinking. Your friend OK?"

"They say he will be."

"Attempted murder will put your guy away for a very long time. I'm on it, Darcy, you know that."

"He's not *mine*—"

"Sorry. I didn't meant that, either. My head's spinning – kids have been with my mom all day and she's been calling me every five minutes. But that's not a problem. *You* have a problem and we're going to take care of it, OK?"

"Thanks, Jess."

I turned off my cell phone and returned to Rich's side, pulling up a chair to sit near him. Fifteen minutes came and went. I stayed and no one complained. I watched Rich breathe in and breathe out. He was alive. At one point I whispered, "I'm here, I love you," just in case he was conscious and could hear. But I didn't think he was or could. Still, he was alive. He would live. When he healed they would unwrap his bandages and we would take it from there.

Obviously now Nat and I couldn't go away. Not yet. (Though didn't we need to more than ever?) I would have to break the news to him and hoped he would understand but something told me he'd be relieved. He had a new best friend and a school he seemed to like. Our lives had almost settled in, but for Joe.

At five fifteen I blew Rich a kiss and left him sleeping with his eyes still open. I wanted to be home when Nat was dropped off. In the elevator down to the lobby I turned my cell phone back on and once it had booted up I saw that I had a message.

Was that Nat's new number? I still hadn't memorized it but it started with the same prefix as his. I played the message.

It wasn't a call; it was a video. From YouTube. A tiny movie began to play itself out on the screen.

The images were dark, fuzzy. It was impossible to focus on them as I walked through the noisy hospital lobby. I found a seat on a bench by the wall beneath a poster of a beach. A beach: what did that have to do with an urban hospital? It took a minute but I figured out how to replay the video and watched it again.

A car traveled steadily along a road. A camera had captured the back of the car as it drove without stopping. A few times the lens jerked and it was clear that the car was somewhere remote, passing trees and open spaces. In the far distance the sky looked vast. But mostly the lens stayed tight on the car. A single driver. A man? The car was a compact hybrid, white – I recognized it because our old car on the Vineyard had been the same model, even color, and there weren't too many of them around.

The car drove. And then there was turmoil. Sudden turmoil, as the car swerved off the road and appeared to crash into a tree. It was hard to tell because the camera suddenly blacked out. I replayed it again and again and again until I knew exactly what I was watching.

Hugo's death.

It was our car in the video. Hugo driving. In the rear window a rolled-up paper moved back and forth with the car's momentum. I hadn't thought of it until now: Nat's science poster had been sent home from school and had sat in that spot for two weeks; I'd kept forgetting to bring it in the house. There it was rolling back and forth in the rear window, back and forth while the driver, a man, drove on a country road. And then swerved very suddenly. And then crashed. Suddenly.

My pulse throbbed in my ears as I was pulled back into the riptide of Hugo's death. That devouring ocean of his loss. Wave after wave of it, crashing through me.

A fifteen second video clip of the end of my world.

Fifteen seconds, just like the clip of my first conversation with Abe Starkman.

Fifteen seconds: was that the limit of a cell phone camera? Only fifteen seconds – the time it took to change my life, twice.

Standing, I dialed the number that had sent the video and indeed it had come from Nat's phone. His voicemail answered. I hung up . . . and tried to think.

Nat's phone was at home in an empty house. Unless he had been dropped off a few minutes early. I tried Henry's home number and got voicemail. So I called Henry's cell and Henry answered, "Hi, Mrs Mayhew."

"Hi, Henry. Could I please speak with Nat?"

"We dropped him off at home a little while ago."

"OK – thanks."

So Nat was at home. I called his cell and it went straight to voicemail again; he had either turned it off or the battery had run out. Where did he get that

video? And why would he send it to me like that?
If he had watched those awful images, why
wouldn't he have called to warn me? He would
have called me; I knew he would have. He never
would have sent it like that, as a curiosity, or for its
shock value.

There was only one person who would be cruel
and calculating enough to send me that video cold.
And if he had sent it from Nat's phone . . .

I ran out of the hospital, down the steps onto the
street, around the corner onto Amity Street, speed-
dialing Jess.

"Darcy—"

"He's in my house."

"Coffin?"

"Yes. Right now. He just called me from Nat's
phone."

"Wait a minute. I left him at his apartment not ten
minutes ago."

"You *left* him?"

"He denies he had anything to do with the
explosion, but, Darcy, if he did, the fire examiner
will find out. We can't pick him up right this minute,
but once we get the evidence, we'll get him, just—"

I hung up and ran faster. Enough *later, not now,
be patient.* Enough! I had a gun in my purse and I
would go home and get Joe away from my son at any
cost.

He was in the house; I knew it. *He was in the house with Nat*.

He had used Nat's phone to call me, so I would answer.

How was it he had a video of Hugo's death? *How was that?*

Had Joe killed my husband? Stalked me. Terrorized me. Frightened my son. Caused a man's death – *two* men – Hugo and Abe. Tried to kill Rich. *Three*. All to get to me.

Who was next? How far would he go? When would he stop?

Never. Unless I stopped him.

I unlocked my front door. The alarm was already off. Stilling my breath, trying to be quiet, I walked into the front hall and paused. Angled an ear toward the living room: silence. The kitchen: stillness. I didn't want Joe to hear me so I toed off my shoes, slid the gun out of my purse and padded up the stairs.

My bedroom was empty.

Bathroom, empty.

I moved, stealthily, toward Nat's room. The door was open. I could see that the lights were off – the blue of his walls and green of his carpet were muted by the grey twilight that filtered through the room's single window.

Lifting the gun just as Gary had demonstrated, just as I had practiced, I entered the room.

Empty.

"Nat?"

Silence.

"Nat!"

Nothing.

His closet was empty except for his clothes, a baseball bat, books piled on the floor. Nothing, and no one, was under the bed.

Only one thing was different in this room since I had been here not two hours ago. Nat's phone: it was missing.

Had I dropped it before? No, I clearly remembered putting it back on the corner of his desk.

I looked everywhere for the phone in case my memory was faulty. Maybe the phone was here somewhere. I looked and looked – no phone.

I *knew* where Nat's phone was: Joe had it. He had been here. And he had taken Nat. Just as he knew that if Nat called I would answer, he knew that if he took Nat I would come.

CHAPTER 13

Driving along Columbia Street to the address I had memorized – it had been impossible *not* to memorize it, Joe had recited it into my voicemail so many times – feeling cold. Shivering with panic that I wasn't driving fast enough, that I couldn't drive fast enough. That it was already too late. Chilled to the bone, even with all my windows rolled up. Evening had fallen and it was dark out. Very dark. The street bumped and dipped and I kept crashing into potholes I didn't see. It was no mystery why Joe had been able to afford it here: it was derelict except for two store-fronts, a bookstore and a trendy bar, where gentrification had sent its tentacles. Lights appeared to have been placed randomly along this forlorn street that edged a mostly good neighborhood with a seedy crust just as it gave way to the East River. The water on this still night looked inky, placid, unmoving. A black mirror separating Brooklyn from Manhattan, reflecting a bright half-moon in a foggy shimmer on the river's surface.

He lived at 65 Imlay Street. I vaguely remembered where that was from my one and only visit to this area, in August, when Nat and I had come to shop at Fairway. I remembered Van Brundt Street as soon as I saw it, and turned. Then, there it was: Imlay Street. I turned again and slowed down to read house numbers.

But before I found the building, my phone rang. It was Nat's number. *Joe* calling on Nat's phone. I pulled to the side of the road near a wide strip of unused land piled with junk: rusted cars, broken shopping carts, heaps of tires, half a dozen of those enormous shipping containers abandoned in a haphazard cluster near the river. Answered the phone: "You bastard!"

Silence. Was he looking at my Nat, holding the phone to his smarmy ear, grinning to the sound of my dread?

"*Joe!*"

Silence. I stabbed the *end call* button with a shaking fingertip. Jess: I had to call Jess. But as I ran down my list of stored numbers, hand unsteady, palm sweating, the phone slipped out of my hand and in an iota of a moment it was gulped up in the space between the front car seats. There wasn't time to fish it out. I grabbed my purse – loaded with gun – and got out of the car, leaving the driver's door gaping and the headlights on so I could see where I was going and also to alert anyone who might come looking for me.

Sixty-five was half a block down, between Bowne and Sebring Streets. I crossed the street to a dilapidated green-shingled three-story house that listed to one side. I remembered that he lived in apartment one, and there was his name at the bottom of a short list of bells: *Joe Coffin*. I pressed the grimy white button and pounded furiously on the door.

"Joe! *Joe*!"

But I needn't have pounded or screamed. He appeared almost immediately, head cocked, wearing the very grin I had just imagined, his eyes weirdly bright.

"Sorry, but you missed your friend." The sarcasm in his tone sent a chill through me. He stood in a gaping space through which I glimpsed a grimy hallway, bare bulb dangling from the ceiling. There were two apartment doors in the hall, one of which was open.

"Where is he?"

"Jesus is long gone." Thinking himself witty, he smiled.

"Not him. *Nat*."

His eyes flickered with thought or more likely calculation and then he smiled and stood aside. I shot past him into the hall. *Urine* was the stink that hit me first, then *mildew*. I ran to the open door and into the apartment.

It was a studio: twin bed pushed into the far corner, small table with one chair against the opposite half-wall of a kitchenette. Tiny doorless bathroom next to the front door. Clean. Neat. An armoire by the bed was the only closet.

"Nat!" I opened the latch of the armoire. The bottom was stacked with books. Atop the books, three pair of shoes. Hanging from a bar were half a dozen shirts and a few pairs of pants. A red tie was slung over the bar next to a brown leather belt.

Joe came in behind me and watched my frantic search. His hands had slipped into his jeans pockets and he stood there calmly, nodding his head as if something had just become clear.

I turned on him. "Where's Nat?" Sweat dripped from my forehead into one of my eyes, turning Joe foggy until I blinked him into focus.

"He's not here."

"You sent me that video."

Joe nodded.

"*You killed Hugo.*"

He shrugged, pathetically, like a child unwilling to settle on truth or lie.

"*Where is Nat?*"

"I told you, he's not here."

Shaking. Heart beating so hard and fast I felt I would collapse. "Tell me where Nat is, give him back to me, and I won't tell anyone about Hugo."

Half a grin crooked Joe's face into a mask terrifying for his mix of docility on one side and menace on the other. I had never seen anyone look this way: like two different people at one time. He was out of his mind. If I could kill him, I would. But the gun in my purse now felt a million miles away. The blue folder had been right: always keep your gun strapped to your body, easily accessible. How would I get to it now without giving him time to intercept it?

"I won't tell you," he said, "but I'll show you."

"Don't play games with me, Joe."

He stepped away, disappearing into his kitchenette, and reappeared – with a gun of his own. It was a handgun, larger than mine. He ostentatiously released the safety before steadying the gun in my direction.

"Come," he said, steering me with the merciless trajectory of the gun to the door and into the hall. I was a marionette controlled by a lunatic. One wrong move and he would kill me; wouldn't he? *Yes*. He had me now and he would do whatever it took to keep me.

The apartment door clicked shut behind us.

"Keep going."

The front door of the building fell shut behind us and we were alone on Imlay Street, facing the waste-land, the river, the star-studded sky. A car appeared around the corner of Van Brundt, rumbling slowly forwards, and I felt the nose of Joe's gun press into my waist. He had one arm around me. I had never been so close to him. He smelled like his hallway, like a urinal, and he also smelled like raw fish. Unless that was a smell coming off the river. We crossed the street and he led me into the rubble-strewn junk heap of neglected land, in the direction of the water.

The air was sharp on my face and I felt the stab of rocks through the soles of my shoes. The fish-stink grew worse the closer we came to the water's edge.

Was Nat here? Here in this wilderness, this graveyard of unwanted things. My heart, a fist, pounded inside the cage of my chest.

No: it was not impossible. Not Nat. Not my baby. My boy. I would do anything, go anywhere, to find him. Even if the chance of finding him alive was remote. I would go.

"What did you do with him, Joe?"

"Shut up," he hissed, then muttered: "You and your *fucking* son."

"Did you tamper with the gas in Rich's house?"

Joe gritted his teeth, a sallow flash in the moonlight.

"You did. I know it. And you took Nat. You thought you could actually have me if you eliminated everyone I love."

"Shut up."

"You'll never have me."

"I have you now," he said. "Don't I?"

We had reached the farthest shipping container, painted beige and dripping with rust stains. Big enough to fit four cars nose to nose, it was the one closest to the river, the only one completely hidden by the others, the one farthest from the street and closest to the glowing darkness of the water. The black mirror: death. It was here. I felt it.

He was going to kill me.

"Don't do this," I said. "If you do this, you'll never have me."

"If I do this, I'll always have you." He smiled at me with the plain enthusiasm with which he had first greeted me at my desk two weeks ago. *He had won*. Then he used his free hand to take a key ring from his pocket, jangle loose a small key and insert it into the bottom of a heavy steel padlock.

His gun dug between two of my ribs and I couldn't help crying out.

"Quiet!" Gritting his teeth, he removed the padlock and slipped it into his pocket. Then he pulled one of the corrugated metal doors, which opened with a screech that could have been a seagull or a child playing but was neither. This was the place, the smell, the sound of annihilation.

It was too dark to see inside the container at first. He walked me in with his arm around my waist, like he was bringing me into a restaurant for a date, except for the gun his opposite hand pressed into my side. If I could only get to *my* gun before he locked me in here! If I tried, he would shoot me first. But if I didn't, I would die anyway.

The smell was appalling – an unflushed unwashed toilet – and I began to gag.

"You'll get used to it," Joe said.

"Nat? Are you here?"

"He isn't here."

"You *bastard*!"

"Darcy?" A frail voice seemed to waft over from somewhere ahead.

My eyes adjusted enough to see a stained mattress on the floor, a card table with a vase of orange plastic flowers and two mismatched chairs. Stacked against one wall were cases of bottled water and canned food. Empty bottles and cans were strewn in front of the boxes.

"Nat? Sweetie. I can't see you."

But the voice had called me Darcy, not Mom.

And then I saw a ghost crawling toward me. Silver

electrical tape had been wound around her head to cover her eyes. Her lips were chapped and bleeding. Her knees were covered in abrasions. That sexy outfit she'd worn on Friday was slit up one side and the transparent shirt hung ripped and open over a camisole soiled with dried vomit.

"Courtney . . ." Degraded. Turned inside out: all the vulnerability she had never revealed now worn as her outer skin.

Joe giggled like a five-year-old. "Told you it wasn't Nat."

"Where is he? I know you have him – you sent me that video from his phone."

"From his *number*, not his phone." As if it should be a given that he would know the tools of an identity thief – soul thief and life thief that he was.

"Darcy . . ." Courtney was close enough now that I could see her face beneath the taped eyes. Her left cheek was bruised. One nostril was caked with dried blood. And her hair, her spectacular golden hair was matted where it wasn't taped against her head. I yearned to reach for her but his gun was still there, biting my ribs. "Don't let him close the door."

Joe then turned and walked quickly to the door that hung open into the night and air and freedom. It was open and we had to get through it before he could lock us both inside this dungeon.

Free of him, I grabbed inside my purse for my gun. He had just started to push shut the door, inspiring that awful screech, when a voice rang out from the distance.

"Mom?"

"Nat!" I hurried toward the door – closing, almost closed.

"Mom! Where are you?"

"Nat – *run*!"

Joe's face transformed from self-satisfied victor into a gargoyle molded and etched on a blade of rage. All the plans and dreams and emotions and hopes and delusions that had led him to this moment seemed to explode beneath his skin as his face twisted into a picture of terrifying determination. He had not worked this hard for nothing. Like dominoes he had felled his obstacles, one at a time: Hugo, Rich, Courtney. And now it was Nat's turn to be obliterated for the cause . . .

"Mom! Are you in there?" His voice was louder, closer.

"Run away, Nat! *Quickly!*"

As soon as Joe abandoned the door, I burst out of the container into the crisp night air and saw the lunatic racing straight for my son. He lunged with overwrought steps, holding his arm stiff in front of him. The gun shook in his hand but never lost sight of its target.

Nat froze in place. He was terrified. I needed to reach him, comfort him, *save* him.

"*Run*, Nat!"

But he couldn't move. Or speak. Or apparently even *think*. He had shut off at the worst possible moment. It was as if his mind had fled his body, abandoned it on the brink of attack. Was that what had happened to Hugo in the moments before he crashed and died? Had he been aware of having been forced off the road by another car? Had he caught a glimpse of Joe in the car behind him and wondered why this nut was trying so hard to rear-end him?

"Nat!" I ran, pausing to switch off the safety of my gun, and then ran harder.

Joe gained speed. He was close to Nat now. *My Nat*.

And then . . . Joe stopped. His whole body trembled as he leveled the gun on my child.

I ground to a halt and raised my gun. Pictured the target. No bull's-eye for me but the real thing: a human silhouette, black as coal, a sinister void.

"She's *mine*." Joe's voice sailed into the sky and spread across the river, trailing three successive echoes: *she's mine, she's mine, she's mine*. As his last word faded, my mind seized on the caving flesh of his forefinger as it pulled in on the trigger of his gun. The creases of flesh below both knuckles. The trigger itself pinching the soft pad of his skin.

A shot rang out, ringing more echoes into the sky. Echoes with the exuberance of chimes. An announcement.

Joe's head spun to face me. I could see in his eyes that he couldn't believe it. It was as if he only now saw that I really didn't want him.

"If you don't, I won't," he said, as if we were bargaining out the final stages of a relationship.

We weren't. My bullet had simply missed. So I shot again.

And this time I hit him: right on the shoulder. He staggered backward as I came at him again, aiming for another shot. My third bullet entered his cheek with fortuitous precision.

Joe's arms flew out to either side as if he were raising his wings. The gun arced out of his hand and landed fifteen feet away, falling with a crash into a pile of stones. His body succumbed to gravity as his wings, having failed to levitate him, flopped overhead then bounced up and down beside him when his body hit the ground. Blood drained out of the hole in his head like oil out of a spent engine. Glassy-eyed, limp, he died before my very eyes, as the sky flooded with angry ghosts waiting to receive him.

I dropped my gun and ran to Nat, down whose face tears were streaming. He was holding his middle as he convulsed with sobs.

"How did you find me?" I wrapped Nat in my arms and felt his arms, shaking, come around my back. We held each other as tightly as the night we lost Hugo, when we thought things couldn't get worse.

"When you weren't home," Nat whispered in my ear, "I got worried. I went out to look for you. When I called your cell, you cursed at me and called me Joe."

"That was you who called?"

"Why did you call me that?"

"Sweetie, I was cursing at *him*. I thought he had you. I came here to find you."

"I had a feeling you did. I remembered his address from the answering machine."

"You're my hero." I pressed my wet eyes into his neck. Soon he would be taller than me. He would grow up and leave me. My little boy.

"I love you, Mom."

"I love you too, Nat. I love you *so much*."

"He was such a *freak*."

"You can say that again."

And then a three-ring circus of sirens and lights blasted apart the silence and vanquished the moon as this barren slice of land was overrun with police. A dozen cop cars must have pulled up practically all at once.

"I called that detective guy," Nat whispered in my ear.

"Good," I whispered back. "That was smart thinking."

Within moments we were standing at the epicenter of a circle of armed police, their weapons uniformly spoked in the direction of Joe. Dead Joe. Funny how much attention he attracted when he posed the least threat.

Jess entered into the circle, breathless from his run from the street. He looked at Joe. Then at us.

"You OK?"

"We're fine. Thanks for coming."

"Darcy—"

"No, I mean it. You're here. A few minutes earlier and you could have had the honors."

"So he had her in there." Jess had spotted Courtney, now sitting outside the container, picking at the electrical tape wound around her eyes. "Someone go help the lady – over there!"

Two officers hurried to Courtney's side. Both crouched beside her. One spoke to her, apparently calming her, eliciting nods. The other gently worked to free an edge of tape and carefully unpeel it.

"He has supplies in there," I told Jess and he knew what it meant though I didn't want to spell it out in front of Nat: it was where Joe had intended to keep me for himself. Obviously he had planned it carefully, organized things for a long-term stay.

The circle of police had slackened as officers

grouped to different tasks. An ambulance arrived. Two EMS workers spoke with one of the cops before zipping Joe into a body bag and arranging him on a stretcher. Others inspected the inside of the container. One came over to Jess, who stood with me and Nat.

"I found the murder weapon," the officer said.

"Don't make any assumptions," Jess corrected him.

"It was self-defense." I couldn't stop the quake in my voice. The officer had called it a "murder weapon". Was that where this would go now? I had just killed someone. But was killing your stalker *murder*?

"You did what you had to do," Jess said. "Don't worry. You'll have to spend some time talking to Homicide but I'll be with you every step of the way. I know those guys and believe me, they'll get it." His eyes settled on the gun in the officer's hand: the small, light, familiar gun. Angela's weapon of choice.

"Nice gun," Jess said with a hint of something in his tone – complicity? "Good shot for a beginner."

EPILOGUE

Names of the Dead
By Darcy Mayhew and Courtney Saks

Brooklyn, New York – As the New York City District Attorney's office prepares to defend itself against accusations of corruption that have shaken City Hall at its highest echelons, the New York City Police Department's forensics laboratory has completed a much awaited analysis of a group of human bones found at a building lot on Pacific Street in Brooklyn earlier this year.

The lot is the former site of a cleaning chemical factory built in 1978 by Tony Tarentino, Sr, the father of Tony Tarentino, Jr who owned the property until recently. The factory was demolished last fall after the lot was sold to Livingston & Sons, a developer, as part of a far-reaching order of eminent domain used to clear over two hundred parcels of both privately and publicly owned land to make way for what has become known as the Atlantic Yards project, the centerpiece of which is to be a basketball arena. Separate investigations have been launched into undisclosed terms of Mr Tarentino's sale of land, which included a total of nineteen lots in the Atlantic Yards footprint, and the provenance of the bones.

Since the discovery of the bones, New York City residents have clamored for information about their origin. DNA testing has now confirmed their identities. An investigation by the *Times* has yielded brief but telling biographies of the long unaccounted-for dead.

Ralph "One Eye" Caruso: died 12 April 1978. A cog in the wheel of the Figaro family crime empire, Ralph ran drugs for Vinnie Figaro whose son Vinnie, Jr later took over as head of the family. Mr Caruso was blinded in one eye while defending himself in a gunfight in which a police detective was killed. Mr Caruso spent two years in prison, from 1975 to 1977, for his role in that incident while another Figaro soldier received a life sentence for the detective's murder. Forensics testing of Mr Caruso's bones revealed a gunshot, probably to the back of the head, based on the condition of upper lumbar fragments found buried in the Pacific Street lot. Mr Caruso was twenty-five years old at the time of his disappearance. Forensics testing of his bones verify that age.

Loretta Amelia Scarpeletto: died 12 April 1978. The fiancée of Ralph Caruso, they had been childhood sweethearts who had grown up on the same block in Carroll Gardens, Brooklyn. Loretta worked as a secretary in the office of P.S. 58, a local elementary school, and planned to marry Ralph in the summer of 1978. A forensics examination of her bones did not reveal the exact cause of her death, but as no elements of her spine, neck or skull were found, authorities believe she was killed with Mr Caruso, also execution style. She was twenty-four at the time of her disappearance.

Lionel Antonio Scarpeletto: died 12 April 1978. The younger brother of Loretta Scarpeletto, Lionel was twelve years old when he disappeared the same day as his sister and Ralph Caruso. Loretta often stayed with him at their home after school while their mother worked. Authorities surmise that Ralph may have been with them at their home when they disappeared. Lionel, known for his sharp sense of humor, was in the sixth grade.

Antoinette Scarpeletto, eighty, was a widow at the time of the disappearance of Loretta and Lionel, her only children. Her reaction to the news that the recently discovered bones belonged to her children: "It helps to know what happened to them and when it happened, but it doesn't change anything. I never liked Ralphie Caruso. I knew it had something to do with him when they all vanished at the same time. I light a candle for my babies every single day at St Mary's Star of the Sea. I'll keep lighting them. Why stop now?"

"Whoa, Mom. That boy, Lionel . . . he was only in sixth grade." Nat dropped the newspaper onto the living room floor and looked at me. We lay head to toe on our blue velvet couch, still in our bathrobes on a Sunday morning. Tonight was New Year's Eve; because we planned on a late night, we'd allowed ourselves a lazy start to the day. Sara and her family were coming for a two-day visit and would be arriving in time for dinner. Courtney had offered to come early to help cook though I was sure that was an excuse; since her abduction she had grown nervous staying alone for long. We saw her often in our Brooklyn house and always welcomed her visits.

I'd told her to come early, but we wouldn't cook. We could order in. I had a better idea for how to spend the afternoon on the last day of the year.

"Poor kid," I said. "He got caught in the middle of something and probably never even knew what it was."

"But, Mom – why does it seem so much worse when it happens to someone young?"

"Because children are precious, pure and innocent."

Nat snorted and rolled his eyes; but I was right and he knew it. He was thirteen, practically a baby, nowhere near as sophisticated as he thought he was. He snuggled closer to me in physical confirmation of what he refused to verbally admit: that no matter how big he got, we still had years together as mother and child. A lifetime.

"Let's get dressed and have something to eat," I said. "Courtney and Rich will both be here in a little while and then we should get going."

"Why Coney Island? It's *December*."

"Exactly."

Two hours later, Nat, Courtney, Rich and I were walking along a deserted boardwalk in the grey winter chill. To our right: ocean. Endless, green, cold water extending to the end of the earth as far as we could see; shivering granite ocean and a cloud-hazy whitish sky barely separated by a tremulous horizon line in the far distance. The boardwalk, which in summer was noisy with beachgoers and amusement park riders, was all ours today. The quiet was exquisite. We might have been on a beach at the Vineyard if not for the stacks of buildings and the swoop and sway of the famous old rollercoaster to our left.

I kept my view trained to the right, toward the water. A wind slapped my face so unexpectedly I gasped and looked at Rich, who walked beside me. Had the sharp gust hurt him? It was hard not to worry about him all the time; but when I turned to him he lifted the good side of his face into his new smile, his *I'm still here so don't treat me like an invalid* smile. Most of his body, beneath his clothes, was fitted with a sausage skin of flesh-covered pressure garments designed to make movement more comfortable and also discourage scar tissue from stiffening him into a living corpse. The good news had been that his burns were treatable by a combination of artificial skin grafts and physical therapy; but all that would take time. Meanwhile he kept moving, kept living, had recently started painting again, and planned to return to teaching next fall. One thing he'd had to give up, for now, were his treasured Wednesday afternoon horseback riding lessons. But it was a small price to pay for his life; in fact, if not for those lessons, he might have been killed when his tampered-with gas oven caused his house to explode.

We still didn't know how Joe had gotten into Rich's apartment – all the evidence had been obliterated – but frankly it didn't matter. He had wanted to kill Rich; that we knew. But Joe couldn't control everything. Just after Rich turned his key in his front door lock, one of his students, who was playing in the park across from his house, saw him.

"Hey, Mr Stuart!" the boy had called out. "Could you get that ball?"

Startled, Rich turned to see a rubber spaldeen bouncing along the cobblestones of Verandah Place.

"Sure, David!" Rich called back. But he had stopped at the art store on his way home and was carrying a heavy roll of pre-gessoed canvas, which he propped against the door. The door, unlocked, opened just as Rich turned toward the bouncing ball. It was the last thing he remembered until regaining consciousness in the hospital four days later. It was also the thing that saved his life. This simple chain of events – the boy, the ball, the roll of canvas – afforded Rich a small but significant distance from the blast, which was immediate upon the door's opening. He was already a few feet away when the blast hit him on his right side and propelled him three yards into the street while the house exploded and burned.

A specially fashioned pressure garment emerged

from his collar, covering the right part of his face and ear and rising into a partial hood that kept it secure on his damaged skin. I'd told him this "new look" made him operatic and mysterious. Even though I was a writer, I didn't know how to express in words how the extra skin he now wore seemed to intensify his beauty in my eyes. *He was alive*. Since most of his face had been left mercifully unharmed, it was easy to look at him and not feel cheated. I still felt a gravitational pull when I was near him; "the accident", as we euphemistically called it, had not changed our attraction or our love.

Being this close to the ocean helped me feel the continuity of past and present because the confluence of water and sand and sky made the earth seem so huge and timeless and my own experiences, miniscule in comparison, fell into perspective. And also because an empty beach reminded me of the Vineyard, where I had lived so long and happily; here, sprayed by chilly ocean mist, I could sense Hugo in the atmosphere. Maybe it was silly of me, but my thought had been to come here as a way to introduce Hugo, in my mind, to our new life. It was more a feeling than a thought, an impulse to show him where we had landed, and with whom. And also to make sure he understood that I now knew the truth about his death – that he hadn't been a careless driver but had been deliberately killed – and that, looked at one way, I had personally avenged him, for whatever it was worth. Looked at another way, I had simply done what any mother would do faced with a threat to her child. When I pulled the trigger and killed Joe, there was no thought of revenge. What I felt was pure terror and that feeling had prompted me to action. The other feelings had come later, in the days and weeks that followed, as I began to grasp the truth about what had really happened to Hugo the night he died. Was murdered, by Joe. I'd stewed in helpless rage for a while; and then, fearing that my anger would poison our lives, decided to somehow find a way to release it. I'd immersed myself in work, trying to shift my energies in a positive direction. I'd sat for hours at my mother's bedside, holding her feather-light hand, offering myself as a conduit to the present while she traveled the byways of her past. And I had been all throughout the city, alone, testing the waters of a world without Joe. Then one day I discovered that Coney Island on a cold, abandoned afternoon was the perfect place to talk to ghosts.

I think Nat felt something special here, too, the way he periodically sprinted like an excited puppy up and down the boardwalk, away from and back to the three adults.

At one point Courtney caught up with him and spoke to him, something I couldn't hear, and then he took off in a fast run straight down the boardwalk. She shouted at him, dared him to run faster as she consulted her wristwatch. Then, suddenly, he collapsed onto the boardwalk with such melodrama that I knew he had staged a fake collapse.

"Wimp!" she called.

From a distance, I could see his belly rise and fall in laughter.

"Get up, kid, and keep going or the deal's off!"

Nat got up and ran half-heartedly, glancing back with a grin meant to tease Courtney.

"What deal?" I asked as Rich and I caught up with her. Courtney was wearing trendy red-and-orange sneakers, tight jeans and a short black puffy jacket with the hood slackened back off her head. Her wind-whipped hair was messy, cinched at the neck by a white scarf.

"I said I'd tell him the best and the worst things that ever happened to me if he could get to the third staircase in under a minute."

"I guess he doesn't want to know," I said.

"Guess not." She smiled, her face bright with youth as always, but less exuberant than last summer when we'd first met. She had never told me her life's best experience and now I wondered what it was. But I knew the when and where of her worst experience and even the grisly what. Joe had used her as a surrogate for me, both to punish her for being close to me and to practice for the real thing. His plan, apparently, was to keep her until he got me; and then he would bury her in the sand through a hatch he had already cut in the floor of the shipping container where he'd held her for three nightmarish days.

"When I saw you walk in," she'd said to me soon after it was all over, "I didn't know if it meant I was dead or alive."

"Alive," I'd reassured her. "I wouldn't have let him hurt you anymore." She knew that was true; after all, I'd brought a gun.

"Listen," I said to her now, "I know you meant well, but don't ever tell Nat, OK?"

"You thought I'd actually tell him about *that*?" She crooked one of her mischievous smiles. "Like I haven't had worse things happen to me."

I took Courtney's hand on one side and Rich's on the other. Walking between them, we moved slowly along the boardwalk in Nat's direction. He didn't get up; instead, he closed his eyes and positioned his face into the next strong wind. It was cold and bracing. Invigorating. And I knew he felt it too: it was time, and we were ready, to begin our new lives.

Turn the page for an extract from
Katia Lief's thrilling page turner

The **12**th
Victim

Also available from Ebury Press

CHAPTER 1

When I walked into Mac's home office he turned and looked at me like I'd caught him surfing pornography, and quickly closed his laptop. "Sorry you saw that."

The image seemed to linger on the screen even after it went dark: the woman's chipped red manicure digging into the loose muscles of a man's hairy back, her face contorted in either ecstasy or disgust; it was hard to tell which.

"New case?"

"Last week. Wife thought he was cheating on her. He's cheating on her. Slam dunk. Next."

I crossed the small room to touch his forehead. "You're burning up."

"I can't lay in bed anymore."

"Some people get a flu shot so they won't—"

"Don't say it again."

Get the flu.

How many times had I told him not to put it off? Our son, Ben; his babysitter, Chali; and I all had our shots two months ago. But Mac, workaholic that he was, couldn't spare the time. Now he was on day one of what would probably be a week of fever, aches, and pains, and already he was crawling out of his skin.

"Go back to bed, dearest."

He coughed. Shook his head. "I've got some stuff to do."

"It's Sunday night. Your client can wait to see those pictures; in fact, you'll be doing her a favor."

"You're right." He shut down his computer and looked at me. It was only eight o'clock, I had just put Ben to bed, but the exhaustion in Mac's eyes made it feel like midnight. "Why do I even do this? I thought I was ready to retire from the police when I did, but now I listen to Billy—"

"Who is overwhelmed, Mac, do I really have to remind you?"

"—and I realize that I will never get another challenging case again."

"You want to be like Billy, chasing a serial killer no one's been able to find for two years? Haven't you been there, done that? Don't you feel—"

"*Bored.*"

"You're sick, you're tired, and now I think you're delirious, saying you wish you had the kind of cases Billy's been catching."

"Maybe I should try corporate security again."

"Come on. Back to bed." I held out my hand. He took it and stood, pausing to steady himself. He moaned and let me navigate him through the hallway back to our bedroom. I left the room dark and steered him into bed. The musty air felt claustrophobic but it was much too cold out to open a window.

"Sleep." I kissed his forehead. "I'm going upstairs."

He was snoring before I closed the door.

With my two men (well, one of them was just shy of

four years old) fast asleep, the house felt peaceful in a way it never did. I crept quietly up the stairs to the second floor of our duplex; it was a typical layout of these brownstone Brooklyn apartments, when you had the lower half of the house, to put the bedrooms beneath and use the high-ceilinged parlor floor for all the social rooms. The floorboards creaked under my bare feet as I passed through the living room. And then, just as I made it onto an area rug, a clatter of noise broke the silence when I accidentally kicked one of Ben's toy trucks toward the opposite wall. I froze, waiting for a reaction from below, but no one seemed to have heard. I switched on the kitchen light and sat at the table a moment, wondering where to begin. An exquisite solitude gathered like fog as I listened to sounds I rarely heard in our home: the ticking of the wall clock, the hum of the refrigerator, dissonant whispers emanating from the radiator.

The dishes: I should do them first. I had made chicken soup, and vegetable skins and crumbs from the sliced baguette were all over the counter. I started by finding a large plastic container to store the soup for tomorrow.

Midway through loading the dishwasher, a text message alert chimed across the room. I turned to look; it was Mac's BlackBerry (mine was in my jeans pocket), abandoned on a shelf across the kitchen this morning around the time he realized he was coming down with something. His phone had been quiet all day, it being Sunday, and the chime took me by surprise. My hands were slick with soapy water. I turned back to the dishes. A few minutes later I closed the tap and looked up—and was startled by my own ghostly reflection in the window that overlooked the back garden. *A tall, crazy-looking woman with messy color-blanched hair stood outside staring in at me.* My heart jumped.

"Get lost!" I waved my arm, and so did she. Then we laughed at each other. Still, she made me nervous.

Mac usually stood here cleaning up at night; I wasn't used to the intensity of darkness directly in front of me and the indistinct mirrorlike reversal of myself. If this was a typical flu, it would be days before he was better. Meantime, I would take on all his tasks, along with my own.

It was still too early for bed, and I had promised myself that before the weekend was over I would quit stalling and enroll in my spring courses. I was eking my way through a college degree while my adult life barreled forward, pretty sure that my twenty-year-old classmates saw me as ancient at thirty-eight. Plus I was a mother. And twice married. My life had been blessed and battered to a ridiculous extent. All I wanted now was to finish school so I could remake my career. Unlike Mac, in-the-thick-of-it police work did not tempt me anymore, even though I'd been good at it, and despite the fact that I now held a private investigator's license so I could work with Mac on the occasional case. The busier he got, the busier I got; but evolving into his work partner (again) wasn't my goal. I wanted to stand outside looking in, which was why I had chosen a forensic psychology undergraduate program.

Well, that wasn't all I wanted.

I wanted, and would always want, *her* back.

Two hers.

Cece, my sweet little daughter murdered six years ago along with my first husband, Jackson.

And Amelia or Sarah or Dakota—the daughter who was supposed to be, but wasn't. She had miscarried, at six months' gestation, eight weeks and three days ago. Giving birth to a lifeless child was . . . I shook away the memory.

I opened the cabinet drawer where we tossed stuff we might need later and rummaged through the mess for the catalog. It was the size of a magazine, easy to locate, but so much junk had accumulated I couldn't resist grabbing a few things—a small plastic fan that was broken, a playbill from last year, an appliance manual for a toaster oven we no longer owned—and tossing them in the garbage. I noticed a freebie pocket calendar that had arrived in the mail almost a year ago, and was about to throw it away when I realized I should check to make sure no one was using it. I was pretty sure Mac used his BlackBerry calendar exclusively, as did I, but you never knew. Good thing I'd decided to check: When I flipped through the pages I saw half a dozen penciled entries in Chali's handwriting. I remembered her asking if anyone would be using the little paper calendar and telling her she was welcome to it. I tossed it back into the drawer and sat down at the kitchen table with the course catalog.

She was supposed to have been born on January first. New Year's Day. Maybe it had been too neat an expectation to foresee a daughter in my future. It was a dangerous hope, as if Cece could be replaced. Of course that was ridiculous and I never said it aloud, but it was a secret wish. I had felt itchy, pregnant with Leah or Elsa or Caroline, as if having her would scratch away a lingering emptiness. But instead of her birth eliminating a void, her stillbirth doubled it. Pregnancy with Ben four years ago had not brought on that kind of inner discord, but he was a boy, and Mac and I were a brand-new couple, and I was amazed just to be alive.

For the past eight weeks and three days, the hours had felt long and heavy.

And now the holiday season was upon us: Christmas was in two weeks, Ben's birthday was just a month away, and I still hadn't bought any presents or planned any parties.

I started reading the course offerings, wondering how I would find the energy to keep up with the work, and Ben, if I took two classes. I had dropped out at the beginning of the semester when I'd lost the baby, but one of the abandoned courses had intrigued me enough that I was tempted to give it another try: The Role of Malingering in the Insanity Defense: An Introduction. I was still interested in examining the vast gray area where criminal intent overlapped with lying at one end and mental illness at the other. So I dragged my laptop across the kitchen table, booted it up, logged into the school Web site and enrolled for the course again. Classes started at the beginning of February. I still had time to decide whether or not to take a second class.

Another text message chimed on Mac's phone. I wondered who had texted him twice on a Sunday night. It occurred to me that it could be important, so I decided to break an unspoken privacy rule and read his messages.

The first was a Silver Alert from the city, advising of a missing senior. The second was from Billy Staples, a detective at our local precinct, the Eight-four, and Mac's closest friend since he'd married me and moved to Brooklyn to begin the second half of his life. His message was simple, and inexplicable (at least to me):

WARREN NEVINS

I carried the phone downstairs, flicking off lights as I went, leaving what felt like a cold, dark void in my wake. We had set our thermostat to lower at eleven every night, and that the parlor floor was growing chilly told me it was late. I was tired. Ben would be up by six o'clock and I was ready to crawl into my warm bed beside Mac.

I could feel the heat off Mac's body as I came around his side of the bed, intending to put his phone on his dresser.

"I'm awake," he whispered.

"You got a text." I handed him the phone.

His face glowed in the anemic light cast by the small square screen. He stared at it longer than necessary to read the two little words. And then he put the phone down on the bedside table beside a heap of crumpled tissues, closed his eyes, and sighed.

Ten minutes later I stepped out of the bathroom in my nightgown, my mouth minty from toothpaste, face moist with cream, and hair static from brushing. And there was Mac: standing in the hallway, fully dressed. His cheeks were pink with fever.

"Huh?" I stared at him; it was the best I could do.

"I have to go out."

"You have to go back to bed."

"I'm meeting Billy."

"No you're not." I took his arm and tried to steer him along the hall, back toward our bedroom, but he resisted.

"You don't understand, Karin."

"Mac, you have the flu. This is absurd. You're not going out in thirty-degree weather to see Billy right now. Whatever he needs can wait until morning."

"This can't." He started toward the stairs.

"Why not?"

He stopped, turned and looked at me. "I'm a big boy, Karin. I can make my own decisions."

"You're really pissing me off right now."

Half his mouth lifted into a wry semismile. And then a sudden coughing fit buckled him over; propping his hands on his knees, he hacked uncontrollably.

I stepped back into the bathroom and returned to offer him a box of tissues. When he could stand, he took one and blew his nose. I touched his forehead, which was even hotter than before.

"We should take your temperature again."

He relented and lay back down on the bed, fully dressed. I turned on a lamp and watched him in the golden light, laboring to breathe with a digital thermometer protruding from his lips. After a minute, multiple bleeps announced that a conclusion had been reached: 104.2. I showed him the reading.

"Still want to go out?"

"I have to." But he didn't make a move to get up.

"Sweetie, what's going on?" I sat on the bed beside him, holding the thermometer in one hand and touching his burning cheek with the other.

"I promised Billy I wouldn't tell anyone, not even you."

"Tell me what?"

I waited, feeling a growing sensation of nervousness. I didn't like it. Finally he took a deep breath, coughed, and looked at me.

"He'll have to understand."

"I'm sure he will."

"I would go if I could."

"I can call him and let him know you're sick."

"Don't call him. Just go."

It was nearly midnight. Freezing out. And dark. "Where?"

"Warren and Nevins streets. You can walk there; it's close. But I'd feel better if you took my gun."

Warren Street, Nevins Street—of course. They weren't far from here, though I never went in that direction. "I won't need a gun."

"White lady alone in the projects at night—"

"No gun." The more I'd had to shoot people, the more I'd grown to hate it. "What's Billy doing over there?"

"Crime scene, probably. He's been having flashbacks at crime scenes, not always, but sometimes. He loses control and it terrifies him."

"Loses control how?"

"Hallucinates."

"Jesus."

"I know."

A year and a half ago, Billy had lost an eye in a rooftop shootout with a woman he loved. The shock and betrayal had been traumatic on every level—physically, emotionally, professionally—but after a standard leave he had returned to work. Some cops seem able to slough off trauma; others crumble instantly; some come apart bit by bit. You often don't know who is who until some time has passed. We had thought Billy was out of the woods, but maybe we were wrong.

"Is he getting help?"

Mac shook his head. "The stigma—afraid he'll lose his job."

Job, full pension, reputation; there was a lot a cop could risk if he showed the slightest sign of vulnerability.

Back when I was a cop and I fell apart, people were kind but they kept their distance, as if they'd catch failure if they came too close.

"How long has it been happening?"

"Not sure. He told me about it a couple of weeks ago. Said he'd send me a code, a location, if he felt one coming on again. The deal was I'd show up, wherever, whenever, and help him handle it."

"You're a good friend."

"Not tonight I'm not."

I kissed his forehead. "I'm on it." Then I fed him some ibuprofen, turned off the light, and went to get my coat.